Baby Boys to Adult Boys:
Equals the Same Boys

Baby Boys to Adult Boys: Equals the Same Boys

ERIC D. JOHNSON

ISBN: 978-1-78324-100-2

Published by Wordzworth
www.wordzworth.com

Dedication

Dear mom and dad, Christine and Dossy Johnson, words alone can't repay you for the enormous amount of loving support and guidance that you have given to your children since birth, so I shall repay you in-kind with love, support and loyalty! **To my daughter whom I've loved from before she was born** and who is unaware of how her mere presence has sustained me, motivated me and given me hope during the toughest times in my life, I beseech God's grace upon you and your mother!

To my aunts, uncles and cousins that I grew up with, I thank you for receiving and maintaining the loving legacy that flows through our clan! **To the ancestors**, seen and unseen, known and unknown, who died, suffered, toiled and prayed, toiled, prayed and sacrificed, and toiled, prayed and prayed and believed that their efforts would not be in vain, I humbly send you my most sincere gratitude!!!

To all of the high-quality, honest, diligent, and compassionate educators **who labor tirelessly to provide an incredible gift to mankind, yet are grossly undervalued, underappreciated and underpaid**, I salute you forever!

To all of the courageous, honest, rational, unprejudiced, hard-working and dedicated **officers who risk their health and life every day** to provide a satisfactory level of safety and comfort to citizens despite being grossly underpaid, underappreciated, undervalued and misunderstood, I appreciate you and thank you for your service! My only request of you is that **you don't remain silent about unethical and unqualified officers or when your brother or sister commits a crime**. Instead, tell the whole truth and nothing but the truth, so that the victim's family and society can experience justice!

The Invitation-Oriah Mountain Dreamer

I want to know if you can sit with beauty
Even when it is not pretty every day
And if you can source your own life
From its presence.
It doesn't interest me to know where you live
or how much money you have.
I want to know if you can get up after the night
of grief and despair,
Weary and bruised to the bone,
And do what needs to be done for the children!!!

Contents

Introduction

All of the **accounts are true,** but the names have been changed to protect the vulnerable!

In this book, I'm bearing witness to the realities I've experienced and the truths that I know! As a result, my prayer is that many parents, grandparents, teachers, faith-leaders, politicians, government agencies, police departments and citizens **will feel compelled to nurture, love, serve and protect all children, strive for excellence and operate with honesty and integrity without regard to race or socio-economic status!**

I have eight years of experience teaching children from K-12th grade. I spent five years and eight months as a detention officer at the seventh largest jail in the Southeast observing and supervising males and females between 17-65 years of age. My sixty-eight months as a detention officer have served as an informal case study of the attitudes, behaviors and characteristics of incarcerated African-American males between the ages of 17-65. Furthermore, it has afforded me the opportunity to **witness and identify common characteristics that are exhibited by students and inmates and multiple factors that contribute to students becoming inmates.** In many respects, human nature is very predictable, for we know that most of our behavior is learned. Therefore, **attitudes, behaviors and characteristics are developed!** This similar behavior reveals that *there can be very little difference in the mindset of the 8-year-old, 21-year-old or 57-year-old.* Working in these two fields has provided me an in-depth look at the crisis educators and officers must combat on a daily basis. It is critically important for these professionals to develop skills and strategies to effectively recognize and cope with sincere ignorance, conscientious malice and stupidity and mental health disorders. **In regard to the proverbial game of life, I've witnessed the beginning and the end!**

This public service announcement (PSA) is for all children, tweens and teens. First, it is very critical for you all to gain a full understanding of the *purpose and responsibilities of loving and responsible parents.* Secondly, you are not smarter than your parents or most adults! Despite what you fully believe, have heard from friends and seen on television, you are incapable of taking care of yourself in a safe, decent and productive manner. Your clear and common sense proof is that history shows that there have always been adults caring for children! If adults were not necessary, I believe that we would had been designed to die after our children reached fourteen years of age. If someone can show me a civilization where the elders are not in charge, I would be very interested. Thus, it is always in a child's best interest to obey the instructions and guidance of loving parents, teachers and positive family, friends and elders.

Chapter 1

Immaturity can last a lifetime!
Robert Half

When I was a child, I spoke like a child,
I thought like a child, I reasoned like a child.
When I became a man, I gave up childish ways!

—1ST CORINTHIANS 13:11

Trays up, trays up, trays uppp! It's 4 am and it is breakfast time at the county jail. Usually you hear an eerie silence, then some mumbling while doors are opening and closing and you see guys walking around in a zombie-like state. Within minutes, you hear *"I got eggs for shank, grits and eggs for a sack, got sausage for a biscuit and got a tray for an item."* Yep, it's 4 am and this is nothing like sitting down at the local Waffle House to fill the hunger in your belly, soak up the liquor and laugh about last night's events! You can't gaze at the table with the scantily clad chicks or strike up a conversation with

1

the good-looking ladies at the other table. In fact, there are no ladies around. A bit of shock hits my brain because I'm a newbie and this is my first week on the job. My brain is still getting used to the fact that I have to wake more than 160 inmates so they can receive their morning meal. If all goes well, the inmates will get up, receive their tray, eat their breakfast and return to their cell within one hour. If all does not go well, there will be considerable whining about the appearance or portion of the food, three or more verbal altercations about childish or illegal activities and one physical altercation. Now, you might be wondering like I used to, *what kind of person argues or fights at 4:30 in the morning.* I struggled for some time with comprehending this behavior until I began to understand the mindset of criminals and their dysfunctional mentality. Then, it made sense to me and I was better able to anticipate and prevent altercations, which made me an effective detention officer. I came to understand that some people **feel resentment and anger for practically their entire day**, so being awakened that early in the morning begins their daily frustration. In addition, if they miss the breakfast meal, they may not receive the next meal for approximately seven hours. Also, for the cowardly thugs and the mean predators, early morning was a beneficial time to attack someone because they could catch the unsuspecting inmate groggy or almost literally sleepwalking.

One of the biggest adjustments for me was *getting used to the enormous amount of daily whining and complaining about petty issues,* such as not having butter, salt or pepper on the tray, cornbread or sandwich bread is bent or broken, the other man has more rice or beans (not about to count rice or beans), his meat is bigger than mine (*you have to speak to your daddy about that*), I want strawberry cookies not vanilla, I want wheat bread, not white, I don't eat ham, give me a turkey sack (sandwich), when are we going to rec (recreation yard), why can't we go to rec today, why can't we stay out longer, why can't we finish watching TV, where is the juice, why didn't we get Gatorade today and on and on and on! Frequently, they asked with a nasty attitude or as if I forgot to serve juice with the meal that they paid for at an upscale resort. Only baby boys get upset about not receiving juice with their meal. I believe that if the *juice was placed inside of a sippy cup*, many of the inmates would had still drunk it. The medical clinic was an area where a lot of daily whining was heard. While taking inmates to receive diabetic medication during the early morning hours, several inmates consistently whined and complained about their conditions and treatment they received. In some cases, inmates would tell the nurse about symptoms and ask for additional medication or sugar tablets. After the nurse politely explains that nothing else can be given without doctor's orders, sometimes inmates would get upset and whine more and louder. Subsequently, I thought how similar their behavior was to babies unable to sleep through the night and wake up crying for their mother. *Surprisingly, I hadn't worked at the jail for two months before I noticed striking similarities between inmates and elementary school boys.* Their similar behavior reveals that there can be very little difference in the mindset of the 8-year-old, 21-year-old or 57-year-old. I have frequently heard that victory is in your praise. I believe that victory lies in your praise and strategic actions! On the other hand, I've never heard anyone say that victory lies in whining and complaining.

Poor ass manners and a stink attitude will cause a person to miss so many opportunities! In fact, it will cause the person to miss opportunities that he is unaware of because many people will not bother to tell him why he missed the opportunity. While growing up, it's important and beneficial for people to become familiar with the concept of at your discretion. Therefore, when you realize that a person isn't required to perform an action, but the person has the authority to do so, it's in your best interest to address the issue in a courteous manner! In most cases, it's just the prudent course of action and sometimes it may require being humble. **Humility** is an important and beneficial characteristic. Many people mistakenly misinterpret humility as being weak. However, you will come to realize that having humility is a strength once you learn the true meaning of the word and how the quality operates during adverse conditions! Frequently, inmates request a new sandwich because the bread is slightly smashed, which happens on a regular basis because of the way the sandwiches are packed. Depending on the manner in which he asks and how busy I am, I will grant the request. In one situation, I told the inmate to hold on, which was the procedure because other inmates were still receiving their meal. However, he asked 2-3 more times for a new sandwich even though other inmates were in line getting their meal. As I was exiting the dayroom, he said "can I get another sandwich now?" in a funky tone. I replied, I know you heard me say wait! He said, "well chuck you then." Since he was impatient and never learned how to wait or chose not to wait, he ended up with a smashed sandwich. Similarly, when receiving a breakfast tray, the cornbread may be broken in half or unusually small. Again, rather than wait a few minutes, inmates usually begin saying insulting remarks, cursing or demanding an immediate correction. In some cases, inmates demand a whole new tray instead of just the item that is irregular. Part of the reason why many inmates behave like that is that aggression is the only problem-solving skill they have developed. Jail or prison is the wrong environment to demand items that aren't required by law. This behavior is a clear example of a lack of understanding of how beneficial good manners are! Too often, inmates fail to realize the importance of communicating in a courteous manner. First, it demonstrates a level of respect. Secondly, it appeals to the officer's sense of generosity and may influence the officer to grant your request. Also, inmates certainly fail to realize how their behavior creates a positive or negative impact on their future interactions. I had no reason to deny their food, especially given the fact that the portions were hardly enough for an average twelve-year-old boy. We're all human and it's only natural to extend a courtesy or bend a rule for a person who is kind and respectful. In this environment, *kindness isn't expected, but respect is required*!

Only a baby boy would plead for one extra cookie or whine about butter missing from his tray, except in this case he was thirty-five-years-old. In this particular case, I'm convinced that this inmate was bipolar. He cursed me out on a Saturday and threatened to spit in my face, which would had brought about severe consequences for him. The next day, I arrived to the floor to give the inmate a citation for his anti-social behavior and threats and I asked him if he would sign the citation. He stuck his middle finger up with one hand and grabbed his groin with his other hand. The following day, I was assigned to work the same floor again and after distributing the sandwiches with a cookie, the same clown inmate said, "Officer Johnson, may I speak to you," in a very respectful tone. I replied, what's up? He said, "if you have an extra sack, do you think I can get another cookie?" I smiled and walked out of the pod. Later, he asked again and even said please. In fact, my biggest shock occurred when I was still a rookie on the job and it involved a cookie. Yes, a single cookie! I had been employed for about five months and I had recently finished being supervised by a corporal and was now handling security duties independently. I had finished serving dinner trays to thirty inmates when an inmate who resembled Kat Williams told me that he did not have a cookie on his tray. I was certain that there was a cookie on his tray when I gave the tray to him. I told him to wait and I would see about getting him another cookie. When I exited the pod, somehow he walked out behind me and called me all kinds of non-dictionary names and threatened to chuck me up if I didn't give him a cookie immediately. As he approached me, I realized that I needed to get into a fighting stance because this clown was really about to assault me over a cookie. Prior to us getting into a physical altercation, my co-worker made a radio call for assistance and back-up arrived before he threw a punch. This verbal altercation that almost became a physical altercation was my early introduction into the severely dysfunctional and violent world of criminals.

The *constant whining like young boys* reminded me of the years I spent teaching in various elementary schools throughout South Atlanta. Anytime an inmate asked about going to rec, I always wondered did he go outside to play every day when he was free. If not, why was he making a big deal about it now? Occasionally, I would ask an inmate if he went outside to play every day when he was home. If he said yes, I said you must not have appreciated it (freedom) or else you wouldn't have committed the senseless crime that caused you to get your recreation time revoked. The main complaint by most inmates stems from them *not getting what they want when they want it and doing what they want when they want to.* This is clearly boyish behavior. Frustration on behalf of the officer results from the irrationality of the many inmates who swear that they behave like an adult. When you contrast the behavior of an adult man with an adult boy, the differences are as clear as daylight. An adult man can acknowledge the truth and accept it--I'm in jail for an illegal act that I committed and this is the small portion of bland food that the jail serves! These are the rules that I have to obey since I gambled away my freedom because of irrational thinking and an attempt to obtain instant gratification. An adult boy rejects the truth and says--"I'm in jail and I didn't do nothin' wrong." Why do I have a little bit of beans on my plate and he has more beans than me? Really! They are grown enough to commit a major crime, yet they whine like a boy about a sandwich missing one cookie from their plate or the portion of beans or rice on their plate. Some of them whine about having a headache and not being taken to the clinic immediately. I've never seen so many adult boys ask female officers and nurses for a band-aid despite their finger not bleeding. I'm reminded of a late night when I was sitting down relaxing my feet, body and mind after a busy and volatile evening when Sgt. Check called and told me to check on the welfare of an inmate because he called his mother and told her that he thinks his cellmate has a contagious disease. I didn't remember his name when I got to the cell, so I intentionally said, "who called their mother?" There was a long pause, then the guy on the top bunk raised his hand. Clearly, this type of behavior is symptomatic of a boy who never outgrew his childhood behaviors and attachment to his mother. This isn't quite the Tupac persona that they normally exhibit.

Similar to a baby boy who pouts, balls up his hands and stomps his feet, many inmates engage in similar powerless acts like pouting, mean-mugging (staring), kicking the mop bucket over, throwing the cleaning brush or spray bottle at the wall, yelling insults and cursing in the dayroom and often from behind large metal doors. For the NFL fan, you've probably seen a football player kick or throw a juice cooler. The locations are different, but it's the same tantrum! This behavior is always silly and sometimes amusing when committed by a boy or girl and even more silly when it's done by an adult boy! They engage in other powerless acts like complaining, stealing and acting silly. As the officer exits the pod to go sit down, get some good tasting food and drink or go home, the inmate is still enclosed in a tiny and often musty room without freedom and limited to no access to family and friends. *Whether at 3, 5, 11, 17, 23, 39, or 55 years old, since no corrective actions were applied during the formative years, the boyish behavior continues.* It's sadly amusing to see and hear a baby boy or adult boy between the ages of 17, 25, 35 and 50 rant and rave about what he's not gonna do, what he is going to make the officer do, along with the infamous statement "you got me chucked up!" Then, he demands to speak to a Sergeant (Sgt.) or Lieutenant (Lt.), but he doesn't know that he won't receive anything that he's demanding. Sometimes they whine and complain for twenty minutes, forty minutes or longer. I'm tempted to say that it amazes me, but I've seen too many inmates over the course of my years who behaved the same way, which is truly reflective of their lack of rational thinking and maturity. However, it is still slightly amusing to see an inmate whine while demanding his release from jail. In this case, the inmate was being held in an isolation cell due to a seemingly positive tuberculosis (TB) test. His initial test indicated that he was positive for TB. When I encountered him, his X-ray results had not returned in several days. As a result, he was banging and screaming, saying "let me out of here. I don't belong in here. Y'all keep chucking wit me...I was supposed to been in court." This adult boy whined and yelled off-and-on for approximately two hours. First of all, I have never seen or heard of an inmate bang or demand his way out of jail. Again, this behavior is a true example of boyish behavior. Secondly, he was arrested for a Failure to Appear (FTA) charge. By not going to court on his assigned day, he demonstrated that he is not trustworthy. Additionally, I've concluded that the court interprets a FTA as a blatant disrespect of the court. Therefore, the court feels compelled and obliged to reward the person with an arrest warrant. The person may view it as a penalty, but I say reward because it's the consequence levied by the court for the person's disrespect of authority and their civic responsibility. Once a person has demonstrated once or twice that she/he "forgot the court date" or "didn't receive the notice in the mail," the court usually mandates that the person stay in jail to ensure their attendance in court. Needless to say, all of his whining was in vain because no jail will transport an inmate who appears to have a contagious disease, nor could he go anywhere before he was transported to his court date.

It was strikingly weird to see and hear a sixty-three-year-old man behave like a five-year-old boy. As I began my shift on the medical floor, Inmate Bubba started banging on the door and shouting "help me, help me, I'm not post to be in here." Immediately, I turned to the corporal who I was relieving and asked her what was his problem. She advised me that his bond was paid, but he had a probation hold (hold) in Clayton County and he refused to accept the truth. Bubba engaged in a tantrum my full nine-hour shift. He banged on the door throughout the shift and every time he saw additional people walk past his cell. Talking a lot, but not saying anything meaningful, he asked the same child-like questions and made the same comments to three officers and two Sergeants. At first, the conversation and questions sounded reasonable, but three minutes after investigating his claim, I realized that his foolish and illogical thinking wasted my precious time! He said that his bond was paid on his pending charge and he wanted to know if the information was posted on the computer and what time he would be getting out of jail (time is the foolish part of the question because repeat offenders know that there is no set time). Well, his bond was paid in full, but he was being held on a probation violation. Just for the purpose of covering myself, I went to his cell and said your bond is paid in full, but you know that you have a hold. With no teeth, he looked quizzical and shouted, where did that come from? Sarcastically I asked, you didn't know you were on probation? Another whining incident happened at a hospital. Another police agency was monitoring a baby boy inmate who looked about seventeen and he had a deep southern drawl. Somehow the inmate knocked over the urinal bottle on himself. He immediately broke into a temper tantrum and began whining loudly. "Damn! I knowed that shit was gonna happen—I been callin dem folk" (nurses)! When the nurse arrived, he said "I'm cold! Y'all need to turn the damn air off!" Then he said to the 300lb security officer, "big boi, call dem folk to come take these cuffs off me so I can shower." He told the nurse, "I'm not gitn back in that bed." She replied, that's the only one we have for you. "Can you get me a tile and some boxers, he said?" She replied, sir, we don't have any boxers. We only have diapers. I'm not puttin' on no diapers, he said. Over the next few minutes, he continued to whine. Again, he said "big boi, call dem folks-where dey at, they shoulda been here by now! They think I'm playin." After 10-15 minutes, a deputy arrived and uncuffed the inmate. The nurse sanitized his bed while he was in the shower and he returned to the bed, put on the diaper and fell asleep in a fetal position. You gotta see this stuff to believe it.

Most inmates haven't put away childish behavior. Everybody grows older, but not everyone grows up! As we know, physical age can be counted by the number of birthdays a person has had. However, emotional age does not always match the person's physical age! Emotional age can be measured by the person's behavior and character. Inmates frequently asked childish questions. One childish question that they repeatedly asked was "do I have any holds?" This question was incredibly childish because he has been everywhere with himself! If an inmate has committed illegal acts in another county or state, particularly if he has a FTA for a court date, he will have a detainer, otherwise known as a hold. Despite having a bond or release date in the county where he is incarcerated, the chances of an inmate being released are about as good as the inmate hitting the Power Ball. In violation of Standard Operating Procedures (SOP), some inmates would press the intercom and lean on the door, climb on the glass or stand on the table as if I would have to address them if they stood there. Sometimes 3-10 minutes would elapse before they kinda realized that I didn't have to respond to the intercom. Then, they would walk away either looking angry or dejected. However, I'm not sure if they ever realized or consciously acknowledged that there was no set time for me to turn on the power for the telephone or TV and no matter how loud they shouted or cursed, they still couldn't force me to turn on the power or unlock the door of an inmate whose rotation time I revoked for violating a jail code. Later, the inmate may come to realize that his homies, crew, gang are powerless to help him. Thus, the lesson is to follow the commands of the officer, obey the rules of the jail and be your own man! Just like a young boy, many inmates choose to engage in playful activities. The first time I sprayed an inmate with my mace, it happened because the inmate was being playful, so he said. Of course, I didn't know his intention at the time of the incident. As usual, an inmate was talking junk to me during one of my security checks and he said something to the effect of I will see you when you come upstairs. When rotation ended, I began securing all of the cell doors. As I walked to this particular inmate's door, he darted towards me as if he was going to attack me. I stepped back, pulled out my mace, sprayed him in the face and shut his door. During the investigation, he stated that he was playing around and he was just trying to scare me. That was a foolish statement because it would never be acceptable for an inmate to scare an officer. Also, it was a silly statement because all of the inmates and staff knew that I didn't play with inmates. Occasionally, I would laugh, but I did not joke or play with inmates! This playful mentality was the cause of plenty of inmates committing violations and getting into trouble. They believe that it's okay to play around in jail, despite the Inmate Handbook informing them that horseplay is not allowed. A Medical Request form is an important document for inmates to use to request a medical appointment at the clinic. Instead of using it for this purpose, many inmates used the form to cover the cell light, cell window or make paper planes and other objects. What do baby boys who don't focus on learning do with the notebook paper that someone spent their hard-earned money on? Yep, make paper planes, spitballs and other objects. Obviously, wrestling and boxing are strictly prohibited because officers can't determine if the inmates are really fighting or play fighting! Yet, many of them frequently engaged in other playful activities, like throwing around their laundry bags, throwing paper balls while another person attempts to hit it with a pencil or a legal pad, or throwing a paper football to a friend. This silly child-like behavior was always on display on commissary day. *Minutes or within an hour after commissary was distributed, baby boys and adult boys would exit their cells smiling, laughing, and skipping like elementary boys while carrying their grocery bag filled with chips, cookies, Kool-Aid, honey buns and Ramen soup! No meat or vegetables in the bag, yet many of them smiled, laughed and celebrated as if they just purchased groceries from Kroger, Walmart, or D'Agostino for a fourth of July cookout!* Then, they would say to each other "I'm eatin' good over here!" I thought to myself, well damn, if he thinks that's eating good, how would he describe a plate of meat, fish, rice, vegetables, potatoes, or macaroni and cheese? To the average mind and someone who is not uniquely familiar with law enforcement or sociology, this type of "normal behavior" is extremely strange. This type of behavior is a unique juxtaposition of how many inmates adapt to their circumstances while others don't engage in various types of peculiar behavior. The mature inmates just quietly carried their commissary to their cells. The flip side of this situation involved the inmates who had sad, puppy-dog expressions or stern looks on their face because they didn't have money for commissary.

Apparently, most of the inmates never learned the value of prioritizing duties, so they choose playful activities rather than responsible or beneficial activities, such as reading or doing homework for their GED class. For example, when inmates return from their work detail, most of them usually plop down in a chair in front of the TV, laugh and tell jokes about officers and other inmates or play cards. Even though the officer advises the inmates to shower first because the cut-off time for taking showers will not be extended, most of them still engage in playful activities rather than complete that important task of bathing. Later, when the officer tells them that it's time to lock down, they begin to give excuses as to why they haven't showered, so they get upset, curse, talk loudly about how the officer is "doing him wrong" and say how it's the officer's fault that they weren't allowed to shower! Frequently, inmates would forget items and ask to go back into their cell prior to the time to return to their cell even though they know it is a violation of procedure. When questioned as to why they forgot the items, they would state childish excuses, such as my friend was talking to me or the officer rushed me out of my cell so I didn't have time to get my soap, medicine, toilet tissue or wash towel. Rarely do they ever acknowledge that their negative situation was caused by their bad, impulsive or reckless decisions. **It is almost always someone else's fault!** Similar to not taking a shower in a timely manner, some inmates would stay awake in their cell laughing and talking throughout the night and go to sleep 2-3 hours before it's time to report for their early morning work detail. When the officer arrives to wake them up, they lie back down in the bed because they are too sleepy and too lazy to get up to handle the responsibility that they requested. Occasionally, after the officer leaves the post, the Inmate Worker will press the intercom and ask did the officer leave? He sure did, I reply. Are you gonna call him to come get me? No. Where were you when he walked to each cell and woke everybody up? "He woke me up but I had laid back down." Well, you made that choice, so you have to live with the consequences. In some instances when the officer did return a second time, the inmate often woke up grumbling, cursing or refusing to go to their work detail. Later, when the inmate has to explain his absence and disrespectful behavior, somehow or some way, it will be the officer's fault as to why he wasn't able to get enough sleep, wear his complete uniform or refused to go to his work detail. This behavior is very similar to those students who say they didn't do their homework because their dog ate it or we don't have a pencil or "pencil sharper" at home. **Excuses are the tools** of those who are lazy, hard-headed and lack ambition! For those inmates who aren't lazy and do have some manual labor skills, they are faced with another serious challenge. Most of them must be carefully supervised because of their inability to work independently without getting into mischief just like a child! Most often, the mischief is intentional, such as stealing food, breaking equipment to make weapons and attempting to walk into rooms and offices that are off limits to inmates. As a result, they get treated like children in that we don't allow them to have any extra materials, including pens, paper, paper clips, magazines, toilet tissue nor soap. Whether intentional or unintentional, the problem usually could have been avoided if the inmate had used some discipline, problem-solving or reasoning skills. Another issue that causes the need for close supervision is that most inmates lack the ability to receive and carry out multiple directions. One direction at a time is usually all they can handle. Their attention-span is as short as a second-grader.

Just like baby boys, an officer can almost always pacify inmates with the TV. The TV was so desired that inmates repeatedly asked officers to leave it on during periods when it was supposed to be off. Most inmates prefer to watch TV, sleep, and engage in frivolous activities for the entire day. These interests are symptomatic of boys and lazy people. Even the so-called thugs will calm down and obey directions when you turn on the TV. This is evidenced by the fact that inmates are on their best behavior on Sunday, football game day. In fact, inmates commit the least amount of violations and violence during the football season because they don't want to be locked down during a football game. The fights that did occur during the football season were usually related to somebody losing a bet on a game. The next best time of the year is during basketball playoffs, followed by baseball playoffs. When an officer turns the TV off, most baby boys start to whine and even the thugs have a temper tantrum! Many of them plead to watch TV "a little longer" just as a baby boy does. Oddly enough, even when the dayroom is on lockdown (their dayroom privileges have been suspended) for bad behavior, several of the inmates will beg the officer to turn on the TV. Again, only the immature mind of a baby boy believes that he should be allowed a privilege (viewing TV) during punishment! During a similar situation where the pod was on lockdown, we let an inmate out his cell to attend his visit from a family member. After the inmate returned from his visit and re-entered the pod, he pressed the intercom and asked me if I would turn on the TV. I said why would I do that? He said, so I can stay out and watch TV. I replied, son, if you would had remained legal, you could be at home watching TV for as long as you want. Once privileges have been suspended, I generally don't think that they should be reinstated before the designated time because leniency and inconsistency cause confusion and causes predators to think that you are weak!

It seems very odd and curious to me how the system enables the inmates by treating them like baby boys. The SOP required the officer to state the rules of the dayroom every day prior to the beginning of the rotation. Since the procedures are the same every day, why should the officer have to repeat the directions every day? If 2-3 new inmates arrive to the pod, they could simply ask their cellmate questions about daily procedures, read the Inmate Handbook or ask an officer. As a former educator, we didn't repeat directions to first and second-graders every day because they were required to remember and follow basic procedures. That is the basis for learning and understanding how to perform a routine! A major aspect of being a responsible adult is obeying rules and doing what is supposed to be done without requiring someone to tell you to do the same thing every day. Adult men follow directions the first time! Adult boys and baby boys require directions to be repeated frequently whenever there is a lack of enforcement. Adult boys and baby boys intentionally disobey directions and procedures. In their minds, that is a cool thing or tough guy thing to do. Unbeknownst to them, after years of disobedience, it's very difficult for them to maintain a quality job because of their inability to consistently follow procedures on a daily basis because it's not a part of their mindset or habit system. Thus, it's an undeveloped life-skill, which is necessary for adequate job performance. One must be able to adequately listen and follow directions, not to mention accept constructive criticism in regard to improving one's work perfor-mance. Developing the mentality to accept criticism is not easy! That's why it is very important to begin the process when children are young. Sometimes, it's challenging for mature adults to accept constructive criticism with a good disposition and make the nec-essary changes, much less an adult boy. Ultimately, he's mentally incapable of accepting and understanding constructive criticism as a critical part of the learning and maturation process! **We are creatures of conditioning.**

Those of us who have children know that boys in Kindergarten through fifth grade stand in a lunch line in the cafeteria to get their lunch. Fast forward 11-50 years later, he finds himself being told when, where and how to stand in line to receive his breakfast, lunch and dinner meals. When these boys began Kindergarten at 5-6 years old, they were taught how to walk in a line with their arms behind their back to help them refrain from touching the person in front of him. For some of the less disciplined boys, they had to get reminded of this simple task again and again and even into the fifth grade. Fast forward twelve years or more, some of the same baby boys find themselves being instructed to get in line to walk with their hands behind their back. It looks cute at 5-9 years old. It doesn't look cute at 17, 24, 37 or 46 years of age walking down a jail hallway! Inevitably, he feels like a boy because he must obey these childish rules. Sitting on a plastic container two inches off the floor inside of a cell and yelling out of the food trap in the door to ask if someone wants an apple for a bag of chips or a rack of cookies for a honey bun must be humiliating on some level. Thus, frustration and resentment from time to time or a weekly basis causes some of the adult boys to act out in boyish ways, such as cursing, shouting, fighting, banging and saying foul remarks. I imagine that some deep resentment and anger stems from a burning desire to feel respected and to have a better life, *yet dealing with the realization that he really has no substantial ideas about how to create a better life!* A really crazy irony is that when the temperature is warm or cold outside, but hot in the cells, sometimes I would see both inmates sleeping with their mats on the floor just like Pre-K and Kindergarten boys. The fact that so many inmates behave so immaturely makes this sight very profound!

Growing up, most baby boys begin their school career riding on a school bus. Ironically, inmates find themselves on a school bus again, except as baby boys and adult boys riding to the local courthouse, jail and prison. Mature men don't sleep in bunk beds at home. Inmates sleep in bunk beds. So again, **boyhood is revisited**. All of these situations from boyhood are present again in adulthood for the adult boys! The lunch tray is divided into sections, including a section for an apple. Now, isn't that a reflection of childhood! It certainly causes me to have a flashback to elementary school, so I imagine that it causes them to have a flashback also. It's no surprise that some of the boys get upset and attempt to resist the procedures of jail and prison because it causes them to feel childish. Yet, very rarely do any of the baby boys and adult boys acknowledge responsibility for their negative choices that put them in this position! This situation is truly indicative of a Shakespearean Tragic Comedy play!!!

The school has a classroom clown and the county jail has a dayroom clown. This baby boy or adult boy spends his days and nights acting silly, joking, laughing, playing and being disruptive and sometimes at the wrong time. He is likely to call you disparaging names and curse you out, then ask you for extra phone time during visitation, an extra meal or to go outside to recreation. This behavior is similar to the young class clown or bully who realizes that you have the best markers or you are having a birthday party with pizza and ice cream in the afternoon and now he wants to be your friend. No, no, no my brother! Your failure to abide by the grade school and church lessons about being polite and treat others as you would want them to treat you has caused you to miss out on a good experience once again. It's the same silly behavior for the same superficial reasons: pay attention to me; think of me as cool, see and hear me because I'm in charge of this pod; think of me as tough; I need attention because my self-esteem is low and I don't know how to gain attention by engaging in positive behavior and being exemplary in my responsibilities. It's very naive for the parent(s) to think that he will eventually grow out of that mindset when no corrective actions were implemented to show the child that his behavior was wrong and that attention can be gained through positive behavior, self-control and effort. Just like boys in school, even as young as third grade, attempt to take advantage of the teacher or substitute teacher by disobeying rules and standard procedures, inmates aggressively attempt to manipulate and take advantage of new officers. It isn't until the teacher and new officer are forced to demonstrate their toughness that the immature boys comply with the rules. Then, their childish thinking compels them to complain to their mother or the Sergeant about how mean and unfair the teacher or officer is. Every so often, I would feel a strong sense of despair, frustration and sadness whenever I thought about the large number of children trapped inside of adult bodies. This sentiment didn't relate just to the inmates, as some of my co-workers were included. My deep sense of sadness stems from the fact that most of these people have children! *How many days, weeks and years of unnecessary debilitating and traumatic situations would these children experience because of the disobedience, stubbornness, immaturity, misperceptions, neglect and dysfunctional actions of their parents?*

Signs of Baby boys and Adult boys

The first and most important step in dealing with a baby boy or adult boy *is recognizing that he is one!* Baby boys and adult boys exhibit the same characteristics as elementary boys. Some of those characteristics include, whining, pouting, tantrums, excessive playfulness, silliness, selfishness; impatience, irresponsibility, immaturity, poor decision-making skills, poor self-control, undeveloped listening and communication skills, undeveloped problem-solving skills, undeveloped comprehension skills, little to no work ethic, easily frustrated, excessive teasing/jonesin', run to a female (officer) to complain and ask for help in hopes of hearing a favorable answer, inability to follow simple directions, combative, controlling, chewing with mouth open (smacking or slurping food), bullying younger, weaker and even elderly and disabled people, attempting to gain access to things that they shouldn't have by way of manipulation or force, and very little to no understanding of manhood.

Instant gratification is a desire to receive what you want right away or as quickly as possible. Instant gratification involves a lack of patience and consideration of consequences in regard to short and long-term repercussions. You will often see this lack of ability in children, baby boys, unruly teens, adult boys and inmates. Baby boys and adult boys are used to instant gratification just like a child. They want what they asked for and they want to receive it at that moment or within a short amount of time. They want to receive the reward or compensation before they complete their assignment, whether it's a matter of waiting for a time-period, completing chores or completing a job. Usually, they were not properly taught how to wait to receive what they want, so they lack regard for circumstances, another person's time or whether that time is inappropriate. Instant gratification often leads to regret because it involves impatience, shallow thinking and unrealistic expectations, which often lead to disappointment, regret, anger and costly mistakes. Examples of instant gratification involve cutting in front of people in the food line, recess or any line that provides benefits or enjoyment and committing illegal acts to obtain money or stealing what doesn't belong to you! A person who has bad impulse-control hasn't mastered delayed gratification. Adult boys must be taught how to focus on short-term planning and avoid seeking instant gratification. There is a valid reason why old folks used to say good things come to those who wait. Patience is a virtue for sure! With respect to shallow thinking, have you ever experienced a situation where someone requested something from you and you said not now, but the person reacted as if you said no? Delayed and denied have two different meanings. Baby boys and adult boys must learn and understand the importance of delayed gratification! Delayed gratification is the ability to maintain patience, commitment and effort, usually for some months or years, until the time arrives for you to receive your benefit or achieve your goal. Delayed gratification is a very important life-skill to develop because it includes, patience, short and long-term planning, determination and focus.

Baby boys and adult boys, like most children, are naturally self-centered because they haven't learned how to share and still feel complete. Both want to control the environment for their satisfaction, despite the fact that their request or demand will inconvenience and put undue stress on others; despite the fact that their request violates rules; despite the fact that they are in an environment where they aren't in control of little more than their behavior. Their consistent attempts to control situations and dictate the terms of the operations are reflective of them never having authority over their lives. Their comprehension is skewed by their self-centered childish mentality and emotions. They engage in childish behavior, such as buying video games and expensive sneakers with their unemployment check even though they have been unemployed for more than six months. His sneaker collection is more valuable than his savings account! He might play video games for ten hours or more a week. Baby boys and adult boys are recognizable because they are easily insulted, which stems from low self-esteem. They become defensive quickly during a conversation because they feel like they are being personally attacked even when the comments are directed to a group. They lack forethought as evidenced by them saying and doing things without thinking about the negative repercussions and the biggest tell-tale sign is that they frequently engage in violence as if it will solve the problem or make the issue go away.

When a baby boy or adult boy isn't raised by his responsible and morally sound father or another man with wholesome characteristics, there is a higher tendency for the boy to obtain abusive traits. Adult boys develop a controlling mentality that fulfills their sad misinterpretation of being manly. This controlling behavior usually stems from them feeling frequently frustrated and powerless regarding their inability to achieve the things that they want in life, as well as their relative lack of progress in their lives! Also, their bloated ego or negative self-perception eventually manifests itself externally. While attending a seminar, I heard a speaker say that the most frustrated people in the world are people with goals that never become a reality. Likewise, some of the most frustrated people in the world are inmates who still possess the desire to do all of the things that a free man can do, but he is unable to do most of them because he gambled away his freedom. As an adult boy, rather than accept responsibility for his flaws and shortcomings, he blames his wife, girlfriend or baby momma. They tend to dominate their girlfriend, baby momma or wife instead of trying to develop a partnership through detailed conversations, kindness, understanding, compromise and sacrifice. Instead of demonstrating patience, composure, problem-solving skills and sacrifice during tough times, he has a tantrum and leaves home to "calm down with another lady," goes to a club or bar to get drunk, smoke weed with his homies or engages in other types of silly and immature behavior that is child-like instead of manly. Rather than sit down and discuss his difference in beliefs and strategies, he ignores or ridicules her opinions and beliefs because they are different from his. It is likely that he will frequently belittle her because he gets satisfaction from making her feel unintelligent, inferior or sad. Isn't that what many children do? Tease their friends or strangers by calling them names, insulting them about how they look, talk, act or a feat that the person doesn't do well or can't do at all. In contrast, a mature boy who has grown into a mature man can accept her opposing views or beliefs and respond with logical and knowledgeable words. Through this type of reasonable conversation, he will be able to determine if he will be able to persuade her, have to compromise, sacrifice the issue for the bigger picture or find a mediator to help reach a solution for a critical issue. He will not try to convince her to agree with him through manipulation or verbal and physical threats. Conversely, in some instances where an adult boy is faced with her opposing views or beliefs, he decides to intimidate her by threatening to use force and in plenty of cases, he does use force. As we know, many women are physically abused by their boyfriend or husband. While working in the Release department of the jail, it's strangely interesting to hear the conversation between the female officers who work in Release and the males who have been charged with domestic battery and are about to get released. The officer may ask the man to recite the special conditions of his release. Then, she may tell him *"make sure you keep your hands off that lady."* Sometimes, the guy has a smirk on his face or says something simple-minded like "she hit me first or she be disrespecting me." Just like a boy, he makes excuses frequently for his negative or abusive behavior. He will likely continue the behavior until sternly punished or he receives devastating consequences for his callous behavior. The consequences may come from her father, brother, court system or her when she reaches her emotional breaking point.

Adult boys are very selfish. Consequently, they are insensitive to the feelings of their mother, girlfriend or wife. One day while I was sitting at the Security desk at a medical facility, just as the elevator door opened, a Caucasian male who looked about forty, walked briskly out of the elevator saying loudly "you wonder why I don't want to have kids with you!" His head was down and his face was flushed, looking like he was having a full tantrum. As the lady exited the elevator after him, she looked around and when her eyes met mine, she looked hurt and embarrassed. He stormed off into the parking lot and left her sitting in front of the building waiting on Uber. This kind of insensitivity and immaturity leads to public humiliation. The logic of adult boys is selfish and irrational, such as he can have female friends, but she can't have any male friends including the guy she knew before him. He believes that he is your be-all-end-all male! His selfishness allows him to accept an expensive gift from a lady even though he knows that he hasn't bought her a gift of similar value, he doesn't intend on having a serious relationship with her, or he knows that it's too early in the relationship to receive a gift of that nature based on the status of their relationship! I witnessed several instances when the smitten lady bought the guy a $200 watch for Christmas and he bought her some perfume from the barbershop. In another instance, she bought him $175 sneakers for his birthday and when her birthday arrived he gave her a $20 set of matching candles from Bath and Body. It usually works out better for the lady when she waits for the man to demonstrate his deep sense of care, love and commitment. Adult boys consistently make a big deal about minor issues. Adult boys hold grudges for lengthy periods or years without attempting to apologize when they are wrong, or resolve the problem or release the issue and move on in a positive manner. On the other hand, mature men easily recognize when an issue is minor and know that it has no major impact on the main situation or their main goal. It is very tiring, mentally and emotionally, for children and women who are faced with dealing with a selfish and irrational adult boy. The children don't receive the resources that they need physically and emotionally because the adult boy (father) is focused on satisfying his wants. The mother doesn't receive the support that she needs because the adult boy claims that he needs time for himself so he can hang with his frat brothers, go to the club, meet his boys for drinks and unwind from the pressure of his job or some other lame excuse. If you were to examine the childhood of adult boys and inmates, I'm sure that you would find that most of them had these characteristics.

Chapter 2

Parenting

I find it incredibly odd how a man and a lady realize that they *aren't compatible, don't have enough values in common, nor love or trust each other enough to get married,* yet they find enough like and confidence **to create a child** that will require an extraordinary amount of conversation, collaboration, trust, love, compatibility, time, sacrifice, finances, patience, planning and compromise for at least twenty-one years. There is something **tragically illogical** about that type of decision-making. Most of the time, *compatibility reduces the amount of conflict that a couple will have.* If they believe in a dual-parent household, mutual respect, honesty, conflict resolution, obligation, the same religion, were raised in the same or similar positive family environment, believe in a strong work ethic, believe in always saving part of their earnings, believe in compromising, believe that a high-quality man and woman are equally important to the success of the family, then the **probability** of their long-term success is much greater. Ladies, when both of you are mature and compatible on all or most of your fundamental values and you are treating him like a king (only if he is treating you like a queen), he will sing *Tyrese's Takeover*! Then, both of you will continue to grow stronger and higher. If you don't hear the sentiments of that song or one with a similar message in a suitable time period, you might consider singing Fantasia's Lose to Win, Bittersweet or Jaguar Wright's Free. Rationally speaking, if he doesn't like, trust, respect, understand and love you enough to commit to marrying you before the baby is born, **how does it seem rational that he will fully commit to his child on a daily basis for the first twenty-one years**? For those adults twenty-five and older, the decision says that we are not compatible and I don't trust you enough to be a committed part of your life. As a result, how is it reasonably logical for others to conclude that the two of you will be compatible enough to make mutually beneficial long-term decisions for the child? Those decisions will require a moderate level of trust. For the girl or lady who says that *she doesn't think that she must have a mutual level of respect, understanding, admiration and participation from the father in order to have a family, I implore you not to place those multiple disadvantages upon the child.*

Having a child or children doesn't qualify you as an adult, nor a good parent. It qualifies you as an adult with a child or in some cases, a *person of child-bearing age with a child*. Likewise, having a car and a license doesn't qualify you as a good driver, nor does owning a rope and a horse make you a cowboy! A few decades ago there was a popular phrase that referred to teens becoming pregnant as **"babies having babies"** and it appears that many people perceived it as affluent and conceited people carelessly criticizing underprivileged people. However, I believe that anybody who disagreed with that sentiment failed to consider the factors of the reality of that situation. Regarding most teens between 14-19 years of age, their brain has not come close to full mental development. Therefore, the adolescent girl lacks the maturity to make all of the responsible decisions that are required to properly raise a baby. Furthermore, most teens in this age group are still having their needs provided for, such as food, clothing and housing provided by a parent or some other adult(s). That being the case, it is very unlikely that a teen will have the ability to successfully provide for the material needs of the child. Obviously, it is not likely that they will be able to provide for the emotional needs of the child because their emotions are not fully developed. Inasmuch as teens and young adults claim to be grown enough to make mature decisions, they usually don't, which was the case of the Georgia mother who left her infant alone in her apartment while she went to run errands. In addition to the horrible decision to leave the infant alone, she was driving without a license. Subsequently, the twenty-one-year-old mother was stopped and arrested by the police. Horrible decisions like this are reflective of someone who doesn't have the maturity, nor good decision-making skills to raise a child.

Children/Gift

It is an extremely special blessing to give birth to a child! For any male or female who doesn't fully recognize the gravity of creating a life and all of the serious responsibilities that are included, therein lies the root problem. Again, we are faced with considering *one's understanding of purpose.* A parent's most critical responsibility is to **steadfastly train the child so that she or he remains a gift** when he goes to school, a friend's home or some other public place. Without the proper nurturing and training, the gift develops into a problem. A parent can send their gift to any classroom and the teacher will gladly accept your young princess or prince. On the other hand, very few teachers are willing to accept your problem, but they are required to do so. Parents only need to truthfully acknowledge that they don't desire to accept someone else's problem, whether young or teenager. I contend that most teachers and adults who have jobs that involve teaching, training and supervising children don't mind accepting a challenging child. However, there are some serious differences between a challenge and a problem. A challenging child requires additional instruction, practice and encouragement! He puts forth minimum to moderate effort to learn. He is obedient, nice, respectful, well-mannered and cooperative. A problem child also requires additional instruction, practice and encouragement. However, he puts forth minimum to no effort to learn! He is disobedient, disrespectful, stubborn, uncooperative and shows no desire to learn! What is a teacher or adult supervisor to do? *No matter how good your seed, information or wisdom is,* **the soil must be good in order for you to reap a good harvest**! No matter how talented the teacher, coach, or painter is, they must be given the necessary ingredients to use in order to produce something significant, beautiful, valuable or long-lasting. Given the wrong ingredients, the product will be basic, lackluster, insignificant or incomplete. Good-hearted people enjoy spending their time helping boys and girls because it makes us happy! But, we feel sad when boys and girls disregard our help because we realize that this behavior will most likely lead to them having serious struggles dealing with the responsibilities of life. Also, we feel sad because it causes us to waste our time! When, not if a person stops helping you, it doesn't mean that the person doesn't like you. It means that they don't like wasting their time and have decided not to waste any more time with you!

In regard to people referring to the 90's children as the Lost Generation, I heard the incredible Andrew Young say show me a *generation of lost children and I'll show you a* **generation of parents who lost them**! I agree completely because parents are responsible for raising children because they are incapable of raising themselves! I've often heard people say publicly, what's wrong with these children! Yet, I haven't heard people frequently ask **what's wrong with these parents**? Family dynamics usually provide an accurate snapshot of the personality traits and foreshadow the behavioral actions and future conditions of the child. Other issues are relevant and necessary to resolve, but secondary to addressing issues related to the root cause, which are family dynamics. This fact is supported by social workers, counselors, psychologists and educators! Children's beliefs are shaped and determined by the way their parents negatively or positively perceive family, friends, education, honesty, violence, drugs, work ethic, society, health, etc. James Baldwin said "the situation of our youth is not mysterious. Children have never been good at listening to their elders, but they have never failed to imitate them." Thus, children are imitating our violence, rudeness, laziness, jealousy, drug and alcohol abuse, mean-spiritedness, ungratefulness, impatience, aggression, bewilderment, slickness, greed, hopelessness, disobedience of directions, rules and procedures, optimism, ingenuity, excellence, kindness, compassion and resilience. As we know, children don't mysteriously appear on earth! They are created and born by the same method that they were thousands of years ago. I contend that the drastic difference is the moral competency level of the parents to which the children are born. Babies should not be used as a means to keep the father connected to the mother in hopes of him wanting to build a family life with the mother and they definitely should not be used as a means of employment for the mother. **Babies aren't born with a don't give a damn attitude**. That attitude comes from a home that has a lot of hostility, animosity, irrational beliefs and treats the child in a discouraging, unsupportive and unloving manner. This is the reason for the scowl on their face while the charges are being read in the courtroom or the disciplinary hearing in middle and high school. Years of bitterness, neglect, resentment, despair and failure are stirring the boy's emotions and fogging his brain. **Babies aren't born using drugs, but they are born addicted to drugs**! How unbelievably sad and upsetting it is for nurses, educators, counselors and responsible family members to realize that a female placed such a serious and possibly permanent disability upon a baby!

Children are soil and we are called to sow into them! If you don't care for your child with continuous love and nurturing, *the child will lack the intimate knowledge of what it feels like to be valued.* Given this practical fact, it's basically indifference and disillusionment on behalf of the family, DFACS and society at large, to behave in a surprised manner when we see and hear about violent and self-destructive behavior! There is a short, but very powerful African Proverb that says: *In a broken nest, there are few whole eggs.*" If the nest is equated to parents, then it is the children's lives that are not whole, but rather incomplete, stunted and severely damaged! They need to be protected from all forms of negative behavior and abuse, including basic neglect of quality time. Children must be nurtured emotionally, spiritually, mentally and physically. The family should be a place of provision, protection and preparation! Credible research shows that many emotional issues originate in childhood! Until corrective actions are implemented to resolve the issue, the issue grows deeper and remains throughout life. Thus, when the child reaches his tween and teen years, he doesn't feel loved. Consequently, he doesn't feel important to people, despite any outward displays of bravado. Inner emotions always supersede and control outer emotions! **Equally tragic to not feeling important to people is the consequence that people are not important to him!** After the horrible crime/"mistake" has occurred, some people wonder why he is in such a dire and irrational predicament at the tender young age of 11, 12 or 14-21. What too many of us don't realize is that the boy/girl has been feeling neglected, abused, frustrated and angry since eight-years-old! Thus, these negative emotions have been simmering for 6-10 years. When you analyze this carefully, the years have amounted to *72-120 months of suffering.* That's a long damn time for most adults, much less children. God forbid that his home environment was so dysfunctional that these negative qualities existed every week. In that case, the same suffering has existed for 312-520 weeks. That's a long, long damn time! Just like a volcano, he erupts! Some physical reactions follow the same laws of nature. In most instances, the children suffer from C.G.R.-Can't Get Right! The children can't get right because the parents are not right, in many instances. If you tell your children that they don't have to obey adults, then they will pick and choose when to obey adults. It doesn't register to you that you are setting them up for failure, but that's exactly what you have done. When you send your cute eight-year-old Pienetha to school with this message "my momma said she don't like men teachers," and she says it with a funky attitude like you rehearsed it with her, you have filled her with all kinds of misguidance that will very likely lead to misfortune in her future. This was definitely one of the shocking moments of my educational career. I was shocked at how adults with children would pour such toxic information into the undeveloped minds of children who are unable to understand how their future is being damaged and in many cases destroyed!

Children require morally sound instruction from their toddler years through the teen years in order to increase their chances of becoming a productive and socially responsible adult. When they rebel against it, the correct response is to stand firm with your instruction, not give in to their resistance. Then, they will learn how to conform to directions and structure. Then, they will learn that they must conform to their parents and authority figures. Too often, I see parents conforming to their children. Children's mentality hardly ever benefit from being appeased in situations where they should conform. This illogical reversal of leadership often leads to wayward and unruly children because they have learned an incorrect perception of society! This gross error is also present in many schools. That's why you hear students using foul and profane language around teachers and you see students walking and brushing into teachers instead of moving out of the way of an adult. **Victory is not accomplished without conflict**! The maestro Barry White said it best, "too much of anything is not good for you." Boys and girls require a consistent balance of love, nurturing, instruction and discipline from their mother, father and other caring adults.

I believe that obedience is the first character trait that parents should teach and enforce upon their child. Once your child learns this trait, he will be able to successfully learn and develop all other positive character traits and necessary skills. Obedience establishes the ability to follow directions! The ability to follow directions during regular situations make it possible to follow directions during urgent situations. Learning and understanding stem from obedience. Trust develops from obedience. For example, trust in you comes from your child obeying your commands. When you hold out your arms and tell your baby to jump off the bed, your baby learns to enjoy this made-up game after you catch her the first, second and third time. You must catch your baby every time! **Consistency** is crucial to building trust. If you ever let your baby drop to the floor, the trust will be destroyed. When you stand your baby up and tell her to walk to you, she will because her small mind has developed trust to believe that you will catch her before she falls down. When the teacher says that you must show your work for the division problems, that means that you must write out each step. This allows the teacher to identify where you need help when you get the wrong answer. You can't just write an answer, as I've seen done on a state test, because you don't want to obey directions or you are lazy.

Parental Qualities

I contend that a *measurable combination of maturity, love, knowledge, respect, power and fear is necessary to raise children successfully.* In most instances, a mother lacks the physical power to control her son(s), whereas a father has the power to control his son(s), in most instances. Of the aforementioned qualities, I believe that a parent must have two of those qualities to effectively raise their children.

They must command **respect and fear**. Both respect and fear are effective methods of establishing boundaries! Ideally, you teach your children to show respect for you, themselves, others, animals and things. As they mature, that respect develops into reverence for you. If you are lucky enough to raise a child who never challenges your authority, you don't have to deal any fear cards and know that you are uniquely blessed. However, most children do challenge their parent's authority at some age and that is when it is necessary to instill fear. Fear is a beneficial quality. When we see our mother or father get upset and then deliver a verbal or physical lashing because of our blatant disobedience, disrespect or bad choice, we learn not to engage in that behavior again. If we see a dangerous animal, such as a pit bull, bear or snake, we stop and walk or run in the other direction. If we see two people or group of people about to get into an altercation, we walk or run in the opposite direction. If we see a house sign that says we shoot, we don't call 911, we ask if we can get our ball out of the yard instead of just walking through the gate. Have you ever heard of a bully picking on someone that was bigger than him or a kid that he thought he couldn't beat? Does a tiger attack a grown elephant or baby elephant? One wolf will not attack a lion, but a pack of wolves will. When I was a kid playing stickball in the street, we hardly ever snuck into Mr. Mapp's yard to retrieve our ball because he was mean and we were afraid of what he might say or do if he caught us in his yard. We wouldn't do anything other than pick up our ball, but this man didn't seem to care for adolescents at all. The interesting thing was that his wife was the nicest lady and didn't mind us asking her if we could get our ball. When people don't respect or fear another person, that relationship is likely to be abusive on some level. A person must have respect for the other person in order to treat the person decently and fairly, or the person must fear the other person and that fear will prevent him or her from attempting to abuse the other person. To my surprise, I witnessed grandchildren as early as the fifth grade

(10 years old) realize that their grandparents are elderly, sickly or both. As a result, the children don't fear their grandparents because they realize that they are too weak to punish them with a whipping or enforce behavior-altering punishment. For the most part, the grands can only make empty threats and pray for obedience and improvement. Consequently, some grandchildren continue being disobedient, disrespectful and become more embolden as they get older. What a sad predicament and stressful burden for "parents" to toss upon grandparents. Now we see how irresponsibility affects multiple people and multiple generations! During my time as a fifth-grade teacher, Greg was failing three of the core subjects. The assistant principal and I arranged for Greg to attend tutoring with me before school began. After Greg missed the first week of tutoring, I met his grandmother in the carpool lane and asked her why he hadn't been arriving for tutoring in the morning. She told me that he would get back in bed with his clothes on after she woke him up. Such blatant disrespect at the tender age of twelve made my head hot. According to his grandmother, both of his parents were drug addicts and her son, Greg's father, was in and out of prison. Her husband was too sickly to help out. Once you factor in the fact that Greg had been held back once and he was still performing two grade levels below the fifth grade, you can foresee that you have the elements of a probable future tragedy!

Even though many inmates disliked me, they respected me enough to obey my commands because they knew that I would deliver the punishment that I said! Even when I didn't say anything to those who chose to disobey, they knew for sure punishment would be forthcoming! They knew that I would lock them in their cell for a day or two. It may happen every time I saw him for a week. They knew that I would write a citation and cause them to lose their commissary, visitation, recreation or all three. Inmates frequently said to me, you must have been in the military. Or they said, Johnson, what part of the military were you in. It's interesting and revealing that they associated my structure and discipline with the military and not with manhood or fatherhood. Every so often, baby boys and adult boys between the ages of 17-35 would "try me" by cursing at me or disobeying my commands. As soon as they started talking loud, simple shid, mean-mugging and grabbing their groin, I could immediately tell by their words and actions that they had not been consistently fathered by a strong, caring and responsible man. Nonetheless, I always thought *they gonna learn today*! It didn't matter to me whether they learned the lesson that day, two days later, two weeks later or two months later, but eventually they learned that respect and obedience were mandatory during my shift! They would have to clown around and be disrespectful on another shift. The important factor was for me to not give in before I broke him! That was when I applied the Biblical saying *"And let us not grow weary while doing good, for in due season we shall reap if we do not Lose Heart."* Galatians 6:9. These boys were unaware that men who were consistently raised by their strong, caring and responsible father, especially when he lived in the household, were trained not only how to defend against various types of challenges, but also to expect challenges! It doesn't matter whether it involves a bully at school or in the neighborhood, two alpha males on the same team, at the same job or a young son feeling himself and deciding to test the rules of his parents. Challenges will happen in life and it's important to know how to deal with them effectively. With respect to parents, particularly the father, after the fear stage goes away when the father becomes older or elderly and he is no longer able to control his son(s) physically, the respect principle remains! This reverence is completely strong enough to prevent the son from disrespecting his parents because it is embedded in his mentality. When a disagreement occurs, most likely it will not involve a level of moderate or severe disrespect. My father has been elderly for a long time. Although we've had some important disagreements, *I firmly believe in the respect principle that he instilled in me.* Therefore, it has never occurred to me to disrespect my dad or attempt to take advantage of him now that he is frail.

Most women are unable to instill fear in their son(s) or daughter for various reasons. It could be because of their size, age, size of their child or moral beliefs. This is a dangerous period to enter because when people lose respect for you, they tend to abuse you subtly or overtly. The son has lost respect for his mother when he stops doing chores, doing homework, going to school, violating curfew, talking back, using profanity, walks away while she is talking, invites rude and unsavory people into her home, etc. I get irritated every time I see a baby boy or teenage boy frowning while his mother is attempting to help him! I've seen it at the auto part store, grocery store, department store (shoe or suit dept), school, jail and the courthouse. Has anybody else noticed this scene? The nerve of him to talk with a scowl on his face and sound disgusted as if the mother isn't helping him with a predicament that he can't handle. If most women can't control and influence children, the chances of controlling a man are highly, highly unlikely. That's basic common sense! You don't need to study human behavior to reach that conclusion. Clearly, the dynamics are totally different in that a man is usually bigger, stronger, probably intimidating and may have helpful resources such as a job, money, car and maybe the skills to repair items on the car or around the house.

I'm reminded of the numerous times that I've heard more than a few mothers say *"he's outta control; I don't know what I'm going to do with him,"* in reference to their child in Kindergarten through fifth grade. Immediately, I'm thinking that she must have some shallow parenting skills since she is struggling to control a child, not to mention a child under twelve. Then, my mind begins to think about the unfortunate struggles that these boys are going to experience simply because of the lack of maturity, preparation, knowledge and commitment of these "mothers and fathers." Mothers and ladies need to realize that it's a gradual progression from the baby boy tantrum to the teenager and adult boy violent tantrum. Discipline requires structure, strategy, control and patience. If a child does something wrong ten times, you should correct her at least eight times. If an inmate is out of pocket ten times, you must check him 9 ½ times. The way that you check your child can vary, just the way I checked inmates varied. Each check doesn't have to be stern! However, if the situation requires a stern check for each incident, then that's just how you should handle it! Sometimes, situations have to be dealt with consistently and harshly for the lesson to be learned or the corrective actions to be effective. Unfortunately, this same lack of control reappears every time you see and hear a mother in court pleading for the judge to have mercy on her "good boy or troubled boy." However, the judge probably reaches the logical conclusion that since you can't control his actions, he may as well receive a sentence that will keep him out of society for a very long time or forever, which will prevent him for being able to hurt other people! On that issue, we've got to maintain our integrity and humility by admitting when our child or other loved one has committed a horrible crime. As a parent, don't give a news interview, get on social media or plead in court that your son didn't commit the crime when his face is on camera, overwhelming evidence demonstrates that he did it or this is his 2nd or 3rd time being charged with a similar crime. Any attempt to deny, justify or excuse an intentional violent act only causes you to appear unsympathetic, unremorseful, and perhaps delusional!

Mom's lack of control was fully on display at the jail on a weekly basis. After a mother completed her visit with her son, she pressed the intercom and said thank you officer. I clearly remember this encounter because of the contrasting behaviors. Her voice sounded pleasant and sincere and it was uncommon for visitors to say thank you. Conversely, her baby boy exited the Visiting Area and walked past three pods throwing up gang signs to other inmates. The fact of the matter is that too many women don't have the natural abilities to influence their son(s) to behave in a mature and respectful manner outside of their presence. My mother's influence extended completely beyond her presence, so much so that the thought of dishonoring her factored into every seriously foolish thought that entered my mind and prevented me from doing it. That was my mentality, not only due to the nurturing and values that she instilled, but mainly due to the reinforcement that my father provided. As a teenager, I knew that my mother couldn't physically hurt me, but I knew that my dad could still bring the pain. Every now and then when I'm in church, this notion of mom's lack of control enters my mind when I see a mother walking into church with one or two boys walking behind her. Frequently, I notice the boy walking reluctantly as if he is being taken to see a judge. The second thing I notice is the boy's sagging pants (jeans)! His shirt is hanging out over his butt as if people won't realize that his pants are sagging. Sometimes, the shirt is worn in a way that the underwear is showing, which should be considered sacrilegious! This is reminiscent of the day I was standing outside the lobby of my job. As a car pulled up, I heard the doors open behind me. As I turned around, I saw a lady exiting the building on crutches. As the lady approached the car, a boy who looked approximately fifteen hopped out to open the passenger door. After he opened the door, he bent over to move something out of the seat and his pants dropped down and his whole butt was exposed. His mother immediately quipped "Jaytron, don't try me!" From my viewpoint, he already did. Subconsciously or consciously, he just showed you his ass! First, why doesn't he have a belt on when his pants have belt loops? Secondly, he knew that he was going to his mother's job, so he should had been dressed properly. Thirdly, when you have complete respect for a person and you know that she or he renders repercussions for silly errors and intentional violations, you always stay on point!

This "trendy style" of pants sagging extends to adult boys also, as I saw a seemingly nice lady who appeared to be in her early thirties, walking with two young princesses in an office building and the apparent father trailing them while holding his crotch because he wasn't wearing a belt to hold up his jeans. This kind of foolery in public is indicative of a high level of ignorance and a lack of self-respect. In general, I can't count the number of times that I've seen an attractive lady walking with her boy(s) and his underwear was showing or his pants were sagging. From a romantic view, I was attracted to the lady, but I was reluctant to get to know the lady because her child's behavior made me question her values! She had to be aware of his attire because I always noticed my child's attire whenever she was with me. This issue simply boils down to a matter of training, respect and discipline. If the son doesn't respect his mom enough to dress decently, then the chances of him respecting me are probably slimmer, especially when you consider that I would engage in constructive criticism by telling him that his behavior is dead wrong. Thus, irrational reasoning will cause him to believe that what he is doing is right because he thinks so or "that's what all my friends are doing" or because his mom allows it! Similarly, a young girl wears her "freakum dress" during the summer and you can plainly see her underwear. First of all, I'm wondering why a high school girl has a "freakum dress," but that's a whole additional discussion. Once she gets older, she's the lady in church wearing the low cut blouse or dress that shows the tattoo on her breast. There's a famous quote that says **everything should be done in decency and order**. When you allow a toddler to do what she wants, she will. When you allow a child to do what he wants, he will. When you allow a person to act a fool, the person will. The same concept applies to a teenager, adult boy and inmate. There must be structure, procedures and consequences in place if you expect to have order, decency, respect, **consistency**, peace, productivity and progress! Some time ago, I had an unsettling experience in church, which was quite disturbing because I usually have a great experience. Shortly after service began, a mother and her three children sat near me and her fifteen-year-old-looking son sat beside me. On 2-3 occasions during service, the pastor instructed the members to hold hands in prayer. Each time the mother had to interrupt her prayer and mine to tell her son to stand up. Then, he would sit down before the prayer was over. By the time we stood for prayer and benediction, he was partially sitting his butt on top of the pew in front of us. Needless to say, I was upset and embarrassed and those are not the emotions that you want to feel when you leave church!

If the mom can't enforce appropriate and decent dress for a holy place, I'm almost certain that the boy will not dress decently for any other place. Now when I was growing up in the 70s and 80s, children were almost always finely dressed in "church clothes" just as their parents were. When you look at photos of African-Americans 1-2 generations ago and even in the early 1900s, you can clearly see by the way they were dressed that they had a **solid amount of pride**. This pride was also revealed in the way they spoke and behaved. African-Americans wore suits, dresses and other fine garments to the movies, nightclubs, dates and meetings. They even wore their dress clothes on a free date, which consisted of walking around the streets of Harlem and on the streets of other major cities. I know this is true because my parents have pictures showing the fine haberdashery of themselves, family and friends. All of us know that they wore their best clothing to church! Church clothes consisted of slacks, shoes, blouse, dress, skirt, tie, suit and white shirt of dress fabric! This appearance was practically mandatory as a demonstration of your respect for yourself, church family and reverence for the church you were entering! This doesn't mean that people were better during that period, but it does show that there was a *mutually general understanding of an appropriate dress code*! It's critically important to teach children how to abide by protocol, so that they aren't inexperienced and look lost as an adult and risk being embarrassed because they are in a situation that requires appropriate dress or following protocol! In my opinion, the belief that you can dress however you want, as long as you go to church with me, sends the wrong message to a child. As a result, he puts on his hoodie, jeans sagging and sneakers. At what age will he learn the appropriateness of business attire? He should know the feeling of wearing a dress shirt and dress shoes other than to a funeral and before high school graduation. The option should be either you will go to church with me dressed appropriately and have a pleasant look on your face (because demeanor is important in life) or you will stay home. If you stay home, you will suffer the consequences. Have you ever seen those Facebook posts where a Good Samaritan helps a teenager or young man tie his tie before an interview? It's a generous act, but odd because it speaks to important basics that aren't being taught, nor required at home.

Dual-Parent Household

I completely believe in the benefits of mom and dad living under one roof. **I believe our roles are mutually exclusive and inextricable!** By nature, we can't create a family without each other. **We need each other for the health of our families!** You don't have to believe me, just listen to the profound lyrics of the song "**Family Reunion**" by the legendary O'Jays! After you listen to it once, play it a second time to really let the message sink in. Then, you can decide if the song is filled with wisdom and accurately describes the importance of the structure of the family! Too often, we behave with a competitive mentality. *Women think, I'll show him that I don't need him! Men think, I'll show her that she will struggle without me!* Sadly, we fail to recognize that this mentality is wrong and harmful to ourselves and moreso to the children. We were and are meant to operate in unison. Whether you analyze the traditional stay-at-home mom, the contemporary stay-at-home dad or the dual-parent working home, I believe it's a necessity for someone to anchor the home! Their primary responsibilities include establishing the foundation of the child, such as nurturing, protection, education, discipline and instilling morals during the formative years. One of the most important qualities a child needs is quality time. Continuous quality time! I don't think it's possible for a man to spend quality time with his children when they reside in three or four different households. Of course, mom has to work to earn money to provide shelter, food and clothing. Nevertheless, this neglect of quality and instructional time is harmful because a child needs his mom and dad to spend adequate time supervising and practicing his homework, supervising his interaction with his brother and sister, instilling positive character traits, demonstrating how to eat properly, perform chores, perform hygiene procedures properly, play fairly, share, solve problems and just listen to him talk about topics that are on his mind! If the most important aspects of parenting involved exceptional housing, clothing, food and money, all affluent children would be problemless and we all know that isn't true! They commit crimes, use drugs, drop out of school and commit suicide just like other children. Another important aspect is for the mother to witness how a caring father disciplines his children with love, especially his son! When a good father raises his boy, he will allow him to cry for good cause, but he will not allow him to whine and pout. No man likes to be around a whinny boy and he definitely can't stand being around a whinny adult boy. A good father will discipline firmly and with intensity when necessary. Tough love is strong, yet flexible and affirming! It's the duty of the parents to correct their child with love for their own good, for it's easier to bend a branch when it is young and undeveloped. As the boy reaches his tween and teen years, he understands that his father's reprimand is backed up by a force that is powerful and one that his mother does not possess. It is unlikely for many women to discipline in this manner because their natural instinct is to be nurturing. In those cases where the mother attempts to firmly discipline her son, she may lack the ability because of her size or the size of her son. Since many women grow up without witnessing this aspect, many women tend to prevent a man from disciplining a boy because they interpret the treatment as harsh. Consequently, the boy grows up without learning how to cope with firm and intense consequences from mistakes or intentional bad choices. These same boys grow up without experiencing how to cope with a stern verbal reprimand from their father, which is totally different from their mother. While teaching, I could always identify boys who were being raised without their father in their lives on a daily basis by the way they responded to my verbal reprimand. Usually, the boy would immediately get angry, have a dramatic tantrum as if someone choked him, cry or yell and sometimes throw items. A definite sign was when the boy said, *"you're not my mother, I don't have to listen to you."* Notice that he didn't say, **"you're not my father."**

Likewise, many young girls grow up without feeling and seeing the love and protection that their father provides to them and the family. They don't witness their father performing his responsibilities along with their mother. They are deprived of seeing and hearing mom and dad talk about daily activities like work, dealing with co-workers, church functions, supporting and evaluating school performance, paying bills, saving money to attend summer camp or how they saved money for vacation as they drive down the highway, walk through Six Flags, Disney World or spend time on a beach. They don't get to see how dad increases his duties when mom is sick, working late; how dad washes the laundry, cooks limited meals or buys fast food for five days in a row, bathes and dresses his children, but doesn't style his daughter's hair. Dad says, I let my sister do that! They are deprived of witnessing mom and dad interact as a team! They miss the opportunities to witness a small portion of a civilized disagreement between their father and mother and then see their dad kiss mom on her cheek later that day or the next. They are deprived of the **consistent** affection, protection and affirmation that a loving father provides. The weekly hugs and encouraging words from dad are invaluable! They are deprived of witnessing all of the fundamental and crucial roles that a father performs in the household. This is why two ladies wrote a book entitled *The Fatherless Daughter Project*. These ladies recognized the significant role of the father in his daughter's life. The daughters miss the many positive influences of a loving and morally sound father. The book explores the negative effects of fatherlessness, such as distrust, anger, abandonment, resentment and self-doubt. The goal of the book is to help girls and ladies to recognize, cope, understand and overcome the various ways that the absence of their father has impacted their life.

Some females see a male and think that he is a good quality man. Months or years after the child is born, she is suddenly experiencing a lot of childish behavior. Yet, it never occurs to her that she was raised without a high-quality man in her life, so how would she recognize the fundamental characteristics of a high-quality man? *How does she know what fatherhood, respect, discipline and compromise look like? How does she know what love, unwavering commitment and loyalty feel like?* As a result, the cycle of single motherhood is perpetuated because a home without a father is all the girls know, so it appears normal and acceptable to them. Her mother operated the household without a father and mom probably didn't encourage her daughter(s) to form a fundamental bond and commitment with a man with whom she could build a family. Just because you don't miss what you have never had, doesn't mean that what you are missing doesn't have a devastating impact or long-term negative impact on your life! Some rural or economically deprived people may not go to the dentist, but you can believe it has a negative impact on their teeth, diet and health.

Simply because something is possible to do and is prevalent (single-parenting, tattoos, smoking), doesn't mean that it is beneficial for you to do it. This is especially true of women having babies before getting married to a responsible man who has specifically told you that he wants to raise children with you. The reason that it's important for him to make this declaration is that you may have married a man who doesn't want to have a child with you. Sure, your mother may have done it, which consciously or subconsciously led you to believe that it was alright to do because you believe that you turned out fine, although you have repeated a cycle that is filled with numerous obstacles and disadvantages; although you frequently complain about being tired, not having any help and how hard it is raising children alone. Now, you are at work trying to juggle your schedule because you won't be home during dinner hours or you are too tired to cook, or you are trying to attend a Parent-Teacher Conference (PTC) or extracurricular event. These are just a few of the times when it would be beneficial to have a husband who would take over when you are feeling tired, sick or overloaded. Then, you end up talking to male coworkers or acquaintances about discipline and respect problems with your son or boys who are now too big for you to discipline. Now that your son realizes that you can no longer hurt him physically, **he decides when and where he wants to obey your rules and show you respect**! Your daughter repeatedly selects negative young dudes to date because she didn't grow up with a mature father in the house, so she didn't get to witness how a responsible and well-mannered man lovingly and respectfully treats his lady or wife and handles his responsibilities.

Children are born, but adults are created! Consequently, *women have to seriously consider how much responsibility they bear in creating baby boys and adult boys, perpetuating the cycle of non-residential fathers and the decline of married families,* **so we can get back to raising Boys to Men**! Many women complain that it is very difficult to find a man who wants to get married or commit to a long-term relationship and raise a family in one home. Yet, these women proclaim that it's fine being a single parent and firmly believe that they are capable of raising a boy into a man. Furthermore, I believe that too many women are under the **false belief that they can adequately**

raise a boy into a man! Most likely, your mother and thousands of other women held this same belief. This pseudo-myth has become accepted as truth over the years in some circles. A generation later, you are creating the same dilemma for a sweet, productive, self-sufficient and caring young lady who is strongly interested in creating a family with a man who has the same good characteristics that she possesses. Which came first, the chicken or egg? Who bears more responsibility, women or men? Can some lady provide me a rational explanation of what a female is thinking when she allows herself to become baby momma number 4, 5, 6, or 7? *What is her philosophy of a family unit? I'm not asking what the male is thinking because I'm sure it is simply catch and release!* In fact, he releases two times and the second time is when he finally lets her go and moves on to the next chick. Why would these guys commit to marrying the pastry chef (you) and provide money for the ingredients to make all of the baked goods when you give him all of your pastries for free? If women don't have unprotected sex, especially with irresponsible men, then the **probability** of having unplanned and unwanted babies are slim. Furthermore, if the man changes his mind about fully participating in the life of the child at any point before the age of eighteen, the mother is usually left with the full responsibilities of raising the child! Females and males must have self-control and limits! So, regardless of his smooth baby-baby talk and bedroom promises, the limit should be not to bear a child or two with an incompatible and irresponsible man who refuses to marry you before you get pregnant.

The crucial dilemma many women and men face is that they weren't raised in a family unit that was loving, nurturing, nor supportive. Thus, they aren't accustomed to receiving these crucial qualities from those who are closest to them, which makes it unfamiliar, uncomfortable and difficult for them to accept and give these crucial qualities when they enter adulthood. As a result, they have a habit of rejecting critiques and criticism even though it is said with compassion by someone who cares or loves them. In fact, they may have received too many insults and discouraging comments while they were growing up, so their mind associates your loving comments with the discouraging comments they received from family members and others who were close to them. Unfortunately, they misinterpret your comments as mean-spirited, demeaning and meant to tear them down, rather than meant to improve them by identifying a character weakness or skill deficiency. Far too many people lack the understanding that identifying a deficiency or problem provides an opportunity for improvement by correcting the problem or strengthening the weakness! Proverbs advises us "**with all thy getting get understanding.**" As we attempt to obtain various tangible and intangible items, such as handbags, sneakers, clothing, car, boyfriend, girlfriend, spouse, friendship, healthy family function, promotion, validation, affection, acceptance, etc., remember that the most important item to get is understanding!

Mother Enablers

When mothers enable their sons by repeatedly coming to their rescue without justification, it prevents them from developing from boyhood into manhood. Consequently, you stunt their independence and they remain dependent! Some unproductive ways in which mothers enable their sons are by frequently paying for driving tickets, paying for vacations when he is unemployed, buying sneakers or clothing when he isn't working or continuously quits jobs, paying for food, clothing and daycare for the second child when you did it for the first child, etc. Hence, the old cultural saying that "black women raise their daughters and love their sons." This adage clearly reflects my position. All good mothers raise their daughters because they are a female, so they have actual experiences to rely on. Therefore, they are able to tell and show them all of the necessary techniques, dynamics and skills to become a self-sufficient lady. Since they aren't a man, they lack the actual experiences of developing from boyhood into manhood, so they just love him, which amounts to continuously spoiling him or neglecting him before or after he reaches adolescence. Every time a mother, girlfriend, woman or wife runs to the aid of a boy, teenager, young man and adult boy without considering the circumstances, **they establish and enforce the mindset and behavior of a momma's boy!** How will the boy or adult boy learn to be accountable? Before giving your boy more responsibility or every request that he makes, consider what has he done to show that he can handle the responsibility in a mature way. If he hasn't shown you more than two times that he can handle the responsibility, your answer should be no. *Saying no is not always a bad answer.* In fact, it is a good answer and the right answer in many instances! You shouldn't give adults responsibilities that they can't handle, any more than you should give children responsibilities that they can't handle. Children must be taught to be accountable just as parents are accountable for their actions and the actions of their non-adult children. There are numerous times in the life of a boy, teenager and young man where he should be allowed to cope with the consequences without his mother, grandmother or some other female intervening to ease his pain, perform his responsibility, explain his deficiency, lack of performance or negative behavior! Pain provides perspective! Whether or not you choose the right perspective is a separate matter. After you experience a painful situation, you will generally consider what went wrong, why did it go wrong, what you did wrong, was it a careless error, was it done prematurely, was it a bad or foolish decision or did you simply disobey good counsel? Hopefully, the new perspective will be beneficial.

Boys should not be babied past their baby years (7). I experienced this over-nurturing while at a picnic with my cousin. During our conversation, she yelled at her seven-year-old grandson and his friend, "don't run so much!" I said why not, they are boys. What else are they going to do? She said they might get hurt. I said getting hurt is part of boyhood, besides, how bad can they get hurt in the grass? Unbeknownst to me, the boy who was playing with her grandson had broken his arm on two occasions while playing sports on grass. I said wow! That doesn't usually happen. The key word is usually, therefore it's generally safe for boys to run and play in the grass without incurring broken bones. It's okay to let boys fall down and sprain their wrist or ankle, crash their bike and knock their tooth out and get disciplined by their full-time mature father. Boys will fall off their bike and skin their knees and arms or brake a bone playing sports. When I was growing up, the boys in my neighborhood experienced all of that and more. If a boy is mildly injured in a fair fist fight, there is no need for the mother to wait at the bus stop and get on the school bus and curse out the other boy. If your son gets driving tickets, he should get a job and pay for them, rather than mom deciding to work overtime or using her savings to pay for his silly mistakes. Whether he pays the court or he reimburses his mother, he should pay for the tickets. To the extent that his mom thinks that he is responsible enough to drive, he must be taught to handle the responsibilities that go along with driving. If he gets incarcerated for an intentional violent crime, she should not go to jail every week to put money on his book (account)! As challenging and scary as it may be to watch our sons and daughters grow up, it is critical to their mental and emotional health and the health of our relationship that we allow them to do so under careful supervision. We can't protect them from everything and we shouldn't try to, so long as it isn't something that will harm them long-term or cause permanent damage. And that may include falling down at the playground or getting a failing grade because of irresponsibility or disobedience on their part. It may include not going on a trip because she lost the money and permission slip, wearing tape on her eyeglasses for awhile because she has broken or lost two pairs in six months.

When a mother who is a high-ranking law enforcement officer uses her title to request a privilege while visiting her incarcerated son and she violates that privilege by smuggling contraband into the jail and gives her son a cheeseburger and cell phone, she has allowed her momma's boy mentality to severely distort her common sense! Of all people, you would think that she would respect and uphold the law! When a girlfriend gives her urine to her boyfriend to submit to the parole officer or for a job interview, she is also establishing, reinforcing and enabling the adult boy. To the extent that he isn't responsible enough not to use drugs while he is on probation, he probably isn't responsible enough to properly care for her on a consistent basis. Clearly, his behavior proves that he lacks self-control and good reasoning skills. Both of these qualities are necessary to have a consistently productive life and to protect and consistently provide for a family on a long-term basis. These two qualities are definitely necessary for avoiding self-inflicted physical and emotional problems, such as frequent bouts of frustration, depression and unstable housing.

Some days at the jail were extremely busy. During those times, an officer may be on his or her feet virtually non-stop for 3-4 hours. On this particular day, just as I sat down for a breather, Sgt. Ben called and asked if I knew whether Inmate Peanut received his commissary. I told him that I didn't know. When I discovered that he hadn't received it, Sarge told me to go downstairs to get Peanut's commissary. I asked Sarge why Peanut couldn't receive his commissary on the next delivery date, which was the standard procedure. Sarge told me that Peanut's mother called and complained that he was hungry. I said hungry! Reluctantly, I went downstairs and picked up two bags of commissary for Peanut. When my co-worker unlocked his cell, I was surprised to see a 40-year-old man walk out with an attitude. I just shook my head and laughed. In order for his mother to know that he hadn't received his commissary, he had to call her. As a result, his mother decided that it was important to call the jail and complain about cookies, chips and honey buns that her adult boy hadn't received because he was in court. This was another interesting example of momma still coming to the rescue of her baby boy who was now forty! There is no way in the world that I can imagine being older than eight and complaining to my mother about cookies and chips. After reaching 8-10 years of age, my brother, sister and I couldn't complain about the snack cabinet being empty. Mom told us we could eat the snacks little by little or we could eat all of them before she went shopping again, but when they're gone that's it. It was that simple! In another instance, a mother called the jail approximately ten times to complain about her son's welfare because he called and told her that he hurt his eye. The irony is that he was convicted of five counts of armed robbery. So, you can't help but wonder whether she had this same level of action-oriented concern prior to him committing all of those armed robberies. Did she make any attempt to sincerely apologize or assist any of his victims? This mother's behavior demonstrates her mentality of babying her son even after he's been found guilty of violently harming people and he is about to serve a lengthy prison sentence. This type of behavior appears to be irrational.

I remember a third-grade incident at a school in college park where I was working a long-term teaching assignment in early 2000. This was at the time that platinum chains were popular with rappers. Little Montrez arrived at school proudly wearing a long silver chain and the rest of his rapper gear. His teacher, Ms. Pat, told him to take it off and place it in his book bag. After frowning up his face, he put the chain in his bag. While Ms. Pat and I were standing outside of the classrooms talking before dismissal, the boy walked to the door and told Ms. Pat that his chain was missing. She asked the class two times if anyone had the boy's chain? In Harlem Boys' Choir tone, they all answered no. Then, she asked each student if they had the boy's chain and once again everybody said no. As I stood at her classroom door, she told all of the students to stand in line with their book bag. Low and behold, she found the chain in RayRay's bag. She politely asked RayRay why did you lie to me? He responded with the famous got caught answer, I don't know. Ms. Pat returned the chain to Montrez and sent a letter home to RayRay's mother. The next morning RayRay's mother arrived at the classroom ready for a Southside showdown, but she didn't know that Ms. Pat was from Duval County! The mother said Ray came home upset because he said that you called him a liar. Ms. Pat explained the events of the situation and told the mother that she asked her son why did you lie to me when I asked him if he had the chain. The mother replied, "I understand that he took the chain, but he was gonna give it back and I don't appreciate you calling my son a liar." The mother didn't say anything about reprimanding or punishing her son for stealing his classmate's chain, but she had a lot to say about whether or not the teacher called her son a liar. Again, any attempt to deny, justify or excuse any intentional wrongdoings only causes parents to appear unsympathetic, unremorseful, and perhaps delusional. In regard to setting good examples for children and creating a mutually beneficial community, it's critically important for people to be able to identify the major issue from the minor issue and cope with the truth of the matter! The truth is Rayray committed two bad acts by stealing the chain and lying about taking it. Rayray's mother compounded the situation by not reprimanding her son for the wrong acts he committed! A similar situation occurred, but it involved an adult boy who was killed while attempting to rob a Pizza Hut with a gun. The boy's mother told the local reporter that she wants the employee who shot her son to be charged for killing her son. How does that make any sense? This is an extreme example of a mother's desire to baby her son and ignore the dangerous and criminal actions of her son despite the possible death of innocent people. Her beliefs provide a glimpse of the type of illogical reasoning she provided her son while he was alive. Her reasoning reveals her delusional mentality and lack of common sense and empathy for other humans.

While working the Evening Shift, my co-worker said that her twenty-year-old son returned home over the weekend. Upon greeting him at the door, she told him that she would hold the door open while he got his bags from the car he was riding in. To her surprise, he returned with a small gym bag. In amazement, she said, son where are your clothes? He replied this is all I have. What do you mean this is all you have? He said, "times are hard mom." He was employed and had been living between his older sister and girlfriend. According to her, he never stated a logical reason why he had so few clothes. In any event, she began to tell me how she was going to "have to" work 60 hours of overtime to buy him clothes. This emotional decision to over-nurture and overcompensate for a healthy-body young man is a natural emotional response for a loving mother. However, it is a bad mental decision for her and him. I could tell from her responses to my probing comments that she had no clue how she had contributed to his laziness and would be further disabling him by compensating him for his irresponsible behavior. Nor did she fully recognize how the additional work hours were going to contribute to her fatigue, decreased work performance and stress level. *Just as momma carries the responsibilities of her baby boy and adolescent, plenty women carry healthy able-body, lazy adult boys!* Any woman who is regularly paying for the needs and most of the wants of a male who is twenty-one or older is providing daycare services! In many instances, carrying a boy or young man doesn't produce a hard-working, self-sufficient man! I'm not referring to any situations where the committed man has been consistently contributing to the financial and emotional health of the family and has gotten sick, injured or laid off. Providing support and coverage in those situations is one of the main benefits of having a sensible, compassionate and responsible queen in your life! It's a beautiful experience!

Some years ago, I dated a beautiful lady who I was truly in love with. I thought that she was the sweetest lady in Georgia. As a result, I felt obliged to do almost anything for her. One day, she mentioned to me that she wanted me to cut her grass. Immediately, I felt disturbed and seriously bothered by this request because her sixteen-year-old son lived with her. He was a very respectable kid with good manners and good grades. His mother had done a great job as a single mom providing for his needs and many of his wants. So, in my mind, I thought that he should be more than happy to help his mother by cutting the grass. All she had to do was tell him. I couldn't ignore my nagging emotions, so I asked her why didn't she have her son cut the grass. She began to explain to me that she told him that it was his chore, but she grew tired of continuously asking him to cut the grass. When you train your child properly, you don't have to continuously remind a teenager to complete their chores. I bet you that you don't have to remind him to eat every day or to ask you for money to satisfy his wants. Also, she thought that it might be too much work for him. To my surprise, she told me that she had cut the grass on several occasions. This information was impressive, yet disturbing because her yard was not small. It was impressive because she was a beautiful lady who could be girly at times and her willingness to tackle that manual labor was reflective of her strong will. Yet, it was disturbing because I immediately recognized this situation as a mother babying her son and a teenager subtly taking advantage of his mother. Subsequently, she hired a guy to cut her lawn. Later, when her finances became tight, she decided that she would eliminate that unnecessary expense. As a result of her inexperience with developing a boy into a man and not witnessing the development of a boy into a young man during her childhood, I was thrust into a mental and emotional dilemma. This seemingly simple request was a mental dilemma for me because I was aware of the multitude of reasons why her son should have gladly accepted the responsibility of cutting the lawn for his mother. First of all, he should have done it as a matter of gratitude and respect for his mother and himself! Secondly, an essential part of developing into manhood involves performing physical chores so that women don't have to do them, particularly physical chores that are atypical for most women and chores that would physically strain their bodies. Thirdly, an essential part of developing into manhood involves increasing one's work ethic. When my brother and I were growing up, we had 8-10 chores! The older we got, the more chores we were given. Our cousins and friends also had multiple chores. For some, that included washing and vacuuming mom's car. These days, many parents don't want to give their children two chores! Then we talk about young people having a shoddy work ethic or how lazy they are. There is nothing wrong with giving children the same amount of chores that many children performed back in the day. Performing chores(and they should be supervised) is the beginning of developing life skills, such as a work ethic, responsibility, listening and following directions, patience, skill development and accepting critiques! Due to the way my father taught me how to work, this situation was mentally tough because I was confident that I would be contributing to her son's weak (lazy) physical and mental work ethic. It requires mental strength to do things that you don't want to do. This is a life-skill that is necessary for boys and girls. It is extremely imperative for boys to get used to these situations during their adolescence years in order for them to be comfortable with them during their adult years. Every time you hear a story about a male athlete being cut from a sports team before the pros and in the pros because of a behavioral issue, it is related to his inability to perform tasks that he didn't want to do, whether it is abiding by the curfew, abiding by respecting females and not assaulting them or a no drug use policy. This same principle applies to a guy receiving a dishonorable discharge in the military. As we develop boys and girls into responsible adults, we instill in them the lesson of seeing the big picture or the value of performing tasks that aren't enjoyable. Cutting the grass eliminates some mental and physical stress from your mother. It also helps to maintain the value of the property, which is the house where you dwell. Exercising and dieting may not be enjoyable, but it helps you maintain a good weight, which protects your health by preventing your diabetes or hypertension from getting worse. Or would you rather be lazy and irresponsible and have the doctor tell you that he has to amputate your toes or your left leg? While escorting an inmate returning from the hospital, he spoke to me about getting all of his toes on his right foot amputated because he didn't do what he should have done regarding his diabetes.

On another occasion, I worked with a lady for a couple of years and we became good friends. She was extremely proud of her son when he decided to join the military. We lost touch for a few years and then we bumped into each other at the mall. We had a good time catching up over lunch. Subsequently, we talked on the phone and she told me about "the need" to send her son some money in a few days. She mentioned several other times when he asked her to send him money. After finding out that he was still single and didn't have any children, I sharply said that he should be sending you money! When I was growing up, I would frequently hear comments about my cousins who were in the military sending money home to their mothers and they had fathers at home. There is just something special and important about instilling values in children to help mom and other loving family members. While having lunch, she asked me to borrow money to pay a bill because she "had to" send money to her son. A pet peeve of mine is the misuse of words or false story-telling. The words "**had to**" mean that you didn't have any other choice, an emergency or an urgent unforeseen situation. Squandering your money and repeatedly disobeying guidance about budgeting your money does not meet the definition of "had to" or an emergency in my dictionary! Terminology is very important in regard to conveying an accurate message! Because of my convictions, I have never felt comfortable contributing to someone's bad habits. As you can imagine, I was very reluctant to loan her the money and I certainly didn't give it to her without telling her my views on developing a responsible young man, enabling young adult men and honoring a good mother.

To the responsible and loving mothers all over the world, **don't automatically conclude that these views and facts are meant to disparage all single mothers and non-residential fathers.** *Instead, they are said to create a dialogue that rejuvenates the traditional perspective and belief regarding the benefits of dual-parenting children, especially boys! No rational person can minimize or diminish the incredible and countless deeds that mentally sound, dedicated and loving mothers have accomplished and still do accomplish.* I'm not suggesting that single women can't raise a boy into a socially responsible and productive young man or that they haven't done it in the past. However, the facts are the facts, as evidenced by the behaviors and conditions of thousands and thousands of children and teens! What I am saying is that when you carefully examine the state of Black men from the 90s until now, the numbers will probably demonstrate that the outcome is more negative than positive. When you examine violence against females, incarceration and recidivism rates, drug abuse, child and family abuse, multiple unwed mothers and absenteeism, you can't help but to logically conclude that **single mothering statistically provides bad results! One study found that 71% of high school dropouts are fatherless;** *girls are more likely to be promiscuous and become teen moms; girls are more likely to become susceptible to exploitation by older boys, pimps and adult boys;* more likely to fall victim to drug and alcohol abuse. All ethnic groups have adult boys! *Dear mothers, I want you to acknowledge* that your efforts to work, grocery shop, cook, clean, drive to weekday football, baseball, basketball practice, attend girl scout and PTC and carefully assist with homework is just **too time-consuming and strenuous.** And I can't forget about driving to daycare! I can't recall how many times I've heard a mother irritably talk about speeding on the highways and streets to avoid the one dollar a minute charge after 6 pm. *Someone or something will suffer and too often, character-building and* *schoolwork are the main areas that suffer, along with mom's physical and emotional health*! Oftentimes, the tweens are home without good adult supervision. Frequently, the tweens and teens suffer mentally and emotionally. They also suffer physically, as reflected by a large number of obese school-age children. Too many mothers and people, in general, have an **I can do-it-all mentality**, which is very misinformed and partly delusional! This mentality was referred to as the Superwoman Syndrome in some magazines. As a superwoman, how will you maintain mental, emotional, spiritual and physical balance while running to and fro every day? According to the articles and what I've witnessed, this superwoman mentality is likely to get you some things: some loneliness, some bad relationships, some bad nerves and some bad health. In many instances, mothers realize that they can't do-it-all and then they feel too embarrassed to ask for help, so they compound the situation by making bad choices or suffering in silence! Then, when they really need help regarding eviction, car repossession, son running amuck in the house and streets, they ask at the last minute, which limits their choices and sometimes subjects them to an option that really doesn't provide a good result or isn't effective. It's very important for people to stop feeling too independent, too embarrassed, too prideful and too stubborn to ask for help, especially teens, parents and guardians. Help! Everyone required help a few times in their life. In some cases, a person should feel reluctant when he is unwilling to help himself or she has abused or squandered previous help for the same situation! Help is not defined as someone continuously performing a task that you are mentally and physically capable of doing yourself. A true demonstration of assistance is when a person or organization provides you adequate training for you to perform the task by yourself in the future. To the extent that you can accomplish "it all by yourself," what degree of effort and quality are you putting into the task because your time and energy are limited? **The fact of the matter is that we can't do it all!** Certainly, not at a high-quality level for an extended time period. That's why we were given the gift of forming relationships and strong bonds with each other. Like-minded family and friends who are rational, peaceful, spiritual, supportive, compassionate, compromising and honest should encompass your support group. **We are and always have been social beings!**

Chapter 3

Fatherhood/Manhood

What is the purpose of a man? We have to reestablish and uphold the **traditional meaning of manhood**! The meaning has been grossly distorted over the past twenty-five years or so and there hasn't been a **concerted effort by those who know better to address this distortion of epidemic proportion**! In fact, it's critical for mainstream society to reestablish and uphold the meaning of several important words, such as family unit, dignity, sacrifice, decency, decorum, mutual respect, work ethic, integrity, justice, equality, etc. Is walking in public places with your underwear showing considered decent? Is walking into church with your pants sagging and sometimes with your underwear exposed considered decent? Or, is this behavior expected to be acceptable under the pretense of come as you are or who are you to judge me? Is shouting out "you lie" in Congress while the President of the U.S. is giving a speech considered proper decorum or despicable? *Indeed, society could benefit from a rebirth of manhood, fatherhood, motherhood, sisterhood and brotherhood!*

I don't know when or how the role of a man was downgraded and relegated to just a male friend, boyfriend, serviceman or repairman!

Call a man when you need your car repaired, tire changed, brakes replaced, faucet fixed, sink unclogged, lawn mower fixed, radiator changed, etc. Not to mention, the decision to call a man to ask for money, borrow money or barter for money! This false and petty redefining of the multi-dimensional value of a high-quality man has led to the demise of families all across America and the dysfunction of all types of relationships, including home, church, children, school, businesses and politics. Historically, I'm not aware of any civilization that thrived without wise and morally sound men participating in the necessary functions of civilization. Christian Scripture teaches that a woman should submit to her husband. My interpretation of that is that *she should have a cooperative Spirit and rely on her discernment.* When a woman knows that her husband is working within his field of expertise or knowledge base, she should defer to his judgment and follow his lead. When he knows that his wife is dealing within her expertise, he should follow her lead. If she doesn't feel as strongly as he does about the issue, she should defer to his judgment. If she feels as strongly as he does about the issue, she should engage in a spirited debate and attempt to persuade him to compromise. In any event, she should avoid a verbal altercation, as that isn't reflective of a cooperative spirit. However, if she doesn't think that she should follow his lead simply because she is grown and she can take care of her financial needs and wants, then that will be a major problem for the short or long-term success of the relationship. Subsequently, she will be sitting around with her girlfriends or talking on the phone to her girlfriends regarding her relationship issues and wondering why she continues to bump heads with her husband or boyfriend. It is because a strong and morally mature man won't allow a lady to be the leader of the relationship. In fact, he cannot allow it because it goes against his cultural and moral beliefs that were instilled in him by his morally sound father. And that may be further ingrained by his spiritual belief. *Any person who feels inferior because she or he is serving in a supportive role to a person of high character and competence might need to evaluate their self-worth.* Before some of you get offended and excited, I didn't say that the wife or lady is not required to participate in the leadership duties of the family. *In fact, most of us know that she is the primary leader of many of the daily family activities.* **Her leadership role is no less important than that of the co-pilot or assistant pastor.** However, in most instances, there aren't two co-pilots or co-pastors.

It is imperative for a boy to be raised by his morally sound father or another morally sound man in order for him to duplicate the actions of a man. In most instances, a boy has to see manhood in action in order for him to naturally and successfully repeat that behavior when he reaches adulthood. In most situations where a boy reaches adulthood, he cannot successfully exhibit the characteristics of a high-quality man without having been taught by a high-quality man. As the boy gets older, dad observes his son's actions and attitudes so that he can provide guidance, correction and encouragement to ensure that they are appropriate. Dad will make sure that his son demonstrates protective behavior around his sister, carries the groceries in the house, washes his mother's car, cuts the grass and completes all of his chores with a good attitude. Sure, through trial-and-error, a boy may eventually find the right path without his father in his life, but consider the number of costly mistakes he could had avoided! At one point during my tenure at the jail, there were three biological brothers in their early twenties locked up at the same time. Clearly, they had very little comprehension of manhood, if any at all, because neither had enough common sense not to engage in illegal activities so he could stay free and employed to help mom support the household. **Despite mom's best intentions, she can't fill the critical role of dad. Likewise, dad can't fulfill the critical role of mom in his daughter's life.** How well do women think the average man would do raising a girl into a lady? How much practical advice could he give her about styling her hair, styling her makeup, wearing different types of undergarments, wearing different shoes or how to participate in and handle girl talk? In most instances, I believe that this can only be successfully achieved through training and guidance by a quality woman or women.

In theory, Father's Day is just as significant as Mother's Day in my eyes, but in reality, it is given significantly less importance. One reason to consider is the large number of mothers who don't know their father or their father wasn't consistently instrumental in their lives. Then, factor in these same mothers who now have children by boys who are absentee fathers or aren't fully invested in the lives of their children. As a result, many mothers bear the burden of supplying the needs of the family. Consequently, *the mother has two highly negative experiences with fatherhood*. For anyone who doesn't believe that these two experiences have a tremendously negative impact on her conscious and subconscious attitude, behaviors and beliefs and provide her a negative or distorted perception regarding men, fatherhood, trust and even her children, you are sadly mistaken. **Nevertheless, the extreme importance of the significance of a mature and morally sound father or man who consistently participates in the life of a boy must be understood and cannot be undervalued!** I vividly remember teaching a second-grade class at a College Park elementary school because of a normal restroom break for the class that ended up becoming a shocking revelation about how early the negative effects of a broken family impact children! As I was standing in the hall monitoring the boys and girls, I heard some boys laughing and running inside the restroom. When I walked into the restroom, I caught three boys playing and they looked shocked to see me standing there. That's probably because there were and probably still are very few males teaching at the elementary level, but that's a discussion for another day. What was even more striking was a boy standing against the wall. After I scolded the boys who were playing, I asked, why are you standing there and not using the toilet? He said, "I'm waiting to use the toilet." I asked, do you have to do a number one or two? He said number one. Without thinking, I said in a stern voice, "boy you better get over there and use that toilet," as I pointed to the urinal! He said, *"I don't know how."* Immediately, a fog entered my mind while exasperation filled my body and then I heard Eddie Murphy say gooney gugu, as I thought *what the hell kind of people are raising children today*! A second-grade child is usually 7-8 years old, and to think that no responsible man, whether his father or some other man, had shown the boy how to use a urinal was completely shocking to me. Could this mean that he was still in the habit of sitting down on the toilet at home? This incident also revealed that his life was filled with females. **Eventually, a boy will need his father or some man to teach him all of the activities and responsibilities of boyhood, manhood and fatherhood.** Without his father, the son misses the chance to run to his dad when boys are teasing him in school, get advice and a demonstration on how to deal with the bully in the neighborhood or at school. All of these interactions are instrumental in boyhood. In regard to the activities of boyhood, I don't imagine that there are many mothers who spend time showing their son how to ride a bike, practice what he learned in the boy scouts, instilling and supervising good bathing practices between 8-12 years of age, practice swinging a baseball bat, playing basketball or showing him what it feels like to be tackled when he plays football. Mothers are not inclined to frequently box or wrestle with their boy. Although this activity begins as fun and bonding between the father and son, it develops into training and self-defense skills as the boy reaches middle and high school. Then, if necessary, he will be inclined to settle a dispute by fighting with his hands instead of picking up a gun and causing permanent trauma to his life and someone else's.

My father taught me the lessons of diligence and sacrifice. The importance of **family, pride and honor** were continuously emphasized. Through his daily actions over the course of my adolescence and young adult life, I witnessed how to morally and legally provide for a family. Fortunately, I saw some of the same characteristics in my uncles who maintained their families in partnership with their wives. As boys mature into manhood, they develop a sense of obligation to provide for their family. Through a learning and maturation process, they learn to feel comfortable with sacrificing their time, money and resources for the benefit of their loved ones! Although some sacrifices may be long-term, strenuous or tiring, their sense of obligation and pride outweigh any feelings of concern or reluctance. When my brother and I were growing up, it was a **serious sin and a crime to be lazy!** Laziness was not tolerated under any circumstances. *A strong work ethic was one of the best qualities that people of limited means gave to their children.* In fact, this quality is so instrumental to a productive life that it is relevant regardless of a person's economic status. My father taught me and my brother to work hard for everything we wanted and to take pride in everything we possessed. When he gave me and my older brother a car, we worked jobs to buy gas, pay for repairs and buy accessories for the car, such as a bra, pull-out stereo and speakers. We kept it clean by washing it frequently. Also, we took pride in our clothes and pets. We never wore dirty clothes. While growing up, we had two dogs. We always took good care of our dogs, partly because our father shared fond memories of how his family loved and cared for their dogs when he was a child. After talking to us about the responsibilities of caring for a dog and hearing our commitment, then he gave us a dog. Thus, it's important to see and hear a person's sincere commitment and consider their past character and behavior before you entrust them with a responsibility, especially the life of a person or creature!

I thought it was very noble and compassionate of my female co-worker to open her home to two male cousins in an attempt to save them from the aftermath of Hurricane Katrina. A couple of weeks after they arrived, she told me that she asked them why do they let the dirty dishwater stay in the sink? One of them confidently replied "that's what we did at home." They left the water in the sink because they could only use dish detergent once a day. She politely informed them that they didn't have to do that in her home. Initially, she felt inclined to give them entertainment money to go see a movie or go to a club. Her biggest struggle was encouraging them to look for employment. After a several months passed, she became frustrated because they wouldn't consistently look for employment. Some weeks, they wouldn't attempt to find a job at all. This began to wear on her mentally, emotionally and financially. Not to mention, her food bill increased drastically, as well as her utility bills. Her feelings were understandable because now she felt like she was taking care of two adult males and she had her own children to care for. The guys were just over twenty years old. Within a year, my co-worker realized that her good and compassionate intentions were probably in vain, as she explained to me that nobody in their immediate family ever worked. I told her that that was the major problem with their lives. They had never seen a work ethic in practice, so they certainly weren't told about the necessity of it during their formative years. Consequently, the chances of them grasping that characteristic on their own or from a relative would be very challenging! Another subconscious issue facing auntie was her gender. To the extent that the guys applied for jobs with their limited skills and education and were not hired, they probably felt some level of resentment, failure, frustration and anger. It takes a high-quality man to effectively relate to a younger man about how to effectively deal with obstacles, failure, frustration and anger. Sometimes a young man or grown man feels a strong urge to release the pent-up aggression he feels. That is when a mentally mature man must tell a younger man not to curse out his girlfriend, wife, or children, not to consider and obey the urge to take what he wants, whether money or material items; resist the urge to fight another man or worse, a lady, just because you are angry. Additionally, the mature man can inform the younger man to consider sensible options, like jogging, go to the gym, lift the weights in the home, go in the spare room or basement and do push-ups and shadow box until you get tired, find a homie to wrestle, etc. He can even invite his homie over to indulge in a small amount of beer or liquor as he vents about the disparities of life and strategize about how to overcome his obstacles. In fact, it's a good idea to discuss his obstacles and strategies with his wife. In the multitude of counselors, there is safety, a wise person told me! Afterward, his spirit shall be refreshed if he is aware that he has options and his brain has the ability to form a plan to reach a happier day. Furthermore, his spirit shall be refreshed and filled with confidence if he realizes that he comes from a race that has survived atrocities and still achieved historical feats! When tough times come around, Bishop Jakes said that you should ask yourself "is this *fate or a state*?" It is critical for a person's mental well-being to realize that you are only dealing with a setback. It's also critical for a male to realize that he is **still a man despite being unemployed or underemployed. The demonstration of manhood lies in the young man's sincere effort to do the best that he can to protect and provide for himself and his family!**

Oftentimes, a boy and certainly a teen, requires the control of his father or a caring man who has the strength and conviction to let him know that we will not tolerate his foolishness, disrespect, laziness, nor illegal activities in this house. That may mean that dad or uncle will have to lovingly whip his ass! Dad will remain firm in his conviction until his son conforms to the rules of the house. On the contrary, most mothers lack the physical strength to control their son when his actions test her authority and violate the rules of the home. Also, due to her motherly instincts, there is a high probability that she will withdraw his punishment early, as soon as he hits her with the sad, puppy-dog face or he pleads with her and says c'mon mom! When a caring father or man is absent from the formative years of a boy's life and from the home, the element of fear is absent. Thus, *the peace of the home and health of the mother and other family members are in jeopardy* when the son becomes severely disobedient and disrespectful. This is evidenced by the many incidents where the son has stolen the money or property from female members or attacked his mother, grandmother or other vulnerable members who aren't able to match his physical strength. I believe that rape, sexual assault and other forms of domestic violence (Baylor Univ. and others/Title 9) perpetrated by boys and adult boys is mainly the result of boys not being raised by a morally sound father or man. Morally sound parents teach their child not to aimlessly hurt children or elderly people. A morally sound father will teach his son that one of his major functions is to protect his sister and mother from harm at all times. *A morally sound father teaches his son to never aimlessly hurt a female* in a way that he almost always abides by. This principle, as an extension, will guide his conscience to protect other females. If for some unforeseen reason, the son does violate this code of honor, there will be a limit to what he does. As a result, it will be highly unlikely for him to verbally or physically assault a girl or lady. I've been on a couple of bad dates. Although I got cursed out for awhile on one special date, I struggled with just the thought of cursing at her. A young man's conditioning reminds him that he must control himself and still protect her, even if that means calling a responsible friend to pick her up, calling a taxi to take her home, driving her home or exiting your own residence for several hours. During the summer of 2016, a twenty-six-year-old Black male invaded the home of an eighty-nine-year-old woman and killed her. This ridiculously shameful incident revealed the violation of a few moral codes. First, you don't make the choice to invade somebody's property because you refuse to work for what you want. Secondly, this incident shows that the killer lacked positive values, common decency and basic reasoning skills! Most importantly, this unnecessary and sad incident revealed that he hadn't been **instilled with reverence for women or elderly people** because if he had those values, he would had run away as soon as he heard or saw the lady. What kind of cowardly and asinine male attacks an elderly lady? **As**

responsible men, fathers and concerned citizens, we must engage in strategies to put an end to that type of madness!!!

Another important lesson for dad or a father-figure to teach boys and young men about is how **empathy applies** to all situations. In every situation, there will always be someone who is bigger, stronger, smarter, taller, shorter, has more money or authority, etc. Consequently, it is never a good idea to take advantage of a person just because you are in the advantageous position, as you will be in a disadvantageous position more than a few times in your life and you will not want someone to abuse you. When I was growing up, grown folks used to frequently repeat the adage, treat others the way you want to be treated. In regard to neglectful and abusive parents, gangs, jails and prisons, boys and young men can and have been molested and raped and they experience some of the same emotions as females, such as embarrassment, depression, anger, guilt, fear and stress disorder. Although I didn't witness a sexual assault at the jail, I did investigate a claim of sexual assault. The alleged perpetrator was a buffed, multiple-tattooed career prisoner and the alleged victim was a baby-face, bantam-weight wanna-be criminal. I clearly remember the shock and fear on the face of the baby-face criminal. I can only imagine some of the thoughts that were rumbling through the boy's mind. Meanwhile, the buff prisoner said all types of simple-ass shid like he didn't know what the boy was talking about; the boy was lying on him because he wouldn't share his commissary. Logically speaking, why would a young teen who weighed 135 pounds wet lie on a muscular 250 pound convict? **All boys and young men need to be mindful of empathy and their protective responsibility towards females** in order to prevent themselves from physically and emotionally abusing females! George Washington Carver provided a great lesson on empathy when he stated: "How far you go in life depends on your being tender with the young, compassionate with the aged, sympathetic with the striving and tolerant of the weak and strong. Because someday in your life, you will have been all of these."

While working in the education and law enforcement fields, my female co-workers would frequently talk to me about the difficulty of finding a mature and responsible man who was interested in developing a serious long-term relationship. Adult boys are one of the main reasons why many women are unable to establish a productive long-term relationship or get married. There is a grave difference between a morally sound responsible man and an adult boy. Too many women have been getting pregnant by and having babies for adult boys. Given that the father behaves like an adult boy, what's the *probability* that he will have some mature and positive characteristics to teach his son and daughter? **An adult boy can only beget another adult boy!** Most adult boys were raised in a female household. As a result, adult boys were not properly taught by their father or some other responsible man how to develop and maintain a serious long-term relationship. This is why he is highly unlikely to commit to you for the long-term because nobody has committed to him long-term, other than perhaps his mother and grandmother. In this case, this experience is *basically irrelevant because the man's role wasn't demonstrated for him to witness*, receive guidance, ask questions and then duplicate. Also, they were not taught how to properly handle the responsibilities and sacrifices of a family. Typically, a morally sound responsible man was raised by his father or another responsible man for his whole life or at least through his adolescence years. As a result, he was taught how to respect a girl and lady at all times. He was shown how to be helpful and protective of his sister and mother. He learned how to get a job and maintain employment by watching his dad go to and come home from work. He may have been fortunate like me to have gone to work with his father during the summer time. He saw his father interact with his mother in a loving, protective and productive manner day-in and day-out over the course of his adolescence years. Most of all, he may have witnessed his parents go through difficult situations together without being combative or giving up on each other. Many adult boys didn't personally witness the benefits of a family unit for the significant part of their formative years, if at all! On the other hand, they frequently witnessed their father not being married to their mother, not living in the home with their mother in a monogamous relationship and having children with multiple women. Consequently, making the decision to engage in a long-term relationship causes confusion, anxiety and fear. On one hand, he isn't familiar with many of the responsibilities that are required for a long-term relationship, marriage or family, such as monogamy, discipline, self-control, sacrifice, strong work ethic, patience, perseverance, honesty, humility, short-term and long-term planning, budgeting, effective problem-solving skills and effective listening and communication skills. On the other hand, he is aware of a few of the main qualities, such as honesty and faithfulness, but he may not be willing to commit to those responsibilities because they are foreign to him and he thinks that the disadvantages outweigh the advantages. Consequently, making the decision to frequently be selfless for the comfort and benefit of a spouse and child is foreign and confusing to him.

Adult boys frequently and consistently exhibit selfish behavior because they are mainly concerned about themselves. This childish quality is the same behavior that they exhibited as baby boys. This is why he doesn't hold the door open for you or open the car door during the first, second and third date, much less the first year. This is why he sits in the chair while you carry grocery bags into the home. This is why you don't get any consistently meaningful assistance with homework, attending PTC, bathing the children, transporting the children to and from their social events, etc. He believes that he should wear fresh clothes while his child is sent to school in worn and dirty clothes. He tells the baby momma that he doesn't have rent, clothing or food money this week, this month; he always has excuses why he lacks adequate and consistent child support money, but he has money to pay for a flashy car with rims;

he has money to make it rain at the strip club; he has money to buy beer and weed every week. It is probably impossible to calculate the number of adult boys who did not and are not paying child support. This massive number doesn't include the number of boys who paid insufficient amounts of money. I've heard stories of guys arguing with the mother about paying $35-$100 a month. That is simply ludicrous! No child in the U.S. can have all of their needs met from $35-$100 a month. In my opinion, the terrible sin isn't determined by the non-payment or low payment, but rather by the fact that the mother and other people can determine that *the father didn't consistently make an effort to do the best that he could to provide for his child or children.* If that means that he needs to take some educational courses to obtain his GED or enroll in college to complete his undergraduate degree, enroll in a technical college or trade school to improve his employment earnings, then those are the actions that a mature man must do. If he needs to stop gambling, spending money on weed, beer and liquor every week, so be it. Meanwhile, if he needs to work two jobs to hold it down until a change comes, so be it! There was a famous R&B song entitled A Change is Gonna Come. It is famous because the message of the song is timeless, powerful and true! A change is going to come, for better or worse, regardless of whether the boy does something positive, negative or nothing at all. Therefore, it only makes sense to engage in positive and meaningful actions so that he can increase the chances of a positive change occurring in his life and lives of his loved ones. At some point, as a young man or grown man, you should realize that it's necessary for you to tuck in your shirt and go to work. "**Nothing in your life will work until you do!**" The Bible says, "If anyone will not work, neither shall he eat." (2nd Thess. 3:10) I can still hear my Aunt Laura saying that "a piece of job is better than no job. Then, when you can do better, you get better!" That's old-school wisdom, yet it is just as applicable today as it was forty years ago when I heard it. *Great wisdom is like a great recipe, it will always be great!*

If you examine the lives of athletes, celebrities and ordinary males who grew up without their fathers consistently participating in their lives, you will see that many of them began to repeat the same destructive generational cycle of having unwed children and being non-residential and absentee fathers. Given that most boys and criminals don't admit to wrongdoings or irrational beliefs, it's very likely that they will consciously or subconsciously pass their negative thoughts and behaviors onto their children. *Too many males are under the sad illusion that impregnating a female and the female giving birth automatically validates them as a man and qualifies them as an adult and a good father*! That assumption is so very far from the truth that it is scary. Having a child gives you the title of parent. **Whether you behave in the traditional manner of a provider, protector, nurturer, teacher, counselor and dedicated loving father is a totally separate issue.** To all of the mothers who encourage or don't discourage their young and immature sons from impregnating a female, children are not toys and they are not objects to fill the void of your free time or provide a second chance for you to be a better grandmother than you were as a mother. Without witnessing that fatherly demonstration that was previously mentioned, how does the boy and teenager determine which manhood characteristics to emulate? Does he naturally follow his absentee father? Does he copy his wayward friends, criminals in the neighborhood, his favorite rappers, athletes or his "slick" older brother? Many times these boys do things to prove their manhood without knowing what actions demonstrate traditional manhood! They wonder should I mean-mug him, fight him, curse at him, carjack him, help him, say what's up, touch her, grab her, hoodwink her, leave her or commit to her. Often, these guys talk about how they struggled with understanding how to be a father and family man. In many respects, why should we be surprised? Absentee fatherhood is all they have experienced! Sure, in some conversations they have heard that it's morally wrong to have a baby out of wedlock and to have babies with multiple women, but visually or environmentally that's all they know. This issue was dramatically covered in the documentary In a Perfect World, by Daphne McWilliams. In this documentary, the director explores the dynamics of what it is like to be a boy and young man who was raised by a single mother and it vividly shows the emotional damage that is inflicted by the absence of a loving father. The children consistently feel abandoned when their father is not involved or stopped being involved in their lives, whether by absenteeism, separation or divorce. This **abandonment causes a child to feel confused, unwanted, angry and devalued**. I encourage everyone who reads my book to watch this documentary. I assure you that you will find it enlightening and beneficial.

With respect to non-residential fathers, *they are still responsible for fulfilling crucial roles, such as spending quality time with their child, establishing legal paternity and providing financial and emotional support on a weekly basis.* Despite living outside of the home, the father should still feel compelled and be allowed to provide the same important qualities of a residential father. He should earnestly contribute to his child's health and well-being by making a diligent effort to maintain a positive relationship with the mother by providing her emotional and financial support and providing his children with supervision, guidance, discipline, emotional support and being a consistent loving presence in their lives. Obviously, the status of the father's relationship with the child's mother will have a huge bearing on her willingness to allow him to fully participate. Being frequently combative or having multiple uncontrollable outbursts in which the father verbally and emotionally abuses the mother will diminish his chances of spending quality time with his child. Regardless of how the mother feels, the father should be able to fully participate in the lives of his children, **so long as his words and actions will not have a negative impact or jeopardize the safety of the mother and child.**

In most cases, a child has to be raised in a traditional family unit with a mother and father who work together to achieve family goals in order to have a clear understanding of the dynamics of a family unit. Then, the child will more likely have the desire to establish a family unit and be able to successfully duplicate all of the positive aspects of a family unit when he becomes an adult. We are creatures of habit and conditioning. When you are raised with love and care, you have a strong mental awareness and an internal desire to duplicate the same situation when you reach adulthood. Likewise, when you see and feel the benefits of sacrifice, you have a strong mental desire and an internal willingness to sacrifice for the welfare of your loved ones. Sacrifice is usually not a pleasurable experience. Given that fact, why would we expect a parent to sacrifice for their child or a child to sacrifice for an elderly parent when that individual didn't see or feel anyone do it for him during his formative years? *You can never give what you don't have* and in most cases, you can't do what you don't know how to do or feels natural to do! Therefore, it may be very, very difficult to show affection to children when you didn't *consistently* receive affection during your childhood years. This was one of the poetic themes fantastically demonstrated by Denzel Washington in the great movie Fences.

In business, there is a slogan that says your reputation precedes you. The same is true of your personal life. People notice how you present and conduct yourself and they usually treat you accordingly. Generally, my respect for inmates and civilians is proportionate to the respect that the person shows for himself or herself. While supervising lunch distribution one afternoon, to my utter surprise, *I saw a one-arm inmate take a lunch plate from an elderly man who had a walker and shove him to the floor.* Any level of respect that I may have had for that inmate was immediately lost! That level of disrespect and abuse was too gross for me. Thus, I believe that you display your view of manhood by the way you talk and act on a daily basis. If you wear your pants below your butt, whether in public or jail, you clearly display your immaturity and dysfunctional behavior in regard to decency and respect! If you disobey multiple directions that are given in a polite and civilized manner, whether at home, school, in public or jail, you demonstrate your irrational understanding of obedience and compliance with rules and procedures. If you disobey multiple directions given to you in a polite and respectable manner in jail, yet you quickly or slowing comply when I give the same directions in street language, that is a sign of your dysfunctional interpretation of communication and manhood. When you stand with *both hands in your pants moving around your groin area in front of another man, not to mention a female nurse, while you are waiting to receive your medication and you act like you don't know that your behavior is rude, lewd and disrespectful, that's a clear sign of a stubbornly dysfunctional mentality.* **This deep level of self-degradation is beyond insulting and highly embarrassing!** Too many inmates are filled with miseducation, minuscule education and anger. These three elements contribute heavily to their devastating plight. Those who are miseducated and fooled into believing that disobeying directions and behaving defiantly, stupidly and aggressively demonstrate manhood fail to realize how foolish they are. I'm reminded of an incident where we were engaged with a non-compliant inmate and Officer Chester repeatedly called the inmate Sir while giving him verbal commands in an attempt to de-escalate the situation. The inmate disobeyed the commands and angrily replied *"why you keep calling me Sir, I ain't White."* His comment sadly reflects such an utter lack of education, ignorance and experience outside of a narrow and dysfunctional world. Demonstrating your ability to be hard-headed, rude, manipulative, slick, disrespectful and violent are not characteristics of manhood. When you curse at me and then mean-mug me while walking to your musty ass cell, you haven't proven to me that you are a thug and certainly didn't show me that you have a clue about manhood. Yet, these guys are the first ones to shout "I'm a grown ass man, you can't tell me what to do!" This type of idiotic behavior stems from immaturity and years of being exposed to false information and dysfunctional behavior. Also, I understood this behavior to be a misunderstood form of bravado or machismo. Bravado is one of the main forms of intimidation that inmates utilize toward each other and officers. In most instances, a male's obvious display of machismo is a fake bid for power by a powerless person, which was frequently demonstrated by inmates to show how tough they are to other people. A powerless person is often an angry person. I frequently heard, "you better check my record" and "open this door Johnson and I'll bust yo ass." Inmates frequently sit or stand around telling fake soldier stories and talking reckless about "how he used to run shid, all of the people who were scared of him, what he ain't gonna do and what he fixin' to do." This childish and irrational behavior usually put a smirk on my face because jail is not the best place for someone to talk shid like that. Oddly enough, in all of my years and hours during the day and night shifts, **I don't recall hearing any stories about how they did anything consistently beneficial for their children, mother, wife or baby mother**.

I estimate that 90-97% of inmates are broke and they know that the officers know it, yet many of them frequently brag about how much money they have or made. As officers, we know that they are lying because the computer system displays the amount of money they have in their book. So, I know that they have little to no commissary money month after month, nor can they afford to pay the low and relatively low amount of bail money. Despite this fact, I've heard plenty of inmates talk shid on a weekly basis about how much "money they got and make" in an effort to belittle male officers and impress female officers. Frequently, inmates would ask an officer to check how much money they have on their book and after the officer said the amount, the inmate would respond by saying "that can't be! Nah, you got da wrong person." In one instance, the baby-face criminal said check it again. Officer Stevens replied "is your middle name Quantavius?" Yeah. You have 79 cents! Other low amounts included $1.38 cents, $2.03 and $4.26. These amounts are just barely enough money for the inmates to order one or two items on commissary, like a pack of peanut butter, two bags of hot cheetos or a honey bun. In Georgia, standard bail requires a person to pay approximately ten percent of the bail amount. I've seen these same "big man on the block" not be able to post bail amounts of $30K, $20K and even $10K. It seems to me that if his hustle was as good as he bragged, he wouldn't have any problem raising $2-3 thousand, much less $500. Simple math and logic tells me that a baller could get ten family and friends with $100 each to post a $10K bond. Yet, most inmates remain in jail awaiting trial, whether it is one year or two years. When this happens, I draw a few conclusions: he is broke and his friends are broke too; his family is struggling financially and they don't have the money; his family is tired of his foolery and wisely decide not to waste their money because he can't be trusted; his family is tired of his disrespectful and criminal behavior and they accept his incarceration as a stress-reliever for themselves and tell him that they can't raise the money; his family believes in consequences and justice and let him stay in jail. For one youngin,' he said can you check my bond officer? Did somebody tell you that they were going to pay it? Yeah, my auntie! And you believed her? Yeah. What's your name? Jeff. Your bond is $700 and it has not been paid! Most likely, auntie doesn't want to pay approximately $85.

With respect to a guy demonstrating his perception of manhood, only an adult boy will date two ladies on his job at the same damn time. In the case of Officer Hitman, he frequently smiles and laughs with his homies when they discuss how good his playa game is. Meanwhile, the two females walk around looking sad and sounding mad half-the-time and talking about how the other heifer is trying to steal her man! Yes, both ladies knew about each other and continued to let him have his cake as they tried to out-do each other! In my mind, they went from being played to playing themselves. How often does that happen? In case you are wondering if these were inexperienced young ladies, these ladies were well past their thirties. *Whenever ladies make emotional decisions when they should be making mental decisions*, it usually leads to a negative outcome. It was all good with Officer Hitman until the day his shiny car got keyed! Damn, damn, damn! I mean it got keyed something awful. You could see that it was artfully done by a scorned woman. Hitman was hotter than the grease after frying two turkeys on Thanksgiving and his face was twisted as if someone had wrapped an inmate's laundry bag under his nose. To make matters worse, he had no idea which female did it because he was swinging with 3-4 officers and nurses. I almost busted my gut trying not to laugh during Roll Call. It was truly hilarious as his "brothers" attempted to figure out the words that were engraved into his shiny whip and determine who the pissed-off sister was.

What kind of guy views himself as a man, yet requests that his future ex-wife pay him spousal support to care for his children from another woman? This irrational request begs the question, what work will he do to provide for his children if he receives the ex-wife's money? No true self-respecting man would ask a lady who he is no longer involved with to pay him money so he can provide for his children's needs. Just the thought of the situation sounds completely asinine! However, this request fits the personality of an adult boy because he believes it is okay to avoid, ignore, manipulate, neglect or flat out reject his responsibilities, no matter how minor or major they are. His lack of development into manhood allows him to *not feel totally embarrassed in shameful situations*. This is a pitiful example of a guy who has no dignity, nor shame! But, I'm willing to bet you dollars for dimes that he will have a girlfriend soon after this fiasco. A further example of shameful situations include baby boys and adult boys filling out emergency contact cards when being booked into jail or getting released from jail. I was shocked at how many boys didn't know their social security number, know the last name of their baby momma, or girlfriend or know the name, but can't spell it. Neither did they know their mother's address or phone number or anybody's number or address. *When people lack shame, integrity, self-respect, loyalty and common sense, we should avoid those people at all costs because they are capable of behaving in any manner.*

Chapter 4

Education/Shakespearean Tragedy

Once upon a time, Africans and African-Americans sacrificed their health and lives to learn and create schools when it was against the law! **Now, young African-Americans sacrifice their lives NOT TO LEARN!** As an elementary and middle school student, they think that they are getting over on their parents, teachers and school system by not doing their classwork and homework and by skipping class in middle school and high school. *All the while, people who care about them are growing frustrated, impatient and beginning to write them off.* **Meanwhile, the school and system concludes another one bites the dust! Next**!!! *Just as the Lord can't bless what you don't do, loved ones, co-workers, teachers, volunteers and Good Samaritans can't assist you with your zero effort,* nor are they inclined to expend their valuable time and energy towards your minimal effort and unwilling attitude! It must be very, very upsetting, frustrating and embarrassing at 13, 15 and 18 years old to realize that you can't go back to the third or fifth grade, nor do you want to, yet you realize that you barely know how to spell, add, multiply or write sentences correctly. As you reach high school and after, you encounter times when you realize that you can't always slick talk a smart girl into helping you write a paper or pass a test. As an adult boy, it's difficult sometimes to take your girl or baby momma to fill out a job application because you have difficulty spelling, writing sentences and your handwriting doesn't look like letters in the English language. Thus, we end up with far too many teens and young adults enrolling in the *School of Hard Knocks*! One of the main problems with the high enrollment levels in this school is that those degrees are virtually worthless in society and rarely lead to good employment opportunities! Furthermore, they provide very little value other than potentially beneficial cautionary tales about the many harsh experiences that the School of Hard Knocks provide. Having been around thousands of students and inmates, it's alarming how **our race and American culture has subtly and overtly decided to accept children volunteering to be illiterate**! In some states, courts require some inmates to attend GED classes while incarcerated. Upon completion of the class, their sentence is reduced by several months or a year. So, for a portion of the African-American race, *we've gone from suing entities in the court system for equal opportunity in education to court-ordered education*. And as crazy as it may seem, some inmates refuse to attend GED classes and choose to serve their full jail sentence.

In response to the rationale by students that school is boring and not fun as a reason for performing poorly or dropping out of high school, I believe that those students have the **wrong perspective of the purpose of school**. The simplicity of the argument relates to its irrelevance. First and foremost, students must understand that education is a long-term endeavor, which means that it provides **delayed gratification**. Secondly, school is not meant to be fun, neither is running suicides for basketball training, running mountains for marathons, doing sit-ups for boxing or swimming multiple laps for the swim team. There's nothing fun about studying for the LSAT, BAR exam, GMAT exam or RN exam. More often than not,

practice or training is tedious. However, ask Jordan if being a legendary player and winning a college and NBA championships is fun?
Ask Gabby and Phelps if winning gold medals is fun? Ask Diddy,
Zuckerberg, Samuel Jackson, Oprah and Earvin Magic Johnson
if their salaries and vacations are fun? Ask Debbie Allen, Kimora
Simmons, T.D. Jakes and Tyler Perry if their salaries and vacations
are fun? There are two primary reasons why school is boring: 1)
You are a below grade level student, so you aren't able to do the
work; 2) Your classes are below your performance level and you
need to be placed in higher level classes. *Learning in school can and
should be enjoyable, but it's not meant to be fun*! When students have
that misperception, it leads to self-defeating traits because they
don't focus on the lessons, nor develop good work habits because
they believe that they are being taught incorrectly, which causes
them to conclude that school is a waste of time! However, with
the right perspective on the future benefits, students will possess a
positive attitude, which generally results in a positive performance.
Learning is enjoyable when students view it as a challenge. From
that perspective, students can receive joy and pride in their ability
to become proficient in each subject that they are given to learn.
Your mindset should say to you, let me see how well I can do on
this task or how well can I comprehend this subject. Rather than
concluding that lessons are too difficult, kids should be taught to
think I just need more understanding and practice. Even all-star
athletes practice prior to games. I've never heard of average athletes
not performing drills in practice. For sure, no all-star or hall of fame
athlete ever reached that status without a lot of practice and dedication! Just doing schoolwork is like only playing in the games. Smart
boys, girls and adults practice over and over until they perform very
well! Consider the accomplishments of Michael Jackson, Jordan,
Venus & Serena, Gabby Douglas, Simone Biles, Mellody Hobson,
Pastor E. Dewey Smith, Mae Jemison and Richard Parsons. Practice
is so essential to the level of your performance and achievement

that Muhammad Ali said "I hated every minute of training, but I said don't quit! Suffer now and live the rest of your life as a champion!" Practice tasks to build academic stamina for testing purposes, similar to exercises that an athlete practices to build strength and endurance! Practice various skills daily for 20 minutes, 45 minutes or 60 minutes. Practice is the only way to obtain progress.

Schoolwork is easy because your mind was created with the ability to do it! We know this because people all over that world have done well academically. The formative years, perhaps three to ten are the most important for creating a positive view of education and building the foundation for performing well in school. The only thing you have to do is pay attention to your teacher, follow directions, practice and display a nice attitude. **Almost all children are eager to learn and want to feel smart!** This fact can be easily proven by observing the energy and excitement of students in pre-k through the second grade. If you are a parent or have ever spent any considerable amount of time around toddlers or children, you noticed that they are filled with curiosity. Well, curiosity is simply an eagerness to know, learn and understand more information! It's important to reinforce the curiosity of children and find ways to sustain it through the teen years! Parental involvement on a daily basis reinforces your child's natural curiosity and desire to impress you and their teacher. You don't necessarily have to know how to do their homework or even understand it. This factor doesn't prevent you from happily watching your child do their homework or enthusiastically telling him "I know you can figure out the answer." At the very least, your child will develop the important mentality of effort! Without adequate parental encouragement and reinforcement, young people assume that learning is too difficult, so they choose the path of least resistance and do the bare minimum or nothing at all. Daily encouragement and support are the best energy boosters for a child's confidence. For some reason, many parents fully understand this concept when it involves sports and other extracurricular activities. Thus, their behavior causes one to question their priorities in regard to education.

The purpose of education, whether formal or informal, is to teach you how to logically think about a problem, clearly articulate your decision and concerns and choose an appropriate or effective way to address it or solve it. Literacy or being educationally sound involves the ability to calculate, read, write and speak fluently. Unfortunately, a lot of underprivileged children and teens lack the ability to express their thoughts and feelings in a clear and logical manner. Consequently, they lack this skill as an adult and experience troubling situations socially and professionally because this skill is important to adult functioning. Informal and formal education are almost always interrelated. Even if a person has obtained a large amount of success through informal education, you can believe that she or he has relied on formal education, either from a banker, an accountant, attorney, etc. I believe that a quality education has a powerful transformative impact upon a person's life. It is very difficult for a person to argue against the benefits of education. Past and present history has repeatedly shown how education provides a means to a successful and productive life, especially by providing multiple options in regard to the things that you have to do and want to do. When you have a true understanding of the purpose of education, you will excel in school, rather than clown around in school as if you are applying for a job at the circus! When you have a true understanding of the purpose of a teacher, you will respect and obey the teacher instead of disrespecting and disobeying the teacher, as many students do on a daily basis every school year.

Based upon words, actions and conditions, we must presume that many people don't know the value of education. I believe that part of the problem with the educational crisis is that *administrators have been operating from the premise that everybody automatically believes in the benefits of education.* A basic conversation with many parents regarding the benefits of education and a one or two day observation of students in class will quickly and sadly dispel this notion. Sure, many people say that they know or believe in the importance of education, but can they identify several instances in their life when education has had a positive impact? Does a parent, older brother, sister, aunt, or uncle who only has a high school diploma or is a high school dropout have any significant personal experience with the benefits of education? If not, they must have faith in the value of education. We must address this false presumption because **parents have the primary responsibility for ensuring that students receive a proper education! Before a teacher, relative, or friend can educate a child, the child must have been taught fundamental values by their parents**. *Fundamental values, such as obedience, respect for self, authority figures and peers, dignity, honesty, right and wrong, manners and the importance of education.* All of these values are necessary in order to be educated. Based on my experience and the experience of many of my former colleagues, too many parents view school as a daycare center! As a result, their children adopt this same belief from their parents, so they go to school without paper, pens, pencils, books, crayons and have the gall to laugh, tease, fool around, fall asleep and disrupt the class several days a week. Unfortunately, some educators eventually adopt the view too. However, it doesn't appear that they have this view when they enter the profession, but after years of unreasonable policies and unrealistic expectations on the part of administrators and school systems, coupled with many, many unsupportive parents, recalcitrant and extremely rude children, they eventually run out of patience. Knowledge is brain food. Naturally, educators become mentally, emotionally and physically tired of trying to feed children knowledge and the kids keep throwing the food in the trash, letting it sit on the desk or worse, spit the food on the floor in front of the teacher.

School should be viewed as each child's job! School is their place of employment! This is the first place they go where they are required to perform tasks on a daily basis and they are evaluated on how well they perform each task. Aside from preschool, this is where children begin to develop their work ethic. We believe that parents should view school as their child's job and by doing so, the children will benefit by having twelve years of behavioral adjustments which should make their transition into adult work easier and successful. This is the student's first job. For all intent and purposes, they are at work! Consequently, many of the policies and procedures that exist for adults at work should be implemented and enforced at school. After all, educators are preparing students to enter the workforce. *If parents went to their jobs and exhibited the following behaviors*: submit substandard and incomplete assignments, fail to submit most of their take-home assignments (homework), sleep during assignments, submit illegible information, make little to no effort to perform tasks on a satisfactory level, tell their manager that you don't want to perform the task, refuse to obey instructions, talk, laugh and play while your manager is giving directions, not be capable of satisfactorily performing many of your assignments, verbally insult your manager several times during the year, frequently leave the meeting to go to the restroom and stay for an extended time while their manager is giving directions and demonstrating how to perform a new procedure, bully their peers, fight their peers, respond by mumbling and sit at their desk and daydream; Would they stay employed at their jobs? No! They would be fired in a short amount of time or almost immediately in some occupations for violating numerous work policies. There is absolutely no beneficial reason to allow students to exhibit these types of negative behaviors! Behavioral problems usually lead to poor academic performance and truancy. You can go to many inner-city K-12 schools and ask the administrators and predominantly female faculty about their daily struggles of attempting to control boys and teenagers. *When young boys and girls lack self-respect and self-control, even the most sincere intentions and efforts toward educating them are unproductive and distressed*! Yet, too many unrealistic parents and administrators expect teachers to work happily under these conditions and perform academic miracles for a majority of the student body. Some educators are good motivators and some are excellent. Through their commitment and passion for their profession and compassion for the students, teachers do their best to encourage children to learn. Their employment contract requires them to teach students to learn. However, we must never disregard the fact that it is **not their responsibility to find ways to force students to learn**. Like good law enforcement officers when faced with conflict, the primary goal is voluntary compliance. A business venue doesn't allow patrons to make noises and engage in disruptive behavior during a professional play. In this instance, security will escort those violators out of the location. If the business doesn't remove the ill-mannered patrons, they are responsible for preventing the other patrons from enjoying the production and receiving the benefits that they paid for. Likewise, a teacher is engaged in a professional production when she is teaching a lesson. It makes absolutely no sense for ill-mannered and unruly students to be allowed to intentionally disturb the teacher's production! These students should be removed from the classroom because they are preventing the other students from learning from the educational production. Also, as citizens, you are paying for the teacher to teach your child and for your child to be sitting in a suitable environment to learn, so you should expect to receive the benefit that you have paid for. Unfortunately, this concept doesn't apply to many inner-city schools. I would imagine that if we conducted a study of how many times a day an inner-city K-12 teacher says stop or don't do that, the number would probably range from 3-10. In school, stop means for the student not to talk anymore without permission, stop throwing crayons, pencils, paper and erasers while the teacher is writing on the board, cease tapping in or on the desk, don't touch or hit other boys and girls and don't disrupt the class anymore! There is an extremely high level of deliberate disobedience and a lack of respect and self-control in public schools, *which leads to decreased learning because of the loss of instructional time* that accumulates from week to week until the end of the school year. Subsequently, this deliberate disobedience and lack of self-control leads to a high level of difficulty or inability to successfully pass standardized exams or function on a job or most types of structured environments. Being recalcitrant and reckless will literally lead to a life of misery and possibly an early and unfortunate death!

While employed on a week-long substitute assignment of a fourth grade class, an ill-mannered boy kept disrupting the class despite my corrective actions and patience. At approximately 11am, *he called me stupid.* I told him to go to the principal's office and he said no. I told him a couple more times to go to the office and he refused. I pressed the intercom to the front office and explained the situation. Then, the assistant principal had the nerve to ask me "are you sure he said that?" It took all the patience I had to say yes in a calm tone. Soon, Ms. Updown sent an office monitor to walk with the boy to her office. About forty-five minutes later, this little rascal opened the class door. I said where are you going? He said, Ms. Updown told me to go back to class. I high-stepped it to the office and told Ms. Updown that he could not stay in the class with me today because he was too rude and disruptive. It's always interesting, frustrating and disturbing when people ask or require you to tolerate people and circumstances that they wouldn't tolerate or doesn't directly affect them. She didn't want to tolerate the rude rascal in her office, but she thought that I should tolerate him in the classroom. Then, some administrators have the audacity to act like they don't know how and why so many teachers get burnt out in a few years. **Who is considering strategies and procedures for reducing and eliminating the heavy burden of stress related to teaching?**

For those parents, administrators and critics who say that it's the teachers' fault because they have poor classroom management skills, that may be true in some instances, but it isn't the major issue. The issue isn't that many teachers have poor classroom management skills, rather the major issue is that teachers don't receive proper training and there aren't procedures in place to help teachers deal with **severely disobedient, disrespectful and rude children**. Even if teachers begin receiving social and psychological training on how to deal with many of "today's children," they still would not have the authority to deal with them effectively because knowledge and procedures are useless without enforcement authority! Receiving knowledge and methods on how to cope with unruly children is as effective as a gun without bullets, car without tires, plane without an engine, rules without consequences, or having money, but no peace of mind. **Teachers join the profession to teach**! Sure, a part of teaching involves resolving minor conflicts and moderate behavioral issues. However, I contend that teaching should not involve dealing with daily major issues, such as deliberate violation of rules, deliberate insults, verbal and physical threats from students and their parents, aggression, assaults, moderate and severe anger, refusal to learn, intentional class disruptions, profanity and other foul language, uncooperative parents, drug and alcohol abuse! I'm not aware of any company, certainly not any respectable and high quality company that tolerates these major issues. Can you imagine if your favorite restaurant had to cope with these issues from their employees and the owner still expected them to provide a high-level of quality food and service? As an alert patron, I submit that you would not expect to have a fine dining experience! All good teachers know that *anxiety and aggressive behavior in children are clearly signs of distress*! Anxiety fogs up the brain, which makes it difficult for the child to think clearly, focus and behave properly. When children are dealing with feelings of abuse, anxiety, frustration and pain, their instinctive fight or flight mechanism kicks in and they begin to display aggressive behavior or fighting. Sadly, that was the case when a **second grade boy began throwing books and turning**

over desks before he began hitting and kicking Ms. Marie, as she attempted to prevent him from hurting other students. Ms. Marie is one of the best educators in metro Atlanta, as she is extremely competent, patient and compassionate. She told me that she had not experienced anything like that in her twenty plus years of teaching. Sadly, she told me that she has noticed an increase in the amount of children who are suffering from obvious signs of distress.

Weeks and years of frustration can lead to aggression for a child who doesn't know an adult that she or he feels comfortable enough to ask for help with what he feels is an embarrassing situation, such as not consistently having clean clothes to wear, suffering from food and sleep deprivation, experiencing verbal abuse, not having a nominal amount of money to pay for the field trip or buy a snack during lunchtime every once in a while or being frequently reminded to tell you mom and dad that they owe a lunch balance! According to the Office of Juvenile Justice and Delinquency Prevention, some causes of violent behavior are physical or emotional abuse, rejection of the child, insufficient nurturing and exposure to violence in the home, community or school. Some studies have shown that chronic exposure to violence can disrupt a child's brain development and cause severe mental and emotional damage! This exposure leads to lasting physical, mental and emotional damage in many cases. Furthermore, teachers don't receive the necessary training, nor resources to effectively deal with the multitude of mental and emotional issues that today's children are experiencing, such as physical and emotional neglect, nutritional and sleep deprivation and homelessness. According to a report conducted in March 2017, Henry County had approximately **1,000 school age children who were homeless.** It is very unrealistic and irrational to expect children who are suffering from these types of major issues and more, to have the mental ability to disregard their crises and focus on learning in school without qualified and strong adult intervention! **Since these issues don't stem from school, schools can't realistically be**

expected to solve them! Teachers can't force children to put forth a strong effort to learn no more than your boss or relatives can force you to clean your home. For example, when you return to your hospital room after surgery, food services is required to give you three meals/lessons per day. The meals are nutritious and designed to aid in your improvement! However, it's not their responsibility to plead with you to eat or tell you over, over and over to stop watching TV or talking on the phone because your food is getting cold. This issue reminds me of the year that I taught third grade and Ms. Geneva was teaching across the hall. One morning, she came to my door and waved to me. Ms. Geneva was a soft-spoken and petite lady from Grenada. She was working at the school through some kind of teaching program for foreign teachers. As I walked to the door, I could see the frustration on her face. She explained to me that a few kids were disrupting the entire class, so she asked me if she could send two of the troublemakers to my class. I said sure. About ten minutes later, Ms. Geneva was at my door with two more students. To my surprise, two more students were opening my door about twenty minutes later. During lunch, Ms. Geneva told me about how her teaching experience in the U.S. had been disappointing and shocking. Basically, she explained to me that she was unaccustomed to raising her voice at students because that rarely happens in her country. Going to school there is a privilege that students and parents take seriously, so students aren't unruly, disobedient and disrespectful. Almost all of the boys and girls are eager to learn and they don't take education for granted!

Reading comprehension is the cornerstone of learning. I believe that reading comprehension is the main skill necessary for good achievement in every subject from second grade through high school. For the students who read below grade level in elementary school and get promoted to middle school, their academic struggle will become more frustrating and their stress level will become more intensified. Their lack of vocabulary and reading comprehension will prevent them from doing well with word problems in math, correctly answering questions in science and social studies and writing essays in language arts. In my experience, a **defeatist mindset can begin to form as early as third grade** (8 years old) and certainly begin to firmly set in the mind by the fourth grade. A student with a defeatist mindset views himself as a victim who lacks control over his ability to perform well academically. He believes negative thoughts about himself, such as I'm not smart, this work is too hard for me to do, nobody wants to help me or nobody likes me. Feelings of inadequacy become associated with specific situations just as fear does. Therefore, a student who feels inadequate about schoolwork will not put forth a good effort to learn the skill or may not even try at all because he has already decided that he won't do well. **A person's self-worth is mainly dependent upon their ability to achieve**! This ability to achieve begins during the toddler years and continues throughout our adult years. I would argue that the formative years and teen years are the most critical periods of establishing and solidifying your self-worth. Remember, attitude determines altitude! Donald Hernandez, a Sociology professor, conducted a study involving 4,000 students and the results revealed that *students who don't read on grade level by the third grade are 4xs less likely to graduate by age 19 than students who do read proficiently on grade level. If poor, the child is 13xs less likely to graduate*. Hence, the profoundness of the adage an ounce of prevention is worth a pound of cure!

Reading is absolutely amazing because it provides so many positive benefits! The most important benefits include increasing your vocabulary, which strengthens your communication and comprehension abilities. Additionally, it helps to keep your memory and reasoning abilities sharp. Furthermore, reading increases your general knowledge. Not only is it educational, but I really like the fact that it is informative, empowering and inspirational. Reading comprehension empowers you by informing you of what your manager and company can and cannot do and what rights you have! Many of us have been involved in a work situation that we felt violated policy or was unethical. When that occurs, as it did to me on a couple of occasions, you must be able to read the policy and accurately interpret it. Then, you will know whether the one page written counseling from your manager is legitimate or wrong and if you should write and throw two factually-based pages back at your manager expressing an accurate description of the incident and their improper handling of the incident. On a lighter note, if you don't have the means to travel to fun or far away exotic locations, reading can take you there! Through words and pictures, you will be able to learn about that location. If you haven't reached the success level that you would like, it's likely that you will read about a person who was in a similar position as you, yet that person reached the success level that you aspire to. If you haven't developed a love of reading or a strong likeness, I encourage you to start reading on a weekly basis! Read or buy a subscription to Essence or Ebony Magazine. Read Black Enterprise Magazine to be inspired to improve your mental, physical, emotional and financial health, for it highlights poignant personal and professional best practices, and many different minorities who are succeeding in corporate America and various types of entrepreneurial ventures, as well as ordinary citizens who are *combining works with their faith* to earn a living by doing what they want to do! I invite you to read some Cornel West, Bishop T.D. Jakes, Iyanla Vanzant, Michael Eric Dyson, Sonia Sanchez, Maya Angelou, Susan Taylor, Toni Morrison, Sister Souljah and Jeanette C. Espinoza, just to name a few. Read some poetry, fiction, non-fiction, a Bible, magazines, comic books or whatever you are interested in.

The real issue here and the one that society and the educational community has failed to address in any meaningful way is the huge percentage of illiterate students in the school systems throughout the U.S. **This shameful literacy condition exists because too many parents, including educators, have become apathetic and fail to engage in necessary actions to solve the problem.** We can clearly determine a person's level of commitment to a cause by examining the time, dedication, effort and money that she or he contributes to the cause. It seems that we've spent an extraordinary amount of time identifying the problems, but not nearly enough time developing and implementing solutions. Ultimately, parents must learn to **stop accepting failure in elementary and middle school**! Almost all children are eager to learn and want to feel smart! The formative years, approximately three to ten, are the most important for creating a positive view of education and establishing the foundation for performing well in school. There is no logical reason for a child to repeatedly fail subjects in elementary school. The only legitimate reason for a child to fail subjects in elementary school is if a professional has determined that the child has a moderate to severe learning disability. Even if your child was diagnosed with a mild learning disability, it would probably be best to express to your child that *you can accept her doing not as well as others, but not failure*. You accept failure not because you performed badly in school or because you dropped out of school or you are a single parent, instead **you accept failure because you don't seriously value education**! I know that to be a fact because I vividly recall a first grade teacher showing me a letter from a parent that said the homework wasn't completed because "yaul give to much homework!" This is indicative of the type of tomfoolery that inner-city teachers have to combat on a daily basis. As a result, you don't create and **consistently enforce** any best practices for learning. For example, you probably didn't create a set time and place for your child to complete homework and practice lessons every day. Also, you didn't require your child to show you his completed work, nor did you require your child to practice their lessons for a sufficient amount of time every week and weekend. Reading, watching and listening are wonderful methods for learning. However, many studies have shown that the best way to learn is by doing. **Students learn through repetition**. Repetition builds competence and competence builds confidence.

All of the repetition can't be completed in school, so it must be done at home or other locations outside of school. The following hours are available to practice and reinforce what was taught at school: Mon.-Thurs. 4pm-8pm; Sat. 9am-7pm; Sun. 9am-7pm or 3pm-7pm if attending church. There are sixteen hours available for practice during the week and at least fourteen hours available on the weekend. If these hours aren't used, they are wasted and it is reflected in the child's mediocre, low, or substandard academic performance. It's very obvious and odd to me how most adults realize that we must practice to improve our abilities, so we practice our work skills on and off the job, cooking skills, nursing skills, computer skills and hobby skills, but rarely think that it's necessary to practice academic skills! Lastly, you didn't tell your child's teacher to tell you the truth about your child's low performance areas. This is critical because it is almost impossible to repair a problem if you don't know what the problem is and how bad it is. **Academic success requires sincere commitment, structure, discipline, supervision, practice and encouragement on a daily basis.** There is very little content that is difficult in elementary school. *Good performance in elementary school is primarily achieved through obedience, effort and practice! Once you create that mindset and habit,* you have established the necessary foundation for your child to perform at a high level. This mindset and habit will continue into middle and high school and your child will excel academically there as well. Then, the main issue that you might have to deal with is identifying and combating any negative peer pressure that your child may encounter. With respect to those mothers who are unable to control their sons and mothers and fathers who accept academic failure, it doesn't mean that some of them aren't nice and caring parents. However, performance abilities and goals require much more than being nice and caring. Several research studies have proven that **positive parental involvement in early literacy is directly connected to positive academic achievement!** So, we must decide:

- How do we convince parent(s) or guardians of the critical role that education plays in determining the comfort and success level in their child's life?

- How do we convince parent(s) or guardians of their critical role in protecting and nurturing the talents of their child?

- How do we convince parent(s) or guardians that their leadership role is a privilege that they should honor and one that will be supported by a team of caring individuals?

- How do we convince parent(s) or guardians of the **magnitude of the disgrace it is to dishonor our heritage by choosing to be illiterate**?

- How do we convince parent(s) or guardians to believe in long-term investment in their child's future and delayed gratification?

- How do we convince parent(s) or guardians that they can raise intellectual scholars without being a scholar, just as a mother can raise an Olympic Gold Medalist (Gabby Douglas) without being an athlete?

- How do we convince parent(s) or guardians that this educational responsibility isn't very difficult, yet **it requires habit-building actions that eventually become second nature**?

Thurgood Marshall graduated from Howard Law School after he was denied admission to the University of Maryland Law School because of his race. In 1954, Marshall argued Brown vs. Board of Education of Topeka to the Supreme Court on behalf of Black parents whose children were forced to attend all-black segregated schools. Marshall argued that the "separate but equal" doctrine was a violation of the 14th Amendment. When those parents went to the NAACP to file their complaint and hired Marshall, I'm confident that they completely believed in the value and benefits that education provides. **Furthermore, I'm sure that they didn't imagine that many thousands of young people of future generations would take education for granted and treat it as if it is useless!** We should honor our ancestors by valuing their sacrifices and obtaining at least a thorough high school level of education. Some years ago, there was a case where a **mother had to serve 9 days in jail** for sending her daughters to a school that had an excellent academic reputation, but was outside their school district. The schools in their district were on the state's list of lowest performing schools. Sometimes, our *principles compel us to do the wrong thing for the right reasons*! This is the type of serious sacrifice and commitment parents should have about the value of education. In this type of case where nobody was physically harmed, I don't fault the mother and I certainly don't comprehend how a rational adult in the justice system could find this offense worthy of jail time. *She should have been rewarded for her act of civil disobedience and celebrated for striving for the American Dream*!

Chapter 5

Ancestors

The Great Migration involved the relocation of approximately six million African-Americans from the rural and Jim Crow South to the northern cities, Midwest and West from approximately 1910-1970. Some of the main reasons for leaving the southern states were violence, harsh racism and very few job opportunities! Aren't these the same devastating conditions that plague some African-American communities today? The first and second World Wars created many jobs in the North, Midwest and West. Blacks recognized these opportunities and traveled to those cities. Although our ancestors experienced prevalent racism and other hardships when they arrived to these cities, it was a significant improvement over their conditions in the South. Thus, the important factor is that there was a measurable amount of improvement, which is the important lesson to me. Sometimes, we are able to improve our lives significantly over the course of years, other times we are able to make incremental progress. Just as our ancestors recognized opportunities, **it's our responsibility to recognize opportunities and take action to become part of those opportunities!** My parents are living proof. Their parents were sharecroppers and they grew up working on farms and experienced Jim Crow racism. Nevertheless, their parents required them to graduate from high school. Later, they migrated from southern states to NY in their early twenties. They met and got married in Harlem. *Filled with mother wit, a high school diploma, aspirations, determination, dignity and a deep abiding faith,* they were able to raise three children, purchase two houses in NY and later buy a retirement home.

With respect to oppressive and violent conditions that plague many inner-cities and rural communities, I can't help but wonder how is it that immigrants who live in another country and don't know our language and culture, are frequently poorly educated, and don't have family in the U.S., are able to conclude to travel to the U.S., albeit illegally, to get away from severe oppression, poverty and crime in order to have a better life, but African-Americans and other low socio-economic citizens who are legally able to live in any of the thousands of cities within the fifty states don't choose to relocate from high crime and poverty-stricken areas? Even if a person can't move immediately or within a year, it seems likely that the person would be able to move within three or five years. I can even imagine and accept him or her moving within ten years. However, I can't think of any logical reason why a person would live their entire life in a dangerous environment and then allow another generation to live in the same environment. Improving one's condition is predicated on the presumption that the individual has the sincere desire to change and has devised and implemented a sensible strategy to reach the goal! This is very possible when you rely on your actions and strengths, the knowledge and resources of people and organizations of good will and you have a cooperative spirit. However, if you are solely relying on yourself and simply wishing that your circumstances improve without a positive social network, your chances of improvement are most likely very slim. Our ancestors traveled to other states and countries based upon faith and word of mouth from relationships they had with family and friends. When you consider the conditions of the Great Migration, it seems apparent that African-Americans were facing much greater challenges, with legalized racism being the worst one! Despite our ancestors living in oppressive and hostile conditions, *they were still able to keep their children moving forward* because they possessed vision and a deep sense of **faith, commitment, perseverance and sacrifice**. By comparison, today's situation makes stationary people look lazier and sorrier because we have the incredible benefit of the internet and social media, which provides a current status of employment opportunities and all other relevant information that one would need before she or he decided to relocate. For me, this conundrum begs the question, are they aware of the history of their ancestors? If not, that's why old folks used to frequently talk about the **importance of knowing from whence you came**! Also, it begs the question of what level of reasoning skills do they have? Do they have legitimate reasons or **excuses** for not improving their conditions? **No Excuses, Speak the truth**! Oftentimes, *the place you are used to is not the place where you belong*! This sentiment relates to those positive, responsible and loving residents who don't move out of negative neighborhoods and inmates who become used to jail and prison. If your current situation is not beneficial to you, *you have the freedom and responsibility to change your situation*. I believe that this is the sage advice that Bishop Jakes provides in his inspirational book Reposition Yourself. Change is basically a three step process. First, you must identify the problem. Secondly, you must identify the solution(s). Thirdly, you must implement the solutions. For many people, it's easier to talk about change than to actually put in the work to bring about the change. "*Progress is impossible without change* and **those who cannot change their minds cannot change anything**," said George Bernard Shaw. Thus, if you change your mind, you will be able to change your circumstances.

I have encountered many inmates and civilians who use the excuse that there aren't any programs for young Black males. Assuming that to be true for the sake of argument, there aren't any programs for poor whites and other minorities either. Yet, I suspect that the violent crime levels for those groups against themselves are less than for Blacks. More importantly, as I recall, there were hardly any programs for past generations, **yet they believed in doing the best with what they had.** As a result, quite a few ancestors were able to overcome their tough conditions and low income status over time and some became successful because they *understood the meaning of the scripture "Now unto him that is able to do exceeding abundantly above all that we ask or think, according to the power that worketh in us*-Ephesians 3:20. If they only had a pig, they ate the whole pig. They didn't have the luxury of wasting food. If they only had lemons, they made lemonade. For those who didn't have lemons, they drank water! Some may have asked a neighbor if they could spare some lemonade. For sure, most of them did not think that their lack was justification to rob a person, store or someone's home so they could buy sweet tea, soda or beer. It is very possible for Blacks and other minorities to rise above their birth conditions because our ancestors and others have shown us that the *happiest people don't necessarily have the best of everything, they just make the best of everything*! Again, it is very important to at least know the basic history of your ancestors or race. Can a person continue an extraordinary legacy without being aware of the legacy? We should know and have confidence in the legacy of "Black Wall Street" in Oklahoma. The Greenwood area of Tula was founded by a freed slave. The community consisted of working class and middle class Blacks. Greenwood grew into the most prosperous Black community during the early 1900s. By 1920, there were over one hundred different Black-owned businesses, including banks, restaurants, grocery stores, doctor's offices and schools. It was a totally self-sufficient community. A similar community was established on Auburn Avenue where many Black-owned businesses were located. Alonzo Herndon was born into slavery in 1858. As a young man, he migrated from rural Georgia to a city outside of Atlanta to improve his economic and social condition. Mr. Herndon learned how to cut hair very well, which led to him owning a barbershop on Auburn Avenue and two other locations. Later, he bought an insurance company and started the Atlanta Life Insurance Company in 1905. His philosophy was based on racial self-help and independent entrepreneurship! By 1960, the company expanded from selling insurance in Georgia to eleven states and had approximately $54 million dollars in assets. Meanwhile, African-Americans were making tremendous strides in the North. The Harlem Renaissance was a socio-economic movement that was infused with intellectual thought, racial pride, art, politics, music and social and economic empowerment. During this period, African-Americans celebrated and promoted their entrepreneurial spirit and excellence in all areas of life! Some people believe that it paved the foundation for the Civil Rights Movement. These African-Americans experienced tremendous obstacles during that time-period. Yet, they didn't frequently shoot or steal from each other, loot stores and burn property to achieve these historical feats! They believed in self-determination and were able to progress because of their can-do mentality! **No excuses and no quitting**! Our ancestors created substantially viable businesses. These simple and amazing accomplishments have shown us and the world that **we have the ability to envision, plan and create everything that we need to live a happy, peaceful and productive life!** Standing on those broad accomplished shoulders, many current ancestors have continued the legacy by demonstrating the ability to envision, plan and achieve their needs, wants and dreams!

Obviously, there is a severe disconnect between the history of our ancestors and the last few generations, particularly many of whom were born since the 80s. *Tradition cannot be perpetuated if you don't know it and haven't been taught its purpose and value!* There seems to be a significant lack of familial respect and ancestral honor for heroes and sheroes like Dr. King, Coretta Scott King, Rosa Parks, Malcolm X, John Lewis, Thurgood Marshall, Maynard Jackson,

Hosea Williams, Madam CJ Walker, Jackie/Rachel Robinson, Hank Aaron, Bill Russell, Harry Belafonte, Ossie and Ruby Dee, Andrew Young, Douglas Wilder, Carol Moseley Braun, Maxine Waters, Sojourner Truth, Harriet Tubman, Nat Turner, Denmark Vessey and others who fought and died for the right to freedom, education and equal rights. I saw a program in which Hank Aaron said that he walked an hour and a half to two hours to school every morning! In 1972, he began receiving hate mail as he approached Ruth's home run record. The threats were so vicious and despicable that he had to be assigned an armed bodyguard by the Braves and City of Atlanta. Despite those severe obstacles to his life and professional success, he persevered and made history! Clearly, if all of us were ingrained with the knowledge of the tireless, physical and psychological fight for freedom and equality by our ancestors, I don't think that so many men and women would recklessly and carelessly sacrifice their health and freedom. Our ancestors recognized the tremendous opportunities that freedom provided. I doubt that many of them dreamt that they would be rich, but **they believed that freedom would give them the ability to make their own choices, earn a living and obtain happiness**! Having those three qualities meant that many other ideas and dreams were possible for them and their children! To a large extent, life is about putting yourself in a position to reach the possibilities that you desire. This entails many different actions, like avoiding self-destructive behaviors, staying away from people with negative behaviors, developing positive habits, being obedient, accepting guidance and criticism from caring and smart people, working two jobs to save money during a time-period, going to school on-line or night classes, going to school to complete your GED or degree, forming bonds with positive like-minded people, establishing a support system of caring people so you can assist them and they can assist you with daily activities and emergencies, exercising for health reasons, etc. As you mature, you learn the importance of not dishonoring yourself, your family nor ancestors. I wouldn't fathom intentionally disrespecting my parents and grand-parents! Our ancestors didn't fight for their freedom to leave the plantation for some of us to live like we are still on a plantation! Some people live like they don't have any value, self-respect, nor dignity; like they are prevented from pursuing an education and success; like they are prevented from obtaining decent housing, food and clothing; like they are prevented from protecting and working to provide for their family! Our ancestors didn't envision that they were sacrificing their blood, sweat, tears, limbs and lives for some of their descendants to steal and hoard miniature bars of soap and toilet tissue in jail to sell to other inmates who ran out of tissue to wipe their butt! Our grandparents and parents didn't work from sun up til' sun down on one or more jobs and struggle to provide a decent roof over your head and food and clothing for the family for some of us to drop out of school at 13, 15 and 17 years old to begin a career as a low-life criminal, violent criminal or corner watchman! This is so, so not what they imagined! The common denominator in all of your situations is you!

Again, one can't underestimate the importance and influence of having a historical reference in order to possess a clear understanding of one's rights, privileges, abilities and potential. Obviously, many young males and females lack a fundamental understanding of the importance of how African-Americans fought to obtain their freedom! I'm a gambling man and I enjoy gambling in Vegas and other beautiful casinos around the world. Obviously, there are only two possible outcomes when you gamble-you win or lose! I learned early that the key to enjoying gambling is to only bet money that you are willing and can afford to lose! Fortunately, I've had some experiences where I've won and lost, but I've always enjoyed the occasion because I stuck to my principle. Clearly, it would be fool-ish to bet the money that I need to pay my rent, mortgage, car note, utilities, food and other bills. As I stated earlier, I like using analogies because they provide a different perspective and in doing so, often provide a clearer and deeper meaning. Whenever people engage in illegal activities, they are gambling with their freedom and health. Obviously, the most important difference between gambling money and freedom is that time can't be replaced. Whether a low-roller or high-roller, you can replace 5K, 50K or 500K. On the other hand, once you get sentenced, you can't replace 5 years, 15 years or 40 years of your life! Once that time has passed, it's parti pour toujours! Ten, fifteen and twenty years in prison are significant amounts of time. To the extent that the father or mother and children are in a mental position to establish a connection, the childhood and adolescence years may be gone. In addition to attempting to effectively work through the disconnection, there is also the challenge of working through feelings of distrust, anger, sadness, abandonment and resentment. These are very serious, complex and time-consuming issues to overcome. It's quite asinine to gamble two of the most valuable possessions you have, unless you don't know that your freedom and health are valuable! This fact was made painfully evident while relocating an inmate who returned from court. As soon as he entered the dayroom, he shouted to his "friends" "I got my time today-I got ten years." Right afterward, he carelessly said to another inmate "K-boog took 15 years." By his careless declaration, I could only surmise that *if you don't value what you have when you are free and don't comprehend that you have anything of value (worth shit),* then it doesn't matter that you will spend a lotta years and thousands of days locked in a tiny ass room with piss-poor conditions, surrounded by sane and insane men performing the same mundane routine every damn day! There is a specific question that I'm conflicted about. I want to know, yet I don't want to know why so many teens and young adults throw their lives away in the midst of committing illogical and violent crimes? What is the probability of a Black male never getting caught carjacking people for several months? What's the probability of a Black male not getting caught selling drugs for five consecutive years? What about ten consecutive years? What's the probability of you participating in criminal activities on a daily basis and not getting killed, almost killed or incarcerated for a large portion of your life? The chances are slim to none and I saw slim at the bus station leaving town! That philosophy of short-term gain is worth long-term pain is totally asinine! A little bit of common sense and basic math will easily show you that the odds are heavily against someone who consistently engages in self-destructive behavior. It causes you to wonder if these type of people have any positive long or short-term plans for their lives. It certainly appears that they do not! That is one of their major problems. I clearly remember hearing a wise professor say "if you fail to plan, you plan to fail!"

Fighting the wrong person or system is like punching the air. Burning buildings and destroying property in Ferguson, Baltimore, Milwaukee and Charlotte is like punching air. The fight is at the mayor's office, governor's office, city council chamber and voting booth! It's incumbent upon citizens to know the integrity of the people running for office and then vote for the best candidate. If the person gets into office and breaks their campaign promises, enacts policies that hurt the average citizen, engages in unethical or illegal behavior, the citizens should take adequate time to develop a strategy to remove the person from office. **The effective strategy will be mental**, not physical! Also, it must be consistent and directed at the correct pressure points. Remember, pressure busts pipes, dams and levies (New Orleans). Pressure causes powerful people to resign, get fired, and civil rights laws to be enacted! Going to the doctor's office or pharmacy and complaining and yelling about the expensive cost of an Epipen won't get the cost reduced. Going to court about a ticket or charge, then yelling and cursing about the outcome and how you were profiled in a speed zone won't change the outcome. Uniting with others who have experienced the same shady, unethical or illegal practice, collecting data and hiring a competent attorney to fight the next case will increase your chances of ending the profiling in the speed zone, stop and frisk, disparate sentencing, and price gouging on medications. Utilizing resources to vote to elect an honest sheriff, county commissioner(s), senator, judge and congressman/woman will change that unfair and illegal activity! A basic understanding of history reveals that improvement stems from continuous struggle! In December of 1955, Rosa Parks was arrested, tried and convicted of civil disobedience. Many of us know that this incident led to the Montgomery Bus Boycott. The boycott lasted one full year. This historical accomplishment that was achieved by leaders and followers who were ordinary citizens, but behaved in extraordinary ways, reveals the power of strategy, vision, commitment, dedication, loyalty, faith, mobilization, unity, perseverance, obedience and courage! Only inexperienced, irrational and immature people and inmates think that the best way to solve a problem is a physical fight! However, reality proves that once you give the legal system justifiable reasons to deal with you, there isn't a damn thing that muscle can do to remedy your situation. The only way to get out of the situation is to think your way out or pay someone (accountant or attorney) to think of a way out for you!

What does voting do? Voting establishes policies and laws that govern practically everything that affects our lives directly and indirectly. It establishes what you can and cannot do where you live (HOA), what fines can be imposed against you, budgets for schools, hospitals, and roads, community and state services for you, children and senior citizens. All of these decisions and more are decided by people who are elected or appointed. Consequently, we should all take a consistently active role in voting and being informed of who our elected officials are. While I enjoy an entertaining and intellectual conversation mixed with street psychology at the barbershop, we have to be careful and challenge negative street psychology. For example, one outspoken barber adamantly stated that "our ancestors didn't sacrifice everything for us (their descendants) to vote, but to have the **option to vote**." To compound his street psychology, he added, "tell me what law says that we have to vote?" I explained to him that our ancestors could not vote because they were prevented by law! So, how does it seem logical that they would protest for years and sacrifice their time, energy, health and lives to gain the option not to vote? They were already in that situation! Choosing not to vote is the equivalent of not having a vote, which was partly the cause of their devastating circumstances. Even after President Johnson signed the voting law, many blacks were killed, beaten and fired from their jobs for voting or attempting to vote. Common sense demonstrates that if voting wasn't important, there wouldn't be so much opposition to minorities having access to voting. *It's not that voting doesn't matter, it's that lack of voting and not actively participating in the political process allows uncaring and unethical people to get voted in impactful offices.* Then, those uncaring and unethical people create laws that provide preferential treatment to the citizens they like and detrimental treatment to the citizens they dislike!

We should consider the past as reference material to help us avoid unnecessary problems in the future! We must gain a full understanding of how the present and future are connected to the past. To a large degree, what happens in the past determines the conditions of the future. For many generations, from Africa to U.S. slaves, to approximately the end of the 70s, **it seems like a high level of pride, integrity and diligence** were passed down from generation to generation, perhaps in our cellular memory and then through oral storytelling. If you've ever seen Roots, read about the history of African-Americans through the 70s or saw movies during that time period, you will recognize what I'm talking about. To the extent that many children, teens and adults are seeking shortcuts in life, it would behoove them to recognize that the legitimate shortcuts have been forged by those who are proficient in the situation they are faced with and have been where they are going or want to go. These old-timers, elders and veterans have the capability to tell or show you the most effective and efficient ways to behave, evaluate or travel! Their sincere and compassionate desire will likely put you in an advantageous position and prevent you from experiencing a lot of unnecessary disappointment, pain, heartache, loss of time, money and privileges! This is the reason for the adage work smarter, not harder! A positive legacy and traditions serve as a foundation that is meant to provide people an advantage to build upon. The benefits of legacies and traditions are that they serve as successful pathways and they provide tried-and-true strategies of how accomplishments were achieved. Also, they serve as a great source of pride and inspiration to all of the dreamers who seek to improve their lives or help improve society! By being aware of the accomplishments of our ancestors and others and being obedient to wisdom from experienced and compassionate people, we can gain the ability to persevere our current circumstances and envision and create a fulfilling and happier future. **It is our responsibility** to be knowledgeable of our legacy of perseverance, pride, excellence, intelligence, determination, achievements, faith and family! Despite the present existence of institutional racism and legal injustice, society and opportunities are significantly better now than it was for our ancestors during the Civil Rights and Jim Crow eras! For that reason, I believe that *many of our ancestors would be severely upset, embarrassed and saddened by the enormous amount of Black-on-Black crime, illiteracy levels, dropout rates, single-parent homes, incarceration levels and squandering of opportunities*!

Chapter 6

Reasoning

We must instill logical reasoning skills in our children so they will be able to strengthen this skill as they reach adulthood. From five years old to teen years and through adulthood, their ability to think through academic work, social and professional situations and make solid reasonable decisions will be a determining factor in the level of comfort, happiness, misery, success or failure that they achieve. Logical reasoning skills provide you the ability to understand the purpose of people, information, rules, behavior, and most things in life. **What is the purpose of a father and husband?** *Can the father's role be effectively duplicated by the mother?* Basically, when you know the purpose of a person, you will respect them accordingly. When you know the purpose of an action, you can determine whether or not it makes sense for you to do it. When you do something, it's always important to know why you are doing it. For example, what is the purpose of shooting a non-resistant person during a robbery? **There is no purpose, rhyme nor reason!** With regard to knowing why you do something, it seems that baby boys and adult boys in every state wear their pants hanging below their butt. Some even tie their belt so that their pants fit snug just below their butt. Every time I see it, I shake my head in disgust and wonder if any of them thought about why they want their butt exposed? I imagine that some would honestly admit that they do it because their friends do it or because rappers do it! Others may admit that they do it because it's a style. Also, I wonder if they know where this "style" came from and does it mean something? For those who don't know, when pants are worn below the butt in jail and prison, that is how a male signifies that he is available for sexual pleasure. I haven't asked any guy on the street why he chose to show the butt part of his underwear, but I'm certain that he has no regard for the concept of common decency. Furthermore, they should develop the ability to generally make advantageous decisions, rather than disadvantageous decisions. However, this is not often the case when criminals are involved. When you watch the TV show First 48, observe the body language of the suspects after they have been arrested. Often, they look and sound dejected, confused, hopeless, exhausted, angry and exasperated. During the interviews, they mumble like a child and it quickly becomes apparent that no logical thought was given before their actions. They say comments like "it just happened, we didn't plan to do anything wrong and I didn't mean to hurt nobody." Such was the case in Georgia when **three cowardly fools** stood outside of a gas station waiting to ambush a lady when she returned to her car. During the carjacking, the lady attempted to defend herself and one of the criminals shot her to death. Although the crime is heinous, I believe that this crime is more of an example of **ignorance** rather than evilness. First, the idiots didn't realize that there were several cameras in plain sight on the premises. Secondly, they didn't realize that two of them could have overpowered the lady and taken her car! Nor did they realize that if they shot the lady, they definitely wouldn't have a chance to benefit from the stolen property. Thus, it's clear to me that no thought was put into this crime other than taking the car. Clearly, the crime of idiots!!! Generally, idiots commit crimes with a minute amount of thought about their actions. As a result, these cowardly fools are likely to receive a life sentence at the age of seventeen.

Osmosis is the method by which the cells of an object (penetrable) absorbs water through the outer membrane without any effort-just by being. **Humans don't learn through osmosis.** Unlike liquid, knowledge and skills don't simply enter into our brains simply by just being. Far too many Americans of all ethnicities and races make the grave mistake of trying to accomplish tasks without reading how to information, without obtaining basic knowledge on a topic, without seeking advice and guidance from elders or experienced and successful people, without receiving proper instruction and training and without obedience and humility! People try to accomplish tasks like raise healthy and productive children, stay happily married, maintain a happy and healthy relationship, start and operate a business, supervise employees, manage millions of dollars, maintain a car and house, interact well with people, solve personal and professional problems effectively, provide good customer service, etc. All of these tasks are virtually impossible to accomplish successfully and with longevity without obtaining prior knowledge, instruction, training and guidance along the journey. *Yet, mainly due to sheer laziness, ego and disobedience, many people attempt to accomplish these tasks and others.* You can't learn how to be a good mother, father, husband, wife, student, teacher, manager or entrepreneur without actively doing some productive things! One of those productive things is being obedient to an experienced relative, friend, colleague, businessperson, mentor or maybe a stranger. Additionally, you must spend hours and hours reading information and talking to experienced people about good parenting skills, **consistently practicing good parenting procedures,** practicing vocabulary words and speaking, so you will gain the ability to express your feelings clearly and concisely and practicing controlling your impulses when you are upset so that you won't say and do things that will have a negative impact on you and your family's lives. There is a lyric in a good ole gospel song that says hold my mule. You must spend hours and hours practicing driving in various weather conditions to become a good driver. My cousin says she is an excellent driver, but she only drives in the day time! She doesn't drive at night, in the rain, snow and she doesn't drive alone! Raise your hand if that describes an excellent driver to you.

I'm a firm believer that it's always important to view situations logically. In virtually all learning experiences from toddler to kindergarten, through high school, to your first job and after, we learn by modeling the procedures or behavior of the person doing the teaching. *Virtually everything people do is a result of formal or informal training that develops into a habit*! It doesn't matter whether you are talking about someone who frequently talks about the Bible, or someone who wears clean clothes or wrinkled clothes; someone who goes to school or work ashy; someone who goes to school to learn or play; someone who is a diligent worker or a lazy worker; someone who slurps or smacks while eating; someone who curses; someone who speaks Ebonics; someone who speaks properly; someone who listens versus someone who talks a lot; someone who plays a piano for years; someone who is a worry-wart; someone who panics under daily pressure; someone who keeps a clean bedroom and bathroom versus someone who keeps a dirty bedroom and bathroom. Proper training requires supervision and correction until the person shows consistent proficiency. It doesn't matter whether you are talking about a thirteen-year-old child or a dental student learning how to pull a tooth correctly. Too often, *people are under the false perception that talking is taught.* They say I told him 3xs, 5xs, so he (child or adult) should know how to do it! I explained it to her (employee), so she should know how to do it. Proper training is not spoken! **Proper training is spoken and taught**! Proper training involves explaining, demonstrating, observing and critiquing on a continual basis. It involves a series of clear and thorough explanations along with complete demonstrations by the trainer. While the task is being performed by the trainee, the trainer is keenly observing the trainee's performance. From that point, proper training involves repeated demonstrations by the trainee. These demonstrations are accompanied by critiques and follow-up demonstrations by the trainer. It's critical for the trainer to supervise the trainee until the trainee's performance shows that he is proficient at the task. Many of us have experienced a person who wasn't a good trainer. This applies to work, employers and parents. The degree to which a trainer is proficient or not, directly impacts the performance of the trainee! Consequently, parents must teach, demonstrate and enforce good manners in order for their child to demonstrate good manners. As a parent, you must supervise your child in the store so that she learns to look and observe without touching. Children must be taught that they shouldn't and can't touch every item in the store. Besides the policy of you break it, you bought it, some items can be damaged by excessive touching. This behavior definitely applies to trips to the museum where this lack of training is evident. Likewise, it is important to supervise children in a restaurant, so that they don't drop their face into their plate for the whole meal. They must be taught to bring their spoon and fork up to their mouth. Also, they must be trained to twirl the spaghetti around their fork, not to slurp their food or drink and definitely stop touching food and licking their fingers at the buffet table! I've witnessed this numerous times and it made me cringe and rush to the other buffet table. Nevertheless, I have a family member who is a fan of the food menu at a buffet restaurant, so I join the member occasionally. For those parents who don't consistently supervise and critique their child's performance, they haven't properly taught their child. You must inspect what you expect. Parents must respond non-violently in all non-violent situations in order for their child to learn how to behave in the same manner. Parents must demonstrate good decision-making under ordinary circumstances and duress in order for their child to possess good decision-making skills. **If it's to live in our kids, they must first see it living in us**! Similarly, parents who maintain a loving relationship and raise their children at home through eighteen years or at least through adolescence, have demonstrated the intricate dynamics of a family unit. Is it logical to think that a young man can effectively model a productive dual-parent family unit even though he didn't experience it? Is it logical to expect a young lady or especially a young man to want to marry a lady and create a family unit when he wasn't raised in a family unit? For those young men who do have the desire to marry a lady and create a family unit, is it rational to believe that he knows how to function properly? Probably not. As a result, he engages in the concept of trial-and-error again!

We have to obtain and emphasize a fundamental and widespread understanding of the slogan trial-and-error. Trial-and-error is only necessary when you are attempting to invent a product or do something that's never been done before. If that is not the case, you should save yourself time, problems and grief and obey the good advice or effective procedure that has been established. Otherwise, my interpretation of the slogan means that someone or some people have already engaged (trial) in that behavior and when the decision-making time concluded, it was determined that those actions were a mistake (error), harmful or not beneficial. Consequently, it doesn't make sense for you and me to perform those same actions and expect them to be beneficial for us! Therefore, if you estimate that 200,000 American males have been imprisoned for selling drugs, how in the world do you think that you will get away with doing it for a long time? You won't. With respect to creating a solid family, this slogan doesn't mean that two young people should have unprotected sex and then think that if she gets pregnant, then they will figure out how they are going to take care of the baby. It is said that a wise man learns from the mistakes of others. As experienced individuals or elders, we see the banana peels in the road. When we tell you to wait, stop, that doesn't seem right or don't do that, we are trying to prevent you from falling! Instead of obeying knowledge and wisdom, too many teenagers, young adults, adult boys and girls decide to follow the mantra can I live. Trying to figure out important or life-altering decisions without caring and experienced individuals to provide guidance and wisdom is often a scary and risky predicament. Making assumptions about how well you will cope with being a single parent, how to be a good mother or father as a young adult, how you will be able to survive as a high school dropout or that using crack and methamphetamine won't damage your life like it did others, are all associated with high-risk results of trial-and-error. Depending on what data you review, the outcomes are significantly more negative than positive. Nevertheless, what isn't disputable is that the number of negative incidents would be significantly less if the people involved had consistent access to caring people who possessed knowledge and wisdom and they obeyed the knowledge and wisdom!

With respect to relying on reasoning or logic, *how do boys know that they've done something wrong or terrible when ladies show them that their behavior is acceptable?* Why would adult boys show honor or change their deviant behavior when their mothers, girlfriends and baby mommas still give them all of the privileges that a righteous, decent, well-mannered, gainfully employed and gentleman receives? As a lady, if you get upset at your adult boy's foolery and you express you discontent by telling him, yelling at him, not cooking or closing the cookie jar temporarily and he has committed the same shenanigans 4, 5 or 6 times, you have accepted his behavior! They say it's never too late to change, but I believe that adage applies to a case by case scenario. With the appropriate support and resources, it may not be too late for you, but it's probably a wrap for him. It's hard to change a playa's game in the ninth inning. For the women in mid-term relationships (4 years or more), this is especially true for you. In addition, many women sabotage opportunities for long-term relationships and marriage by giving an adult boy "employee" all of her benefits without carefully evaluating his character and performance before the probationary period is over! Within seven to ninety days, giving a guy the key to your home, letting him frequently drive your car for social purposes, giving him your debit card as if he is a tenured employee who has shown his value during several years of service to you, are all actions that will most likely lead to gloom and doom! If your young husband frequently spends the household money partying with homies on the weekend, going to socialize with the shoe models or gambling on sports and you continue to find ways to work longer hours, borrow money and cut back on necessities to cover his immature and irresponsible behavior, you are perpetuating and reinforcing his boyish behavior!

The majority of visitors that a male inmate receives are females. Obviously, this is related to most women's natural character to be nurturing and emotional. Conversely, you rarely see a grown man or father figure visit a male inmate. Why don't males visit often? This can be attributed to absentee fathers and to a degree, fathers and other male relatives who are incarcerated, on probation or have open charges. When your son, boyfriend, adult boy or husband goes to jail or prison multiple times for intentional crimes and you faithfully spend your time going to visit and placing your hard-earned money on his book, instead of establishing a strategy and deadline for him to behave like a mature and responsible man, you are perpetuating and reinforcing his baby boy mentality and behavior! As a result, he firmly believes that some female will rescue him or assist him, whether it's momma, grandmomma, baby momma, or his shawty. In fact, consciously or subconsciously, he believes that it is their duty! This mentality and behavior was on display when Tony was being released from jail at 4:30 am. Upon being released, inmates are allowed to make two phone calls. Per Tony, the first number he asked me to dial was his baby momma. With the phone on speaker, the phone rang several times before the answering machine came

120

on and I heard the sweet voice of a baby babbling on the message. After five minutes, he asked me to redial the number. Again, no answer. He said "damn, where the hell she at?" Then, he asked me to dial another number. A lady answered the phone and he said "momma, I just got out. I need you to come and get me." Groggily she said, no bay-bee, William has the car. With shock and anger he said, "how am I supposed to get home then?" I was thinking that he probably got arrested without his mother's involvement, so he should be able to get home without her involvement. While looking sad and pouting, he mumbled words as he walked out of the exit door into the cold morning air.

Reciprocity is critical to the understanding and success of all relationships! If you consistently give 95% effort and he consistently gives 45% and 65% during a good stretch of time, why would he feel compelled to give 95% despite your yelling, twisted face and complaining? When people disobey your rules or standards, you should treat them the way their behavior dictates they should be treated, in order to get them to understand their inappropriate behavior and hopefully help them improve their behavior. In my years of experience, I've found that people usually respond well to reciprocity, regardless of whether you are dealing with children, teens, adults, nice people, rude people, civilians, criminals or co-workers. Almost immediately or over time, this practice usually creates a mutual level of understanding and respect. Warning, this practice is probably a little dicey with your boss who has the authority to terminate you for insubordination. At one point before my daughter was grown, although she thought that she was grown, I carefully explained this concept to her. I told her that when she gave me 35% effort, I would give her 35%. If she gave me 50%, I would give her 50%; if she gave me 85%, I would give her 85%. If she gave our relationship 100%, **I would give her 200% because that's how a loving father behaves**!!! Her compensation package rivals that of any high-powered CEO. She can call me early in the morning, afternoon, evening and even in the wee hours of the early morning. She can borrow five dollars, five thousand dollars or my last dollar! She can call me to talk, to listen or get advice. She can lean on my shoulders, cry on my shoulders or stand on my shoulders! No valley is too low, no mountain is too high and no distance is too far for me to come to her rescue! I am not her friend, yet I can be her friend! Whether she gives 25% or 100%, she will receive a lifetime of protection! Her protection detail is better than the CIA, as I would sacrifice my life for hers at any time and I don't get paid to do so!

In that same vein, women who find it offensive to have some "old-fashioned values", engage in some old-fashioned behaviors or feel embarrassed when their peers call them old-fashion, must not confuse these sentiments with being a progressive woman! Paying for a vacation for you and your boo to celebrate your short-term relationship is not being progressive. That is being impatient and irrational! Generally, mature women possess the ability to hold out for delayed gratification rather than immediate gratification. Rational thinking and effective communication on the part of the mature woman will provide her the ability to suggest a vacation and determine his desire to vacay with her. There's a cliché that says *boys do what they can, men do what they want*! If he wants to go on vacation with you, he will make plans to pay for it or make some good faith effort to make a significant contribution to the trip. Likewise, if he wants to marry you, he will ask you and make sincere and reasonable plans to do so! Asking a man to marry you is not progressive! Nor is it old-fashion for a woman to wait a reasonable amount of time for a man to ask her to marry him. It is traditional and many traditions carry important intrinsic values! I've heard a few women say that they don't see nothing wrong with asking a man to marry them. Well, Kelly said "I don't see nothing wrong with a little bump and grind." If you follow that sentiment, I don't believe that it will provide you any substantial results. I would suggest that some women have sight while others have vision. The women with the vision understand that there is a grave significance to the tradition of a man asking a woman to take his hand in marriage. Traditionally, it indicates several very important aspects. First, it reveals that he loves and honors her so much that he wants her to be his wife. Secondly, it reveals that he trusts her enough that he is willing to commit to a permanent relationship with her. Additionally, it indicates that *he has decided that he wants to be her protector and provider and build a family with her.* These are traditional roles that apply to a morally mature man. Whether or not he violates these aspects during the marriage is a separate issue. A woman should give careful consideration to whether or not this man has shown the potential (for young couples) or demonstrated the ability to be a diligent and faithful provider and protector before accepting a marriage proposal. All of this, notwithstanding the current divorce rates, a good marriage has been shown to have many positive benefits.

Good logical reasoning skills will help girls and ladies to know that every cute boy and fine man is not dating material and **definitely not fatherhood worthy**! The converse is just as true. She needs to be aware of this fact before he leaves the baby in a hot car in the summer or leaves his guns and cocaine on the sofa while the children are curiously walking around or puts the baby in a hot oven. I have personally encountered one of these criminals and I didn't notice any remorse. The thought of knowing that I had to interact with this guy in a professional manner was very disturbing to me. Again, there is something very enticing and unpredictable about the street psychology expressed at your friendly neighborhood barbershop. In this case, we were discussing sports in the barbershop in Douglasville when some clown loudly and proudly said *"I got 7 kids and 4 boys—I know at least one of 'em gonna go pro, so I ain't sweatin' workin'*! My lady get stamps and I hustle on the side." After I felt a constipated look come over my face, I wondered whether some people really create babies believing that "one of 'em will go pro?" Is this really a segment of the fatherhood population? Then, I thought don't the children need food, clothes, shelter, toys, books, birthday gifts and money for the school trip and book fair before they reach the pros. Not to mention, there is no decent guarantee that any of them will make it to the professional level! That statement was so ignorant to me that I never went to that shop again! This is proof to owners that your clients do have an impact upon your business in terms of how their positive or negative and foolish words and actions affect your clients.

Good logical reasoning skills will help you respond correctly to situations like if I point this gun at myself or cousin, it might discharge. If I take these drugs, I might not wake up. Is this fraternity hazing sensible or dangerous? Is this what it appears to be or is it nicely disguised? Is this situation good for the short-term, but bad for the long-term? Is she fine on the outside, but can't cook and lacks maternal instincts? Is she built like a charger, but leaking oil (money) every month? Does she think being beautiful is her employment? Is he built like a new black escalade, but his engine (brain) is damaged? Is he very handsome, but has never held a good job for more than two consecutive years? Do you have long-term plans of graduating from college and he says he doesn't care if he gets you pregnant before then? Does he hum like a Mustang? He makes good sounding promises, but his actions rarely match his words. Too often, a large number of males and females *make emotional decisions and then attach logic to the decision afterward*. I believe that it's generally beneficial to make logical decisions and then attach emotion to it afterward, if necessary. For example, when you decide to spank your child, it should be a logical decision and then your emotions will kick in and tell you when to stop because of the love that you have for your child. It's very difficult and sometimes impossible to get some people to understand that their thoughts or actions don't make sense because their mentality doesn't usually function by logic. They generally make decisions based on how they feel. Oftentimes, emotions don't include logic or they outweigh logic!

This was frequently the case regarding the female visitors who came to visit inmates. In the case of Shalonda, she looked seventeen but was twenty-two years old. She arrived twenty minutes late for a thirty minute visit. The female officer explained to the baby-face girl that she had missed most of her visit and asked why was she so late? The young girl sheepishly replied, "*I had to get my medicine from Kroger because I had a miscarriage today.*" Suddenly, the female officer and I stared at each other in astonishment! After a long pause, the female officer asked the baby-face girl why are you here instead of home resting? The girl replied, he told me to come see him today! That was the whole explanation. C'mon, we must use common sense in all situations! Unfortunately, this was another sad example of low, low self-esteem and emotions outweighing logic. Initially, it was very shocking to see so many "mothers" who brought their toddlers, children and even newborns to jail on a regular basis and in all types of cold weather, cold rain, heavy rain and snow just to visit for thirty minutes. Yet, many of these same mothers don't find it necessary to go to school to observe their child's performance in class, have lunch with their child or attend PTC with the same frequency or at all. At that time, I didn't have the opportunity to ask the young mothers why they thought that it was okay to take newborns, toddlers and young children outside in inclement weather. On multiple occasions, grandma accompanied the young mother, which demonstrates dysfunctional values on her part too! Thus, providing visual confirmation of the adage the fruit doesn't fall far from the tree. The grandmother, daughter and child visiting jail under these circumstances almost certainly prove generational dysfunction.

Emotions have a tendency to go suddenly out of control more so than logic! In many instances, this concept applies to a lady who decides to have an unwed baby. Emotionally, she thinks that they will be in love forever; he will always be with her; he will be a very good or at least a supportive father and a bunch of other happily-ever-after thoughts. We should not be driven by our emotions.

Too often, people make decisions and engage in actions based upon anger, fear, dislike, frustration, greed and jealousy instead of a solid balance of mental and emotional consideration. We need a balance between our left and right brain--rational mind and emotional mind. Logically, she realizes that she hasn't dated him for even twelve months, neither of them have a good paying job, she has caught him cheating multiple times in less than twelve months or two years, he hasn't shown her that he knows how to be a responsible father, he has two other unwed children and he hasn't **consistently** provided the necessary support for them, nor their mothers; she's forty with three kids and he's 30 with no kids or he has an impending jail sentence that may last for a considerable number of years, yet she decides to have children with him! These types of situations or worse, typically have a measurable negative impact on the children and sometimes long-lasting. As a result, 7, 12 or 18 years later, your son or daughter is dealing with abandonment issues and you will be clueless or wishing you had chosen a better mate or angry and placing blame on others. Sooner or later, you realize that you got entangled with S.A.M. Could it be that having an unwed baby is like paying a contractor in full before he completes building you a house? Subsequently, the mother is left wondering whether the father (contractor) will show up every week to perform all of the necessary actions with diligence and passion to complete building the child. From a logical perspective, this seems like a risky proposition when you consider the small percentage of people who would work diligently to complete a long-term project after they have already been paid!

In my experience, I've often heard single mothers and some advocates say "we need help with our children or we need more government programs for our children." Well, I respectfully submit that we need to redefine and re-emphasize the meaning of good parenting. The *first aspect of good parenting is obtaining a solid understanding of the major requirements of good parenting, which includes parenting*

24/7 365, continuous nurturing and planning, nonstop attention to details, continuous training and discipline, continuous compliments and critiques, **maintaining sufficient food, clothes and shelter,** *maintaining positive relationships with family, friends and teachers, asking questions about concerns and best practices and obeying solid advice and wisdom. Then, we would know without a doubt that government programs were never designed to help people raise children!* **Nobody owes you anything** other than respect, equality, civility or a service that you have paid for. The government doesn't owe you anything more than **equal treatment and protection under the law.** To the extent that the government provides tax subsidies and clean drinking water to one community, the government must provide the same resources to all communities. A celebrity does not owe you a picture or autograph! They don't owe you a two minute conversation. It would be nice on their behalf, but they are not obligated!

Is it possible that having a child is like owning a home? You make plans to own a home. For most people, they just don't jump up one day and decide to buy a house. They make specific plans to get the resources to buy and maintain a house. They determine how much money they need, how long they will have to save to raise the down-payment money, how much overtime they will have to work before and after they buy the house and whether they will have to work two jobs for a time-period. Like a child, you have to take care of the inside and outside of the house, roof to bottom floor, front, side and backyard, cleaning, sweeping, mopping and painting inside and outside of house if it is not brick. *As a good parent, you are responsible for making sure the right food, beliefs, and ideas are placed on the inside of your child.* You must fill them with love, confidence, compassion and pride. On the outside, it's important for you to dress them appropriately for the occasion and in clean clothes. Make sure their teeth are brushed daily, body washed daily, hair is cleaned and combed and their clothes are properly washed. A reasonable person wouldn't attempt to buy a second and third house when she knew that she was struggling to properly maintain the first house. The house will appear unkempt and dirty on the outside and will likely be that way on the inside. The grass isn't often cut, weeds growing around the house, toys and junk in the yard, stains on the house, the house is in need of painting along with broken cabinet doors. Similarly, boys and girls arrive to school hungry, wearing wrinkled and dirty clothes, ashy faces, arms and legs, dry and nappy hair, crust in the corner of their eyes, in discomfort from sleeping on floors and sofas and worst of all, damaged mentally and emotionally from neglect just like the house! Almost always, you buy a home when you become an adult because all reasonable people know that a child does not have the mental, emotional and physical capacity to properly maintain a home. Likewise, a pregnant child does not have the mental, emotional, physical and financial ability to properly raise a child. Therefore, as rational citizens, we must do a better job of discouraging teenage pregnancy! For those males and females who don't feel like advancing their education after high school, they should not conclude that they have free time to have a child! On the contrary, they should keep their options open with the mindset that maybe I will change my mind and attend a college or trade school to improve my employment skills in the future.

A former co-worker has two children and was working a full-time and part-time job and taking three classes online. How is that situation supposed to work out well? Of course, she frequently mentioned that she was tired, overwhelmed and needed sleep. **Ladies, accept 2-3 men in your life who are old enough and wise enough to act as your uncle. Get 2-3 brothers in your age range who can keep you up on the current game of adult boys and young men.** This is particularly important for ladies who don't have male family members in the city where they live or lack productive male family members. Between the brothers and uncles, you can ask questions and gain knowledge and wisdom, so that you don't put regular gas in your car that requires premium. As a result of your independent attitude (stubbornness), now you are faced with an unnecessary repair bill. These are brothers and uncles who you can call when your car breaks down at night, who you can call to help you move instead of me hearing a story of four grown women helping another woman carry a table and sofas during a move; A man who can give you an inside scoop on your boyfriend or fiancé's behavior; Men you can borrow an occasional $50-$200 from without wondering if you will have to pay it back physically; Men who can come over when your boyfriend starts talking sideways like a punk who takes advantage of a weaker person; A man who can accompany you with buying a car or examining a house you intend on renting or buying. Between the brothers and uncles, you have some men who will provide nurturing, consistent training, guidance and discipline to your son, attend PTC, sporting events and most importantly, a duplicable example of how an **honest, compassionate and morally sound man conducts himself**. Between the brothers and uncles, these men will provide the same qualities for your daughter. *You should have good reasoning skills, discernment and counselors when you select these brothers and uncles.* This is very important because a former co-worker of mine chose a man with bad character and it was very evident to the other good men that he had questionable character. Later, there were some allegations of foul behavior between him and her daughter. Had she asked me to evaluate him, I would had clearly told her that his character was shady, not worthy of dating and definitely not marriage material! So, the risk of allowing him to father a child would had not been a consideration at all! Whether or not she would have heeded my warning is a separate issue. Women must remember that men have access to information that women don't! If we have a personal or working relationship with a man, it's likely that we've seen him do things or heard him say comments that represent his character in a positive or negative way. Then, you'll be able to say he was the best thing you never had.

When I was growing up, occasionally I heard an aunt or uncle describe someone as being *wrong and strong*. It meant that the person's choice or behavior was wrong and he or she was forceful about their position. Also, I remember the elders used to frequently say a hard head makes a soft butt. A peculiar aspect of human nature for many people is that they rather be independent and wrong, instead of obedient and right! I recall hearing a wise person say "the prudent sees danger and hides himself, but the simple go on and suffer for it" (Proverbs 27:12). The ego is so powerful and distorting, coupled with our socio-economic and cultural misunderstanding of the meaning of words that it causes many people to suffer unnecessary problems, setbacks, failures and sometimes life-altering trauma because of the false belief that being *humble means that I am weak, asking questions and asking for help means that I'm not smart; obeying guidance and wisdom means that I'm not an adult; I'm not independent; I'm unimportant or I'm inferior.* **Yes, you are inferior in that situation,** on that subject or that specific incident, **but you shouldn't feel like you are inferior as a person!** Furthermore, you are no longer inferior in that specific area now that you have gained that experience! We must recognize and accept that we gain knowledge, know-how and experience by going through experiences as a novice. In this case of wrong and strong, a twenty-two-year-old inmate got into a physical altercation with an officer and required stitches for the back of his head and forehead. Yep, young thugga caught a two piece and a biscuit! Yep, he tried the wrong officer. I was working in the clinic that night when they brought him in. The youngster received two ice packs and waited awhile before he received stitches to his forehead. I don't recall the reason for the delay, but the youngster requested to go back to his cell and rejected stitches for the back of his head. After he signed the Medical Refusal Form, I escorted him to his cell. When he returned to the pod, an officer familiar with the youngster asked him why he didn't get stitches in the back of his head. The youngster said he didn't want to wait any longer. The officer asked what are you going to do? The young inmate said "I'm gonna put toothpaste on it." Now I realize that inmates develop creative ideas to help their circumstances, but this one sounded like a different type of foolishness to me. This statement sounded like an immature youngster doing what he thought would make him appear to be a tough guy, despite jeopardizing his health. Shortly after I returned to my post in the clinic, an officer brought a female inmate in and she was complaining of body pain and sickness. While answering questions from the nurse, the inmate hesitantly admitted that she was addicted to three or four different narcotics. After examining her and determining that she was suffering from basic withdrawal symptoms, the nurse told her that there was very little that they could do to alleviate her pain and sickness. Upon hearing that news, she began crying, whining, moaning and pleading for the nurse to give her any type of medication. The nurse asked her if she was aware that those drugs were harmful to her body and possibly deadly. Through her sobbing, she said yes, "but it hurts sooo much." So then I wondered, why wouldn't she expect to be in pain while going through withdrawal? This was a vivid lesson in the opposing elements of life. You must be able to handle the good and the bad, highs and the lows!

All rational people know that it's best to attempt to solve an issue as soon as possible once it is discovered. **Ignoring it, rejecting it or denying its existence doesn't make it go away.** Most of the time, the problem gets worse, whether it involves finances, child behavior, adult behavior, health, abnormal relationship or academics. Inevitably, a day will come when you will be forced to deal with the issue you were ignoring or denying. Ignoring a problem is like a tire that has a nail in it and it's causing a slow leak. Every so often, the air leaks out weekly, bi-weekly or monthly, as a reminder that something is wrong with the tire. Then, you have to keep putting air back in the tire for it to function properly until you decide to spend the money to fix the problem! If you are proactively avoiding the problem, every day or week you smoke weed, drink beer or liquor to prevent your mind and emotions from dealing with the slow leak--aka baby boy, adult boy, unhappy marriage, unhappy job, volatile temper, bad children, criminal-minded boyfriend, abusive relationship, low self-esteem, self-destructive behavior, sometimey friends, back-stabbing co-workers, unqualified baby mama or daddy, low educational level, criminal friends of your child, obesity, bad work ethic, etc. *Almost all problems require corrective action*! As a result, it is **critically important to engage in proper training, constructive criticism and strategies to combat irrational reasoning at an early age**. If not, the same irrational reasoning is deepened by the young man's testosterone, misperceptions of manhood, peer pressure and other negative influences. Thus, this irrational reasoning causes him to believe that it makes sense to not put forth the effort to master the lessons in school, despite multiple teachers and staff telling him the importance of education. It causes him to think that he won't have to cope with severe social and economic consequences from dropping out of school. It causes him to think that it's okay to commit a violent assault against a person, commit an armed robbery because he doesn't have any money, he wants to buy some Jordans and designer jeans, a gang member told him to do it, or to "buy clothes for his child." This is the same irrational reasoning that causes him to believe it's okay to kill a person or have the unmitigated balls to kick in the front or back door to your home as if he is responding to an emergency! "*The way of a fool is right in his own eyes*," according to Proverbs 12:15. This was clearly the case regarding Inmate Smooth. Inmate Smooth was charged with murdering a teenage boy and he was housed on the maximum security floor. Subsequently, Inmate B murdered a teenage boy who happened to be Smooth's younger brother. Ironically, Inmate B was housed on the same floor as Inmate Smooth. As I supervised Smooth while he was performing Houseman duties, Smooth sincerely expressed his sadness at the loss of his brother and told me that he recognized Inmate B from the news. His expressions had me feeling sympathetic, as he told the story from the perspective that his brother was the victim of a random crime. Two days later, I found out that Smooth was found guilty of murdering B's brother. Of course, he never told me that while he was relaying his sob story. As I thought about the manipulation, I wondered why Smooth was mad at B. Did Smooth really not comprehend the obvious elementary, yet tragic tic-for-tac circle of criminals? Had he not heard of kill my dog and I will kill your cat? Had he not heard of karma? Or, was it the classic psychological case of I'm the victim no matter what? Most of the time, when you do dirt, you get dirt! It's just a matter of time.

Baby boys and adult boys are haunted by impatience and foolish thinking. These two traits lead to foolish comments and actions. At approximately 12:30 am, I notified an inmate to pack up to go home. At approximately 1:30 am, he hadn't been picked up from the dayroom. He pressed the intercom and said, can you turn on the TV? I said no. He replied, "what I post to do, sit here and do nothin!" I said yes or you can go back to your cell and go home tomorrow. He chuckled and said i-ight. I wondered what made him think that I should turn the TV on in the wee hours of the morning when inmates were sleeping. Also, did he not realize that his only option was to sit and wait for the officer to pick him up? Impatience and foolish thinking also applies to free people. While working the Administrative Segregation pod (the hole), five female mental health counselors arrived to the floor to conduct mental health evaluations of the inmates who were housed on the floor. The counselors had more than nine cells to visit. I explained to the counselors that we should travel together in one group or we could go in two separate groups. The purpose of following this procedure was so I could monitor their safety and deter any lewd acts by the inmates. One counselor twisted her face in typical sister style and said, it will take too long and we have time-constraints. We will walk individually. In my mind, I'm thinking that she is a professionally trained social worker and she isn't new at this job. Therefore, she must know that inmates in the hole are unpredictable sometimes and usually engage in perverted behavior when they have the opportunity. I told them that we can follow her suggestion as long as you know that I can't deter the inmates from engaging in perverted acts. Having issued my disclaimer, they agreed to conduct their evaluations individually. Within fifteen minutes, they finished their interviews and we existed the pod. As we were walking towards the exit of the floor, two counselors told me that they wanted to report two inmates who masturbated while they were conducting the interviews. Both ladies had a look of disdain and disgust on their faces. Nevertheless, I tried to sound concerned as I recorded their complaints. However, I felt a bit confused because their knowledge and experience should had told them that there was a high probability that one or more of the inmates would engage in such behavior without an officer standing next to them. Being bold is okay sometimes, but being bold and impatient is usually a recipe for disaster. Later, I issued citations to both inmates.

One night while I was escorting a seemingly harmless and friendly fifty-four-year-old man from the medical floor back to general population, he stated "I get out on the 19th Johnson." I said good. What are you gonna do? He replied, go home! I said, I know that! What are you gonna do as far as staying out of trouble? He replied, "I don't usually get in trouble, *I had a good reason for stealing!*" As my ears began burning, I said what do you mean you had a good reason for stealing? He said, I got fired from my job and I got two young ones at home to take care of. Sooo, I replied! There is no good reason for stealing, to which he responded, "yes there is." "I gotta take care of my kids." I asked do you live in a house or apartment. He said that he lived in a house. Good, I said. I got a homeboy who has a good reason to steal. Give me your address so he can rob your house. He laughed and replied, hell nah! Now do you see my point, I said! If it's not okay for someone to steal from you, then it's not okay for you to steal! Obviously, his reasoning skills were elementary, selfish and illogical. Unfortunately, illogical reasoning is prevalent on a more devastating level among those males who engage in senseless gun violence. If a person **believes that their best choice is to get a gun** or some other weapon to address a verbal dispute, commit a violent crime, whether home invasion, carjacking, robbery, without regard to jeopardizing their health, life and freedom, that should be deemed a mental health disorder because that type of reasoning is abnormal in a civilized society! We must reasonable reach this conclusion without even factoring in the callous disregard for the health and life of the adult victim, not to mention the children and elderly people who are victimized! By no means am I suggesting that these violent cowards are incompetent and don't know what they are doing is wrong. The majority of them know that their behavior is wrong and illegal, but their parents and environment have taught them that it's the cool thug-thing to do or this is the only way to survive. *Somewhere along their growth process, nanna, auntie, Sunday school or a school teacher told them that certain behaviors were wrong.* I'm reminded of the evening when I responded to an emergency call over the radio. As I ran to the location, my adrenaline was high and my heart rate was faster than normal because I remembered that a petite female officer was performing security duties at that location. I was the first officer to arrive and just as I reached the door to enter the pod, the punk inmate ran up the steps to his cell and shut the door. He was a true example of a cowardly clown! During the incident, he walked up to the officer and stood in her face and verbally threatened her. Fortunately, he didn't physically assault her. He still got dealt with. **They know right from wrong**, but they have no positive reasoning skills, no empathy, pride, self-worth, work ethic and very little self-control because most of their lives they weren't required to control their impulses, tantrums and outbursts. However, under strong and quick supervision and the right environment, believe me when I tell you that they learn to refrain from disrespectful and negative behavior rather quickly. The harder heads fall in line soon enough!

Mentality is directly related to preparation, preparation is directly related to actions and actions are directly related to results! Unless a person has worked extensively in an inner-city public school, rural school or in law enforcement, *most people have no clue how prevalent ignorance is in society*! Is anybody able to identify the time-period when it seems like it became uncool and an embarrassment to work for a living? It's intriguing how this mentality spreads across multiple ethic groups. Oddly enough, it seems more prevalent among low-income and high-income groups. When I used to conduct a security check in the am hours, regardless of whether it was 1 am or 2:30 am, inmates would often stand at their cell door or sit up in bed and say, "Johnson, can I work for you in the morning?" This meant that they were pleading to be the clean-up guy to keep the floor clean throughout the day. This was the last thing on my mind at that time in the morning because the daily activities didn't begin until approximately 8 am. I've often wondered, if I say yes, will he sleep better? Shouldn't he have more important issues on his mind? After the inmate finished sweeping, mopping, cleaning windows, distributing laundry bags, and collecting trash, the officer would pay the inmate with extra food-two sandwiches and two apples. The incredible irony was that some inmates would plead to work for food in jail, but refused to work for money when they were free in society. Within thirty days to a year, some of these same boys would be back in jail for robbing or stealing. Adult boys fail to understand that they can't fix their problems until they **fix their thinking**! Once they resolve to seek and obey guidance from knowledgeable and wise people, put in the commitment and effort to get educated, treat people decently, respect themselves and others and refrain from illegal and negative behavior, they will be able to resolve their obstacles and problems in a beneficial way. Everybody can get mad, curse and act a fool! However, everybody can't get mad and then find a legally productive solution to the problem that caused them to get mad. Which group are you a member of?

To these criminals, I would ask have you ever given any basic thought, much less analytical reasoning, as to why the government "exhausts funding" for educational programs, social service programs (job training, mental health), unemployment, but never exhausts funding for jails and prisons? Hmmm! That's why the Creator stuck a brain inside of our melon. The **purpose of the brain** is to provide a person the ability to solve problems in a reasonable manner and to analyze whether a situation is beneficial or detrimental. This purpose was made ever so clear during a conversation I had with an inmate while he was on a cleaning detail. Inmate JuJu relayed a sincere story of being released from prison in Florida and moving to the Atlanta area to get a "new start and stay out of trouble." JuJu said he met a nice lady who had some questionable family members, but they continued to date and attend church and they eventually got married when he was twenty-six-years-old. Shortly after getting married, a so-called cousin or family friend began spending questionable time with his wife. Then, JuJu said that he began to hear rumors about this man and his wife fooling around. When he questioned his wife, she swore that nothing was going on. Yet, inappropriate calls and visits continued to occur when he wasn't home. When a person has undeveloped reasoning skills, it doesn't make a difference what city or state he moves to for a new start. **Wherever you go, there you are**! You think the way that you think, whether you are on TV or just watch TV, in a classy nightclub or a hole-in-the-wall, attend an urban or suburban school, on church grounds or off, in an upscale hotel or regular motel, in politics or on the PTA, a celebrity or regular person, have a lot of money or a little money. When faced with an untrustworthy person who puts you in dangerous situations, even a spouse, he should had logically concluded that he needed to get away from her because she was jeopardizing his health and potentially his freedom because he was on probation. At thirty-years-old, JuJu admitted to me that he realized that his wife jeopardized his freedom, but he didn't realize it at that time. I told him that he should had realized that immediately since he had already spent time in prison! Also, he should had realized that something negative usually happens whenever two Black men have an on-going dispute. At the time, JuJu said that he just thought about "not letting this man disrespect me" and trying to fight for his marriage. After some time, another verbal altercation happened and the man attacked him. They tussled and JuJu shot the man. When JuJu told me his story, he had not gone to trial on the shooting charge, but even if he wins his self-defense claim, he will still have to serve time for having a weapon as a convicted felon. He also admitted that he didn't know his father and never had any positive men in his life who could have given him wisdom to make wise choices regarding some situations. Wise elders and mentors are very beneficial to a person's life. If JuJu had formed a relationship with some elders or mentors, I think they would had told him that he was in a volatile relationship and all relationships can't be saved. Maybe they would had told him that all relationships are seasonal and perhaps JuJu would had realized that the season of his marriage had ended and he should walk away before he is carried away in handcuffs like he was in Florida.

From a psychological view, what causes many inmates to think that they are still entitled to the same rights as if they are not incarcerated? In one instance, an inmate believed that he could decide when he would be discharged from the hospital. On a basic level, why couldn't he understand that that was solely a medical decision that was within the authority of the hospital in conjunction with the law enforcement agency? This same guy asked me why I was reading his information contained in the folder given to me by another officer. I explained to him that when he is in custody, all of his property becomes the jail's property. We read, inspect and review everything that is provided to him, except legal and medical documents. He didn't seem to understand that basic concept. After providing examples and explaining it for the third time, I told him there was no need to discuss the matter anymore. Another right that some inmates think they have is privacy. *Privacy* is one of the main privileges an inmate loses when he's incarcerated. Usually, it's a new inmate that has this false expectation because experienced inmates know that privacy doesn't exist. In fact, the veteran inmates will attempt to have a conversation with you while they are sitting on the toilet. Some would yell "hey Johnson, I was talking to you." That was one of the craziest interactions to me. I'm reminded of the time when an inmate was waving frantically from his cell and banging on the door. When I arrived, I asked what's the problem? He said, "I need to get out cuz my roommate is taking a dump." I said oh no my brother, you are stuck in there with that booboo smell! As I walked away, he shouted that's chucked up Johnson! On another occasion when I was locking the doors one night, an inmate walked out of his cell and casually sat at the table. I asked, what's goin on? He replied, "my roommate is taking a dump." I said, And. Then I said, I will allow it this time, but that is a violation of policy. Many times, I would require the inmate to enter the cell anyway. First of all, I believe that the inmate chose to sacrifice his privacy when he willingly decided to commit an illegal act. Secondly, they are in the cell for more than fourteen hours a day, so it's a fact that they've already used the toilet with each other in the room, so now is no different.

There seems to be a serious disconnect between reality and their view of life. Additionally, *psychological dysfunction is evident in most inmates by their constant attempt to rationalize their illegal and violent acts.* They make statements such as, "I have babies, but I ain't have no money and no job; There are no programs for Black men; I didn't have no choice; I took a charge for my homeboy; I didn't have nothing to do; I didn't know they were gonna stick up the store; They were talking about me, so I shot him; She didn't say stop; I was getting that money," which means chump change. *Forethought* is a critical part of analyzing a situation that many people lack, especially baby boys, adult boys and inmates. Although hindsight is 20/20, foresight shouldn't be 20/70, which is equivalent to low vision. Low vision is defined as not having enough sight to do whatever you need to do. It's a darn shame for a person to have poor physical vision and mental vision. Forethought will provide you the ability to realize that just because you are the getaway driver for the robbery, it doesn't guarantee that you are too much safer than your three immoral and irrational cohorts who are going to commit the robbery. So, as she sat in the driveway still not deterred by all of the possible terrible results, she was shocked when only one cohort came out of the house and he was bleeding. Shortly after her arrest, her living nightmare was exacerbated by the fact that she may be incarcerated for the rest of her life. **Oops, I'm sorry, I didn't mean for it to happen, I wish it never happened, please forgive me, is of little to no consolation after you have intentionally killed a person**! None of those recited remarks ease the pain of the victim's family not having their loved one around because of another person's inability to control their anger, frustration, greed or use good decision-making skills! Here are several scenarios involving a lack of forethought:

During the early years of the millennium, educational professionals noticed a trend among some parents of troubled students and coined the phrase "school-hopping." This phrase referred to parents who transferred their child to a different school at the end of the school year for two or three years in a row. This was a naïve and petty attempt to conceal the child's difficulties because the child's academic records are transferred to the new school. Whatever academic and social problems the child has, they will arrive at the new school on the same day as the child! This situation is akin to the family moving and the mother driving her dirty car to the new apartment. It's at a different residence, but it's the same car.

While teaching fifth grade, I had an unnecessary and unfortunate encounter with Rerun. For some reason, his mother didn't like me. It could have been because her son didn't like me or perhaps she

didn't like me because I gave her an honest assessment of his defi-
ciencies. As the school year progressed, she wrote a couple of letters
to the assistant principal and phoned the principal and claimed that
I was the cause of her son failing badly. She claimed that her son was
an A student in math and other subjects prior to being placed in my
class. Rather than accept my assessment and make a professional
determination, the principal decided to appease the mother. I don't
recall whether the mother or principal decided that the boy should
take a math chapter test in the principal's office with all of us present. Needless to say, the mother was very embarrassed after her son
scored a 45 on the test. ReRun had that same frustrated expression
on his face that he often had in class. His mother babied him into an
embarrassing situation! Mothers cannot and should not attempt to
protect their boys from all consequences. Consequences are meant
to correct you, direct you or protect you. Consequences notify you
of your mistakes, disobedience (hard-headedness), ignorance,
weakness, impatience, foolishness, bad choices, laziness and inexperience. Fifth grade math involves basic counting and approximately
ten formulas, about half of which are taught in the fourth grade. So
my position was, all during the weeks of the mother challenging me
and receiving questions from the administration, if he knew how to
count prior to being placed in my class, he should still know how
to count and he wouldn't be failing! The fact of the matter was that
the boy was not proficient in multiplication and division. This was
another sad and drastic example of a mother engaging in irrational
behavior that revealed her shortcomings, which subjected them to
unnecessary negative consequences. The mother knew that her son
was a cry-baby with a sour attitude and that she didn't consistently
supervise his academic studies outside of school. This was also a
drastic example of the *unnecessary pressures that good quality and
dedicated teachers have to endure!*

Inmate Nippy, a fifty-three-year-old man, got sentenced to ten
years in prison when his son was fourteen-years-old. While escorting

him and a few others to the clinic to receive diabetic medicine at 4 am, his friend asked how he was doing. He replied, "I can't sleep cause I'm madder than a motherchucker. I called my wife last night and she said that my son (now 24) is talking shid to her and hitting her." Then, he said I spoke to her the day before New Year's Eve and she said that my son pushed her down and stole her money to buy drugs. Now, Nippy is stressed and upset about the situation and he is feeling angry and guilty because he can't protect his wife! All he can do is try to comfort her through the phone. This situation is a glaring example of an a*dult boy* lacking forethought and reasoning skills. Nippy failed to realize that one of the **essential roles of a mature man is that of a protector**. Mature and responsible men realize that they must maintain their freedom and be present in order to serve their critical and irreplaceable role as protector of the family! I can't imagine the frustration and agony I would feel knowing that someone was abusing my wife or mother and I couldn't protect her because I was locked up! I know that the agony would be compounded by knowing that I was locked up for the foolish choice I made. Again, you shouldn't undervalue the incredible importance of freedom!

An inmate pressed the intercom at 8:30 am on a Saturday morning. He said, "I gotta get a new cell, me and my roommate ain't getting along." What's the problem, asked the technician? "He said I fart too much." Get out of here with that foolishness, she said as we laughed. Then, his cellmate came to the intercom and said, "I been here seven months. I can do my time, but I can't do it with him. He makin' my time hard! I know his people on the street-I know his auntie, uncle and cousin. I just talked to them on the phone the other day and I told'em sumthin wrong wit ya kin folk for real! He be fartn' all times of night and da man don't even say 'cuse me cuz he think I'm sleep." This story may sound unbelievable, but it's totally true. This is the type of trivial foolishness that a detention officer is forced to address on a daily basis. Yet, I had to contact the Sergeant with that silly situation because it appeared that it was going to escalate to a physical altercation. Who knew that a person tends to pass gas often as he goes through cocaine withdrawal, as the inmate so politely informed us. The lesson of this story is that a person has no clue what type of roommate he may have in jail.

Late one night, I responded with the nurse to a call for medical assistance. When we arrived, the adult boy began whining about the lack of medical attention he was receiving and how he was also mistreated in another county jail. After we arrived at the clinic, it was determined that Inmate Neckbone was obese and suffering from high blood pressure. While at the clinic, Neckbone complained that the medical staff and I weren't concerned about his serious medical condition and that we didn't value his life. Ironically, my view was that he didn't value his life, nor view his condition seriously or he wouldn't have had criminal charges in two counties. Is it rational to expect people to appear overly concerned about your personal issue when your actions clearly indicate that you aren't seriously concerned about the issue? I contend that it is **foolish to expect someone to show a higher level of concern about you than you have for yourself**. It amazes me the number of people who always want people to show them the utmost respect, yet they demonstrate almost no respect for themselves and others. Common sense dictates that freedom is very important when a person has an on-going medical condition. Common sense also dictates that Neckbone should had given some thought to the necessity of access to medical treatment as a free man before he engaged in criminal activities in two counties. As usual, he was quick to emphasize that his charges "are only a misdemeanor." Nevertheless, the charges were serious enough to get him incarcerated and lose his freedom. Neckbone went on to stress that he had a family and career. It appears to me that having multiple charges in different counties is counter-productive to valuing his family and career!

Little Jeff was a baby boy inmate who was about twenty-one-years-old and he had a habit of threatening to jump off of the mezzanine rail anytime he didn't get his way or got upset about something. On this day when he pulled this stunt, I was the officer on the floor. After I asked him to get down two times and he refused, I just calmly called for back-up. Little Jeff had no clue that sitting on the mezzanine rail and threatening to jump because he was mad about his situation was not hurting me. For the other boys, threatening to break the phone, slamming the cell door as hard as you can, threatening to flood the cell or actually flooding your cell and the dayroom doesn't hurt me or any officer. In fact, it might help me by providing overtime money to my paycheck if there aren't enough staff to supervise the cleanup. Inmates would frequently threaten to flood their cell or pod as if they knew that an officer had to mop the water. Not only did the baby boy usually cause water damage to his property, but also the property of the other inmates who were usually surprised to see water pouring under the door into their cell! All of this childish behavior is sadly amusing and swiftly disregarded by a mature man. This boyish unruly behavior and damage to government property almost always resulted in punishment in the form of suspension of some or all of the inmate's privileges. Again, the inmate has engaged in another sad example of irrational thinking and self-destructive behavior by thinking that aggression is the best answer to all of life's problems!

I remember having to work on July 4th. It was probably my third year on the job. I remember it clearly because it was a beautiful day and my friend was having a cookout and pool party. I really wanted to call-in sick because I wasn't able to get the holiday off. So, I improvised by going to the cookout and having a little fun before I went to work to deal with the boys. I arrived at work two hours late. Not too long after I arrived to my post, I saw the nineteen-year-old kid-thugga walking around the pod acting frustrated. So I said to my co-worker, what is his problem today? She told me that he was mad because his family was late. Right after she finished speaking, kid-thugga pressed the intercom. When my co-worker answered, he said "is my people here yet?" She said no. I told you when they get here, I will tell you. He said "damn, they post to been here." A short time later, rotation ended and it was time for everyone to enter their cell. After I entered the pod, everyone began entering their cell except you know who. I looked at him and said what are you waiting for? He said "I ain't goin' in Johnson." I said why not? He said, "cuz my people ain't come see me" along with some heavily pronounced curse words. I tried to reason with him by saying it's the holiday and they probably went to a cookout and got tired up. Try not to sweat it and I'm sure they will visit on your next day. That didn't help. As I was securing the cell doors, I said you know how I work, so go inside and try to relax. He said "chuck that" and kept pacing around with his fists clenched, pouting and cursing. He even threw water cups at the wall. He had a full-out seven-year- old tantrum with tears in his eyes. I just shook my head and walked out of the pod. As a detention officer, it's very important to have sharp decision-making skills. I knew that baby boy needed some time to finish pouting and his energy level would decline after some minutes. When it was time for the other inmates to begin their rotation, I flashed the pod lights on and off two times and clicked his door and he slowly walked into his cell. He seriously believed that his family was obligated to visit him, rather than enjoy the holiday. It appears that many inmates don't give any consideration to the fact that life goes on for their family and friends who aren't incarcerated. In retrospect, he may have been more irritated because I know that I smelled like hamburgers, hot dogs and chicken.

I recall starting my shift one night around 11pm in mid June and an inmate said, "my cell is too hot ... I can't breathe in the cell ... I got asthma and I'm not going back in the cell." I said where do you think you are going? He said "man, I'm telling you I'm not going back in that cell. "You gonna have to call ya folks." I said, I will and you're going to be right back in that hot cell, so you might as well walk in alone. He remained stubborn and as soon as a few officers arrived and he realized that his whining wasn't going to change his circumstances, he walked into his cell. This was another glaring example of a lack of forethought and no wherewithal of consequences. It seems to me that a potential criminal should give some thought to the high possibility that the jail and prison conditions will be worse than his conditions as a free person. More often than not, negative consequences result from negative actions and your only two choices are to accept the consequences peacefully or reject them and suffer the consequences. Constantly getting upset and whining about the consequences hardly ever eliminate the consequences. After the temporary halt in whining, the inmate still finds himself in isolation, a hot or cold cell, eating bland tasting food or having visitation and recreation privileges canceled.

Upon returning from court, many inmates are sad and angry. Who cares! Now, it's their turn to feel hurt and angry even though they aren't innocent like most of their victims! They frequently talk to each other about how the prosecutor and judge did them dirty regarding their sentencing. Yet, no thought was given by criminals about being caught a second, third or fourth time and being prosecuted by the same prosecutor that dealt with him previously. Likewise, no thought was given to appearing again before a judge who has presided over a previous criminal trial. Consequently, the prosecutor and judge are immediately aware of whether his actions reveal a pattern that is unchanged and likely to get worse. So, it comes as no surprise to anyone except him and his family when the judge renders a stiff sentence! In one memorable case, the judge sentenced all five members of a neighborhood gang to life plus twenty years. The oldest criminal was twenty-six and the youngest was eighteen. All of these boys, by choice, just eliminated themselves from the game of life. Runnin' amuck in the streets and engaging in foolish and destructive acts is similar to the inevitable outcome of rolling dice at the dice table in Vegas. **Eventually, you will Crap Out!** Their behavior and comments are indicative of no thought given to the consequences of their actions. Then, when sentencing time arrives, inmates are filled with shock, anxiety, anger, depression and sometimes suicidal. All of these emotions are reflected when they board the bus to return to jail or within days after they return to jail. Deputies report that some inmates are so emotionally distraught that they don't return on the main bus for safety reasons. Part of the shock stems from their delusional rationale that causes them to think that they can beat the case at trial despite the overwhelming evidence, which sometimes includes one of the co-defendants testifying against everyone who was involved.

On one occasion, a sixty-year-old Inmate Worker touched the arm of a civilian worker and told her that he wanted to kiss her juicy lips. I'm not sure whether he had a senior moment or whether he's just a nasty old man. What I do know is that wisdom is absent from where it should be present! He was immediately removed from the workforce and returned to General Population. The next time I saw him, he was upset and whining about being housed in General Population and the possibility of receiving a new charge of sexual harassment. I just shook my head and walked away because if he makes piss-poor decisions and lacks self-control at his age, there really wasn't anything beneficial that I could have said to him. Similar to the old man lacking wisdom, Inmate Pookie lacked the least bit of common sense. I locked Pookie in his cell for insolence. Subsequently, he managed to get out of his cell, perhaps during medication call. He pressed the intercom button in the dayroom and asked me to check information about his charges. That's like a criminal going back to the crime scene while the police are there. His foolish behavior caused me to investigate how he got out of his cell, which led to me discovering how he had jammed the lock on the door. As a result, I gave him a citation and suspended his privileges longer than before.

It's completely irrational to promote and glorify gunplay, as many rappers and so-called thugs do. Then, when the shots hit you, your family and homies, you say "it was senseless, foul, he never did nothin' to nobody, he was just tryin' to provide for his family; or when the shots hit your friend or family you say "the hood is chucked-up, they was just tryin' to make a livin'; he didn't deserve to die like that." Usually, a rapper lives in the hood that he claims is chucked-up and it was all good because he was rep'n the hood all over social media. Now that the crabs have pulled someone he loves down to the bottom of the barrel, the hood ain't all good. You know that there are no positive guarantees to a criminal lifestyle. Consequently, you consciously or subconsciously accept all of the possibilities of that lifestyle, including a colostomy bag, tracheotomy tube, paralysis, partial blindness, critical stabbing, risking your family's health, a ten year sentence, life sentence and death. Until somebody checks you about the correct qualities of manhood and toughness and you begin to demonstrate those qualities, the hood will remain dangerous. Manhood and toughness have nothing to do with bragging about stealing, robbing, trappin', shooting someone, killing someone or your crew stomping someone out for no reason. Bragging about violence proves two things for sure. First, it proves that you were raised without any decent human values and common sense. Secondly, it proves that you were primarily unloved as a child and you suffer from so much bitterness, resentment, anger, delusion and self-hate that **you don't recognize the incredible blessing of a human life**! A similar situation plays out in jail every few months. Frequently, inmates who have committed violent crimes are quick to yell and curse when they are in pain, sick or are fearful of being beaten up by other inmates. Yet, these same people had no problem inflicting pain on their victims and will have no problem inflicting trauma on future victims if they have the opportunity. It's interesting and ridiculous how abusers and criminals have no hesitation when they violate children, women and adults, but give animated pleas and react like it's a cardinal sin for someone to violate them. In one instance, I recall an inmate charged with rape and four counts of aggravated sodomy began getting teary-eyed while pleading with the officer to save him by moving him to another floor because some inmates were threatening to beat him up. Now he's pleading for protection, but that didn't occur to him when he was violently harming his innocent victim! These fake thugs get into trouble, disrespect officers on a daily basis, hold their groin, masturbate in front of nurses and female officers and when they write a check that their ass can't cash, then they want the officer to save them. They make comments like "I know you police don't give a damn about my health or life, but I do." Ironically, his actions and mentality strongly suggest that he doesn't give a damn about his health or life! In response to one thug's request, I recall a funky veteran officer telling the soft thug, what goes around comes around. I'm not Officer Save-a-Hoe! In a separate but similar situation, I discovered that Inmate Bonehead rigged his lock and got out of his cell. Just as I was telling Bonehead that I was going to relocate him, Sgt. Burnt walked up. Now, Bonehead begins to whine, "Sarg, I been in that pod since I got here and I don't have no problems." Sgt. Burnt replied, it's too late now. You should have thought about that before you damaged the door. With fear in his voice, Bonehead said, "Sarg, you don't understand, I got like a high profile case and I don't feel safe moving." Ain't this some shid, I thought. Now, he doesn't feel safe and he wants the Sergeant to be concerned about his safety. Indeed, it was the responsibility of the officers to protect the safety of the inmates to the best of our ability, but I hardly ever showed a trouble-maker inmate that I was concerned about his well-being. The expression on my face would be expressionless.

In 2015, three teens in Georgia committed a home invasion. They kicked in the front door of the house and shot the male resident. As the wife clutched her baby and ran towards the rear door, these baby clowns ran through the house and shot at the lady. Supposedly, all of this happened simply because the nineteen-year-old clown asked the 18 and 16-year-old boys if they wanted to make some fast money. Had they possessed reasoning skills, they would had asked what do we have to do to make the money? If they were told that they had to break into somebody's home, they should had decided that it would be wrong and not worth the risk. Subsequently, the three of them were found guilty and sentenced to 18-30 years in jail. The two youngest baby-face boys could pass for 14-15 years old. I'm certain that they are not physically nor mentally prepared to safely and positively cope with prison. Unfortunately, when they reach that realization, it's going to be extremely too late for them or anyone who cares about them to protect them from the physical and mental wounds they will likely receive. For some, the closing of the cell door on the first, second and third night is very scary, confusing and intimidating. Their anxiety-ridden minds and bodies are intensified by the strange noises during the night, such as arguing, party-style laughing, sexual moaning sounds and fighting. Jails and prisons are filled with mentally and emotionally abnormal people who completely believe in preying on weak and immature people without any regard for consequences or the temporary or permanent harm that they are inflicting. Entering prison between 18-23 years of age and weighing between 120-150 pounds is probably a dangerous scenario. One day while I was conducting a security check on a minimum security floor, I did a double-take because the inmate was so short and young looking. He stood about 4'6" with braids. His eyes were watery and he had such a baby-face that he looked 14-15-years-old. I really thought it was a mistake and maybe management was checking to see if officers were performing thorough security checks. Therefore, I stopped and asked, how old are you? Seventeen, he said. Later, I found out that he was wanted in New Orleans for a violent felony. My sympathy immediately evaporated. Suddenly, I began to think that his lack of forethought may place him and others like him in situations in prison that they may never recover from or cause their family members to make weekly payments of protection money!! I imagine that many of these boys find themselves in defensive situations only to realize in the final moments that there is no gun to shoot. Suddenly, he is faced with getting beat with a sock of dried soap or magazines! Now, he's forced to defend himself with his hands and I don't think any of the boys in the younger generations learned how to box. Growing up watching Ali, Frazier, Holmes, Sugar Ray and Hearns made me and many of my peers want to gain boxing skills! We would run outside before or after a fight and practice "throwing our hands" and some boys even took boxing lessons! At various high schools and neighborhoods, some guys would be known for being good with the hands. That's how we defended ourselves.

In a manner similar to what goes around comes around, it seems that there is a similarity between some politicians and inmates. The attitudes and behaviors of many Republicans mirror those of adult boys. Often, I heard various Republicans say that the Democrats should be cooperative and act professional, yet they rarely exhibited a cooperative and rational demeanor regarding a multitude of policies during President Obama's administration! Many of them around the country lacked basic self-discipline to demonstrate professional decorum! Quite a few Republican congressmen said that they were doing what was right when they opposed President Obama's policies. I think that their actions and comments demonstrated that they engaged in obstructionism for approximately seven consecutive years of Obama's presidency. Now that Democratic congressmen are opposing policies of the current president, for just cause, most of the Republican congressmen are accusing the Democrats of obstructionism. *Anytime words and actions are wrong only when another person does it to you and not because it is simply wrong to do, that is a clear sign of immaturity, hypocrisy and illogicality!*

I recall hearing a situation wherein a father claimed that he really loved his son and wanted to be with him on a regular basis and that was why he was really stressed out by the on-going custody battle. After he "lashed out" and committed a tragic crime, he probably eliminated his ability to ever be able to spend quality time with his son. Basic reasoning skills should reveal to you that you must pick your battles after careful consideration, *for all battles are not worth fighting*. Also, many battles often require patience. It's important to know that when you are going through misfortune or fortune, neither condition has to be life-long. Misfortune won't last if you accept guidance, learn the lesson(s) from it and have a sincere desire to do better! Fortune certainly won't last if you squander and abuse it. This has been proven by the many athletes and celebrities who have squandered millions of dollars. Also, you should realize that as long as you are alive and not severely impaired, you live to overcome another day! Lastly, all solutions involve a logical strategy. Another example of a clear lack of basic reasoning skills and reverence for life, women and children involves the clowns who began shooting at the Mother's Day parade in California. Foregoing the callousness of the crimes momentarily, these actions clearly show a lack of reasoning skills. These adult boys are clueless of the permanent trauma and loss they cause! They are clueless of their loss of freedom that they will soon encounter, not to mention the unforeseen dangers of the prison environment that awaits them. A similar unbelievable incident occurred in Kentucky when boys shot people who were celebrating in a park on Thanksgiving Day.

During an unusually slow Saturday, I encountered an inmate who appeared upset. As I walked by, he asked me if I could help him. I said maybe, what's your issue? He asked me if I knew how he could file a complaint against his probation officer for revoking his probation. Why did he revoke your probation, I asked? The inmate said that his probation officer "revoked me because I didn't report to my scheduled weekend program in DeKalb County. It wasn't my fault I didn't report." I asked why didn't you report? He said that he didn't report because he was locked up in Gwinnett County for driving with a suspended license. He seriously stated this to me as a legitimate reason and believed that his probation officer did him wrong.

Who's coo-coo? Did he not understand that it was his responsibility not to get arrested while he was on probation? Subsequently, he gestured to me two times with his thumbs up as if to say, I'll ask him for something one day and he won't provide it. It was an amusing gesture in that it demonstrates the psychological disconnect that inmates have regarding the relationship between officers and inmates. We are not equally positioned as many inmates believe and strongly state. Many inmates believe that officers are required to listen to them and are required to obey their requests. For some, this false belief is based upon their misunderstanding that officers must obey them because they are required to obey our commands. This conclusion is evidenced by their frequent statement, "you want me to listen to you, but you don't listen to me." For some reason, those inmates didn't realize that it was not a reciprocal relationship.

Again, I can't understate how much information I have been exposed to and how intriguing it has been to work in the fields of education and law enforcement. One intriguing aspect to me is the percentage of males who have feminine names. I suspect that the femininity of these names is most likely reflective of the boy's father not being a committed man during the birth process. More than likely, an involved father who possessed maturity would had protested a feminine name and required a masculine name. I contend that these names reflect the presence of a female-headed family, including the grandmother. In the minds of some ladies, especially young mothers (teens, early 20s), naming a baby boy a "cute name" is justification for a feminine name. However, no realization is given to the stigma associated with the negative self-esteem and possible anger issues that may result from consistent teasing, as early as the 1st or 2nd grade. I'm referring to names like Chantelle, Laquinta, Ashley, Tandy, Brandy, Larelle, Lavelle, Latrell, Shantae and Leslie. These names aren't any more masculine than Franklina is feminine. I'm not sure if many men would give their sons a feminine name. Whether parents realize it or not, acknowledging a person by their name and pronouncing it correctly has a positive or negative impact on their identity, especially during the early childhood and teen years. This assertion can be evidenced by the facial expressions of students in school every time the teacher calls the roll. Many teachers can attest to this. I remember the happy and surprised expressions of Latino kids when I pronounced their names correctly because I know a little Spanish. Conversely, I remember the embarrassed expressions of African-American and Caucasians kids whenever I mispronounced their names and their classmates began laughing. Nobody likes being laughed at, especially children! While this might seem minor, it is another unnecessary burden that the child has to bear from their parents. I would imagine that a boy who has a girl's name, according to U.S. tradition, probably would develop some level of anxiety, frustration or defense mechanism after having his name called so many times from K-12th grade. In some cases, this issue doesn't end during the teen years. Haven't you met an adult who seemed just a little hesitant when she or he said their uncommon name during an introduction? Similarly, what's the reason for a parent sending a boy to elementary school wearing an earring? Does the mother think it's cute or the father thinks it's cool? Either way, it is senseless because it doesn't serve any beneficial purpose and causes an unnecessary distraction for the boy. From his first day in school, the boy sees that most girls are wearing earrings, so the question becomes why am I wearing an earring? When you have an accurate understanding of the meaning of purpose and a sense of respect for purpose, as it relates to objects, your life and the life of others, it will usually guide your actions accordingly. Upon returning to school after Christmas recess, little Joe returned to school with an earring in his left ear. I was truly perplexed as to why someone would put an earring in the ear of a third-grader. As I sat at my desk, I wondered was this on his Christmas list or his mom or dad's list? It's a scary thought to consider that it may have been on the boy's list. Now, many of the boys and girls are focused on his earring.

Of course, Joe spent the week showing it off to his classmates instead of focusing on his lessons. By the second week, the earring had been misplaced 3-4 times, which was another unnecessary distraction. Children don't need any irrelevant distractions in their lives and definitely not in school.

It's extremely important for many people, particularly young people, to get out of the habit of acting and reacting without giving basic and adequate thought to their words and actions because as sure as night follows day, **consequences will follow sooner or later**! It's critical to determine or estimate whether the consequences will be beneficial or detrimental, minor or major. In the case of an inmate who refused to return to his cell after breakfast ended, he told the officer that his cell was cold and he wasn't going in until he got another blanket. The officer asked then told the inmate several times in a nice manner to return to his cell. Then, I politely told the youngin' to go in his cell. The baby-face eighteen-year-old mustered up as much bravado as a twenty-year-old and told me, "I ain't goin' nowhere 'til I get a blanket!" I asked the youngin' if he was familiar with how we work? I said you can walk by yourself or we can help you walk and he replied, "man, I ain't studin' what you talkin' bout!" Soon, the 6'4 sturdy, bald-headed Sgt. Tripp arrived and ordered the baby-face gangster to his cell and he suddenly began walking after a slight hesitation. Afterward, the young buck received eight hours of confinement to his cell for disobeying the commands of an officer. Instead of being able to walk around the dayroom for several hours, the youngin' would be locked in the cell that he said was cold, all day and night with his extra blanket. Gotta be mo' careful! What did he prove to the other inmates who were staring out their door? I don't know. Did he learn a valuable lesson? I'll know the next time I see him.

Chapter 7

Slickness/Forethought

Many wayward teenagers, drug dealers, violent criminals and white collar criminals are constantly scheming on ways to prey on people and out-slick the system. These miscreants are obsessed by the "11th commandment, thou shalt not get caught," says Dr. West. To a large degree, this is the fundamental belief of most inmates. If you can recall the history of an adult boy or you examine the history of adult boys, you will find that this lazy, deceitful, predatory, unethical and selfish mentality and behavior began in his baby boy days. He thought, let me see how I can get over on my mother or grandmother, fool my teacher, my girlfriend, my wife, my boss, the probation officer, police officer, investors, voters, church members, nurse, correction officer or female civilian worker to get contraband into the jail. Several mayors and congressmen have tried to live by the philosophy of slickness. It doesn't matter the position, the common denominator is that greed, cockiness, power and ego fooled them into believing that they were slick enough and powerful enough to get away with their illegal actions! A lack of historical knowledge also contributed to their demise. If the mayors had remembered

157

what happened to the other mayors and politicians before them, they could had reasonable concluded that the **probability** of getting away with the illegal and illogical activities were slim. **Nothing lasts forever**! There is a serious reason why this saying has been around for many years. You can keep trying to come up the fast way and ski-mask way, but you can rest assured that one day you will come up short like an air ball! Based on my experience, I've determined that "Slick's" criminal lifestyle will end one of three ways. He can end it, the streets will end it or the system will end it, but it will end!

Assuming a "slick" criminal made $10k selling drugs on the corner, a bank robbery or luxury carjacking, how much did he benefit after he gets charged? Once he receives a five year sentence, he has earned $5 per day; three year sentence-$9 per day. He could earn that amount of money sweeping the floor at the barbershop or standing on the side of the highway begging and not have a criminal record. More importantly, he would not injure a person, damage their property or traumatize someone for their entire life! Assuming he made $25k from criminal activities and later got sentenced to fifteen years, he would had earned approximately $4.56 per day. $4.56 per hour would be sad, but per day is just downright absurd. Assuming he sold drugs and made $2 million and later got a twenty year bid, he would had earned approximately $273 a day. I must admit that $273 is a good per diem. But now he has to ask himself was the money worth losing his freedom for 7,300 days and dealing with all the negative aspects of being incarcerated? It's extremely important to use forethought to evaluate short-term gain in exchange for long-term pain! He could get violated, assaulted repeatedly, killed or be forced to kill another inmate and get a longer sentence. If you gave me a choice between $273 per day or freedom, I would choose my freedom every time! The main reason I would choose freedom is that **freedom allows for your circumstances to improve**! Therefore, I can think of a way to legally earn $273 a day. You can be down to your last dime one week and doing extremely well the next week. You can have no water and plumbing one week and be living with water, juice, plumbing and good food by the end of the month. In contrast, your circumstances can barely improve in jail or prison. The second reason why I would choose freedom is that **I have the authority to make my own choices** even if they are very limited. Although inmates and prisoners have limited choices, all of them are provided by the jail or prison. We tell them when it's too hot or cold for them to go outside to play! We tell them how often and what day they can have their friends and family visit! We tell them when to wake up and when to return to their cell at night (go to sleep)! Who wants to spend three years (1,095) days or 5,475 days playing cards, checkers and watching TV; eating the same bland meals, wearing semi-clean clothing, sharing a shower with 20-30 males or sitting on the toilet with a guy standing twelve inches away from you? I just can't imagine how that situation could be better than their home life, but I know that it is possible in some cases. In most instances, jail or prison isn't better! So, the logical conclusion takes you back to **a matter of choice and a grave ignorance of the value of freedom and the many beautiful possibilities of life**!

All of the inmates on the minimum security floor who are in the drug rehabilitation program join hands in a prayer circle and give each other a hearty congratulatory hug immediately after the social worker leaves. Many inmates in the drug rehabilitation program behave in a very sincere manner when the counselor is conducting the program. Just based upon appearance, some even look and sound focused and dedicated. Yet, for many of them, the lessons and wisdom don't last past the counselor's departure from the pod. Within two minutes, some of them are engaging in negative behavior, such as entering another inmate's cell, jamming their door lock, asking me silly questions that they know are a violation of policy, not going to their cell in a timely manner and ignoring my commands to promptly return to their cell until I talk to them harshly or threaten to suspend their privileges. When I respond to their misbehavior and begin talking about invoking consequences, some of them start cursing at me, which prompts me to say how do you curse at a person three minutes after praying? Didn't you learn anything about positive behavior, self-control, obedience and good decision-making during the counseling session? It occurred to me that all twenty-eight of them are in this court-ordered program because none of them know how to manage freedom. When they are out in the world and they are free to do as they want, they choose negative and illegal behavior like using illegal and prescription drugs, breaking into cars, stealing, committing simple battery, domestic violence and cruelty to children! Learning how to look serious and say the right words isn't fooling me, the counselor, nor the judge. We will judge you by your actions! When you appear before the judge again within two weeks, three months, eight months or a year after being released and I see you in general population again, we know for sure that you were faking the funk! "How you gonna win when you ain't right within," said Lauryn Hill. It's highly unlikely that an inmate will participate in a self-help program and continue to disrespect officers and engage in illegal and negative behavior in jail, yet engage in positive behavior in society. A changed mind, heart and spirit can happen wherever you are!

There is some allure to this slickness mentality that attracts all types of people from all walks of life. In 2015, there was a NYC police officer who was arrested for operating a prostitution ring. Even after he was officially stopped by officers for a driving violation, he continued to act as a pimp. Soon afterward, a wiretap was authorized and he was busted. This is another glaring example of another person's irrational belief in slickness! In 2017, a Caucasian female detective of the Chicago Police Department had been arrested two times for shoplifting, yet she was still working at the department. It wasn't until a news station covered her second arrest and began asking management why was she still employed that they finally terminated her. This incident of slickness is very troubling because it's impossible for police departments to have a good reputation and credibility among citizens when they engage in deception regarding the misdeeds of officers and don't uphold the law towards officers as they do against citizens.

One of the funniest stories surrounding slickness involved Inmate Bonehead's account. Bonehead asked me to check the money on his book. After I told him that he had 54 cents, he had the serious gumption to say "my money is missing. I need you to track down my $150.00." In his infinite wisdom, he decided to mail two money orders to the jail in anticipation of turning himself in. He claims that the jail "messed up his money because the jail gave him the wrong identification number." When I asked him his full name and ID number, the computer showed the same number since 1997-15 years earlier! This is another example of slickness gone awry! I'm curious to know what convinces criminals to completely believe that they are smarter than every other criminal or person in law enforcement. If he did mail money orders to the jail, this clown probably wrote the wrong ID number on the orders and now some other inmate was happily spending that money on commissary and wondering how that money got on his book. It's a hard-knock life for sure when your thinking ability is very low. Another half-baked scheme involved people moving into vacant or foreclosed mini-mansions and claiming ownership. I encountered this slick clown on the Mental Health floor when he requested a blanket. I told him that he couldn't have a blanket because he wasn't authorized by the medical staff to have one. The inmate said "but everybody else has one," despite not being able to see into any other cells. I said that's the problem. You are concerned with everybody else's business. Only do you, I said! He smiled and said "you right Officer Johnson." Somebody told me that before, but I'm a Moor. Do you know what that means? I said yeah. He said why do people look at you like you are crazy when you tell them

161

that you are a sovereign citizen? I said it depends on what context you use it in. I should get a blanket because I'm not bound—stop right there. That's why people look at you like you are crazy. This is the United States of America. You can't live in this country and claim that you don't have to abide by the laws. And you certainly can't move your property into a vacant home and claim that you own it. You certainly know that I can't go to your home uninvited and eat your food and take your money simply because I believe that I'm a sovereign citizen and I don't have to obey the rules of this country. If you are a U.S. citizen, you can't go to China and tell those folks what they can't do to you because of the rights you have in the U.S. Furthermore, who told you that you are a sovereign citizen, I asked? That's what's on my paperwork. No it's not! "It do!" Where were you born? Trinidad. Well then, go back to Trinidad and you can do all the shid you want to over there! Maybe you will have better luck.

I remember several times when an inmate would pick up the phone to make a twenty-five minute call, but there were only fifteen minutes remaining in his rotation. If the inmate knew that he wanted to talk for the full twenty-five minutes, he should had waited for another time or day to make the call. However, they had a tendency to think that they were entitled to the extra time or they were going to manipulate the officer into allowing them the extra time. Ten minutes may be a long time in a sporting event, but it is a very short amount of time in law enforcement and depending on the circumstances, it may be necessary for the officer to use that time efficiently to complete other tasks. This slickness mentality led to plenty of unnecessary verbal altercations. The officer is not a hoe or witch ass ninja when she or he doesn't allow the inmate to stay out ten minutes past rotation to finish a phone call. Some officers recognize game. It is up to the officer's discretion. Similarly, some inmates utilized the same slickness regarding their visitation. Inmate Macdaddy pressed the intercom and said to the female officer, "I'm fixin to see this lady and I ain't seen her in awhile, so I wanna know if you could let me get a little mo' time." How much time, Officer Lew asked? "Bout twenty minutes, Macdaddy said." Without answering him, Officer Lew looked at me and we both laughed before she told him to go see his visitor. Obviously, Macdaddy failed to see the irony in his request. He was indicating to a lady that another lady was important to him, yet she wasn't important enough for him not to engage in illegal activities. Now that he can't spend time with her, he wants to spend mo' time with her. As you might imagine, inmates frequently use slickness to manipulate each other. Sometimes, it was amusing to see how career inmates or slick talking inmates would manipulate young or unwitty inmates to violate policies. I recall a situation where a baby-face thug refused to return to his cell at the end of rotation because of a discrepancy with his commissary order. I told him two times to return to his cell and he could try to resolve his commissary dispute the next day. Instead of obeying my commands, he followed the chants of the "tough" inmates who were standing behind their doors yelling "yeah man, later for that ninja! Don't listen to that ninja! Stand up for ya rights," so he calmly went and sat at the table. The following day, his supporters were going to rec and walking around the dayroom while he was on lockdown for disobeying commands from an officer.

I believe that a person is foolishly arrogant and abundantly stupid when they concoct a simple scheme such as "I forgot my baby in the car" and think that most rational people will believe the story. Most people would agree that a baby is the most precious gift in the world. When you truly love your baby, your baby constantly stays on your mind when you are with your child because your brain stays in protective mode. You think to yourself, am I driving safely, am I driving too fast, did I buckle her in correctly and I hope no one hits my car! Many parents frequently talk and sing to their child during the commute. In most instances, just by the natural position of your body when you exit your car, your eyes are positioned towards the front and rear seats when you shut the driver's door. It is virtually impossible for a loving parent to "forget" their child in a car and not remember within minutes. As a side note, I'm always concerned about the welfare of a toddler when I hear the PA announcement of a lost child in a mall, department store or amusement park. What parenting information or class doesn't tell you to hold your child's hand or keep your child next to you when you are in public places?

Slickness doesn't only apply to poorly educated criminals. A mentality of slickness and arrogance applies to highly-educated white collar criminals. Somehow your experience as a banker or accountant, combined with your greed, lack of self-control and impatience causes you to believe that you can embezzle money and not get caught. However, your greed and illogical thinking prevent you from realizing that you aren't the first person to figure out a crack-brain scheme on stealing money. More importantly, your off-balance ego prevents you from realizing that law enforcement officers have banking, accounting and financial analyst skills. So, it probably won't be difficult for them to unravel your semi-slickness and follow the trail straight to you! In one case, a former lottery security director was facing a twenty-five year sentence after being found guilty of manipulating the computers to win and cash lottery drawings for six years. How long did he think that he could outsmart all of the other security personnel of the lottery association? Then, there is the case of the Caucasian CEO who boosted the cost of a medicine by approximately 700%, according to a published report. Another report stated that a CEO increased the cost of a two-pack of Epipen injectors by 550%, which made the store price about $608. Why did these people engage in these greedy, idiotic and immoral tactics without thinking that they would attract the attention of concerned parents, citizen groups and government agencies? It doesn't matter whether it's a Ponzi scheme by a former pro football player, a shiesty financial adviser or corporate identity thief, it's just a matter of time before they get caught, just as it is for the everyday criminal.

Manipulation

We must recognize and remember that character controls intelligence and authority! Intelligence doesn't control character. As we have seen, there are plenty of intelligent people who have shady or bad character. Trusting knowledge is risky because criminals and other immoral people have knowledge. Many schemes are performed by people with knowledge. How many times have you seen or experienced being mistreated by a person with an above-average level of intelligence? How many times have you seen or heard of a person being treated wrongly or abused by a person in authority? Have you ever had an interaction with a smart person who had a nasty attitude? Exceptional or good character compels you to treat people fairly and kindly even though you have the strength and authority to take advantage of them. Generally speaking, people are more willing to give you the benefit of the doubt or an undeserving opportunity based upon your good character. Whenever I can, I choose good character over knowledge because I can trust character!

People are manipulated due to a variety of reasons, such as gullibility, naïveté, age, poor reasoning skills and greed, but the primary reason why people get manipulated is due to low self-esteem! Their low self-esteem prevents them from understanding and considering the illogicalness and sometimes, the downright foolishness of the stated information (scam), dangers of their actions, the lack of common sense of their actions and the probable and often likely long-term impact of their illegal actions. Violent criminals have manipulated and coerced females and males into committing all types of irrational and illegal acts, such as smuggling food, liquor, drugs, cell phones and tools into jails and prisons, providing personal and classified information, committing outside crimes and even marrying them! Inmate manipulation is a continuous presence. For me, as a matter of common sense and knowing history, it made absolutely no sense to trust the "friendly officers." During my tenure as an officer, three detention officers were investigated and terminated for providing contraband to inmates. It's critically important for officers to hold each other accountable and for management not to be out of touch with the personalities of their officers! Shortly after I became a detention officer, I was surprised to hear when I arrived to work that a female nurse was fired for kissing an inmate. Why did she sacrifice her job, career, reputation and risk getting arrested for an adult boy who engages in criminal acts? Rather than a lapse in judgment, that's a lack of common sense! According to the evidence presented against one civilian female employee, she provided tools and other contraband to two violent inmates who later escaped from a prison in New York in 2015. Also, they allegedly told her of their plot to murder her husband. Her mental and emotional instability endangered the lives of officers inside and outside of the prison, as well as innocent civilians in the surrounding communities. When the shid fell apart, she was left holding the bag. Given all of the obviously senseless, illogical and fanatical aspects of this situation and others, it begs the question of the competency and mental health of women and men in regard to having extremely low levels of self-worth, heighten levels of frustration, fantasy, delusion and greed. As a result of these factors and others, I think that these people lack the confidence to believe that they can obtain a life filled with happiness and peace. Dreams are meant to be inspirational, shared and achieved! Dreams are not meant to be bought from a slick-talking person! It's bad enough to get bamboozled, but **when you play yourself, it is even worse**!

Chapter 8

Behavioral Conditioning

Habit is either the best of servants or the worst of masters!!!

—Nathaniel Emmons

Allow me to share with you a very powerful saying that probably isn't widely known, but occurs in life every day: According to Dr. Phil, **When you choose the behavior, you choose the consequences!** This concept is extremely important because sometimes consequences can be traumatic, long-lasting, permanent or deadly! For example, if you play with fireworks, you might get your hand burned or your finger blown off. If a student doesn't do his schoolwork and pay attention in school, he will not learn! Notice that I did not say that he will fail. I didn't say that because a lot of times some schools will pass a student even though he is failing. As a result, he or she will be semi-literate, will not have good employment skills and will probably not get a good paying job! If you excel in K-12, you will likely be eligible for an academic scholarship. If you engage in slickness and a life of crime, someone will likely victimize you or you may get incarcerated for many years. Sometimes, consequences are intangible. You may damage or lose the trust and respect of family, friends, a spouse, a manager, co-workers and citizens. In some instances, these consequences are just as unbearable as physical consequences. The strange and ironic aspect is that some people get upset with you for not trusting them despite the untrustworthy acts they committed. Likewise, some people get upset and want to challenge you verbally or physically because you give them the least amount of respect. I didn't extend trust to some officers because of their friendly behavior with inmates. Depending on the crime that an inmate committed, I extended no more respect than giving him proper commands and calling him Sir. Earlier in the book, I mentioned the inmate who took the plate from the elderly man with the walker and shoved him to the floor. His actions demonstrated that he didn't deserve more than a morsel of respect.

I'm all for compassion, sympathy and second chances depending on the nature of the crime, **but none of that eliminates the purpose and need for consequences.** There was a classic TV show in the 70s called Baretta. In the theme song, there was a very interesting and poignant verse that said, "don't do the crime if you can't do the time." In my experience with civilians and inmates, many of them don't want to accept the consequences of their actions. Therefore, people need to have a fundamental understanding of opposing qualities, such as win/lose, happy/sad, joy/pain, dry/wet, cloudy/sunny, loose lips/sink ships and reward/punishment. Too often, people don't want to enforce a consequence and they really try to avoid a consequence. Most often, you can't experience one quality without the other and if you attempt to avoid or deny it, you'll create an unrealistic situation that will worsen the negative aspect. A friend of mine who is a Human Resource Director told me of a case involving Simone who was late 35xs in one year, yet she claimed that the write-up and termination were unjust.

While escorting inmates and riding in the elevator with them after returning from court, inmates frequently say "those folks be trippin! "Wanna make a ninja cop a plea, take probation for five years and it ain't even all that; or I ain't even do it!" I'm wondering who's delusional. It's his 2nd or 3rd time getting arrested for the same type of crime or the police have overwhelming evidence, yet he's upset about the sentence that was imposed. Then, there was an inmate who was convicted of attempted murder, but he consistently complained that the system did him dirty by giving him a fifteen year sentence. In another instance, some guys sold drugs for ten years, but they don't think that the thirty-year sentence is fair because they were convicted of a non-violent offense. *The purpose of punishment is to deter and punish*! Therefore, the prison sentence must be compounded by the length of time they committed the illegal acts. Then, you must factor in punishment for the tax evasion and probable money laundering. Finally, if they participated in the drug trade for multiple years, someone died because of the drugs and someone was killed because of the drugs. That is almost a certainty. Once you consider all of these basic elements, it's unreasonable to expect to receive a one year sentence for each year they were "in business." Adult boys unwittingly participate in their own subjugation.

Punishment or consequences are a teaching tool and self-control mechanism for children who are learning about good and bad choices and teens who lack self-control and are still developing good reasoning skills. Punishment teaches people that the majority of society does not approve of immoral and illegal behavior. It teaches people that illegal, immoral, unethical and irresponsible behavior will often result in some form of punitive action, such as incarceration, employment suspension or termination, school suspension or expulsion, monetary fine, eviction, etc. Consequences serve as a reminder of the right way to do something, the wrong way to do it, when to do it and what you shouldn't do at all. Punishment protects society from people who make threats of committing violent acts, people who are prone to committing violent acts and people who have committed illegal and violent acts. Punishment acts as a deterrent for most people. It prevents people from committing wrong and illegal acts, which they might do were it not for the punishment that could be imposed if caught! I'm sure there have been thousands of times when people were desperate for money and jokingly made remarks about robbing a bank. However, the possible consequences of getting harmed, shot and incarcerated deters plenty of people from attempting to make that illegal withdrawal.

In many respects, human nature is very predictable, for we know that most of our behavior is learned. Therefore, **attitudes, behaviors and characteristics are developed**! The rationale of behavioral conditioning is that *almost all behavior is learned*. Humans don't truly have a natural instinct not to harm or take advantage of another human. That is a *learned condition*. If you've ever seen toddlers and children playing, one child will walk over to the other child and take the toy or candy when she wants it. An older girl will take or snatch her doll from the younger girl. You may have even seen a child push another child down on the playground, at the park or at home. This is the time when parents should begin teaching their child how to share and that it's bad manners to take an item from a person's hands without asking! Thus, as sensible and compassionate parents, we begin teaching our children to ask for what they want and not to take items, nor push or hit someone. Hence, the mentality of the child, teen or adult is almost always reflective of the mentality of the parents and family. All of us have probably seen babies and toddlers play with each other. If you simply consider that children don't even know their eyes from their nose, much less anything about racial or ethnic groups, we should all reach the conclusion that **children (little adults) are taught to dislike other races by their parents and family members. To argue otherwise is to defy all logic**! Whenever rationality is in direct opposition to generally acknowledged rational reasoning, there is true reason for concern and related individuals should intervene in some manner. Related individuals include coaches, teachers, church members, family members and friends. *Any parent or person in authority who is still promoting the ideology of a race being superior to all other races in the 21ˢᵗ century* **is stuck in a delusional and pathetic time warp**.

In relation to the family's mentality influencing the child's mentality, I walked in on my female co-worker while she was answering a question from an inmate. I remembered this (23 years old) young guy because of an abnormal normal comment he said to me the prior day and because he had a mild-mannered personality. As a result, I pressed the intercom and said what's up my man with "all the family down the road" (in prison). He smiled and said, "hell yeah, been like that all my life." I replied, they have fine women, delicious food, money and sunshine outside, but you prefer to follow in their footsteps? He replied flatly, "my daughter gotta eat!" My daughter gotta eat too and so do all of the other daughters out there, I responded. How is your daughter eating now? My moms, he proudly and carelessly said. I said, two people gave birth to her, but only one person seems responsible for feeding her. How does that make sense? *"It don't, but that's just the way shid is,"* he calmly stated. As a result of his conditioning in his family environment, he developed the mindset of resignation, struggle and survival of the illest as his path in life and going to prison did not seem wrong nor abnormal to him. It was as if he was looking forward to seeing some of the male members of his family. For those people who are knowledgeable about behavior and experienced in various types of behavior, it is fairly easy to identify statements and actions that indicate hopelessness! Several days later, I thought about him when I was dealing with a fifty-five-year-old male who was housed on the medical floor because he used a walker to get around. This inmate was always very mannerly to me and he appeared to be a nice seasoned gentleman. I thought that he was probably charged with the usual revoked or suspended license, no insurance or DUI. However, on the morning that I escorted him to the Transport Area for court, I learned that there was a violent side to this well-mannered gentleman. He was charged with armed robbery! Later that morning when I had some down-time, it occurred to me that it must be difficult for some children and grandchildren to obtain wisdom from their elders when the elders are being incarcerated. Sometimes the elders are using the same drugs and committing the same crimes as the young relatives. Sadly, this was the case in Decatur, Georgia in 2017, when a father and son were arrested for robbery and murder.

During rotation, some officers allow inmates to stand by the door where the intercom is located even though that is a violation of policy. When the officer turns on the intercom, he can hear the inmates talking. Once, I heard a 45-50-year-old inmate bragging to a baby boy about how he's a "vet" and he can do certain crimes and nobody will know. First of all, it's a foolish and irresponsible statement for a middle age man to say to a younger man. Secondly, he can't be much of a good criminal because this is the second time he's been incarcerated in three years. There's an important facet to receiving wisdom from an elder or older family member and having accessibility to model positive behavior! When wisdom is absent from a child's life, the child can only think like a child. Back in the day, granddad and grandma, Aunt Hellen or Uncle Jesse would tell the younger relatives when they did something wrong or their shid was beginning to stink. They were able to declare when the kids were wrong because they had experience and wisdom from living honest and productive lives. *Also, they felt obligated to tell us because they loved us and they knew that it was their responsibility to guide us in the right direction and not sit by silently while we went down the wrong path.* Those of us who obeyed them benefited from their wisdom. An interesting aspect of this wisdom sharing is that it seems that we seldom accept peer to peer guidance or counseling even though our long-term boyfriend, girlfriend, family member or spouse has experienced our behaviors first-hand. For this reason, we should give their criticisms careful consideration. Perhaps they lack the knowledge to suggest proper resolution strategies, but they can probably explain those behaviors to a professional who can suggest resolution strategies for you to implement.

On another occasion, an inmate completed his visit and then demonstrated his upbringing. Immediately afterward, he pressed the intercom and asked Officer Jones if he could have more time. She told him no because other inmates were waiting to go to their visit. When the inmate returned to his pod, he pressed the intercom. Officer Jones answered, how can I help you, Sir? He said, "you a real witch," and walked away. He said it in the exact Too Short tone. We both shook our heads. Suddenly, the intercom rang from the Visitation Area. Again, Officer Jones answered, how can I help you? A lady said, "you a witch—you coulda given my son more time." Officer Jones said thank you ma'am! We looked at each other in amazement and then laughed. This incident reminded me of that poignant Biblical verse **He saw, too, that the fruit originated with the root!!** (2nd Tim 1:5NIV) Similarly, men and women, particularly women arrive to jail to visit an inmate, but are inappropriately dressed despite two signs outside of the entrance that describe the dress code and it is listed on the jail's website. One sign is posted on the door in memo form and the other is a 4ft tall wooden sign. Yet, girls and women still arrive in see-thru tops, low-cut tops that partially expose their breast, short skirts, no bra, profane language on shirts, etc. When an officer tells the lady she is in violation and cannot visit, she demands to speak to a supervisor and sometimes says, "I'm not leaving or "you gonna have to put me out." How foolish is that? This is a jail—that would not be a problem! When we encounter noncompliance, we will use various types of verbal persuasion, but when that fails, we will use force compliance. Even as a free citizen, your demands do not supersede the decision of the law enforcement officer. Apparently, dressing provocatively wasn't only related to visiting the jail. In 2016, I attended my father's regular doctor's visit at the VA hospital where I was stunned by a mother's appearance mainly because her daughter, who looked about ten, was sitting next to her. Immediately after I sat down in the waiting room, I noticed this lady, who appeared to be at least thirty-five-years-old, wearing a low-cut halter dress that exposed two tattoos covering her breasts. Once again, Houston, we have a problem! This can't or shouldn't be an appropriate demonstration of proper dress for a young girl. Once the parent shows a negative behavior as right, the child will interpret it as right even though the behavior has no positive value and is as wrong as two left feet. **Parents always lead by example**, regardless of whether the example is good or bad, advantageous, disadvantageous or downright destructive. Consequently, it is very important for parents to be thoughtful about their behavior because they are almost always the most important positive or negative influence in their child's life. Maya Angelou said it best—"All you can do is what you know; And when you know better, you do better!" Hopefully!

In terms of behavioral conditioning, the thoughts, values and habits that are instilled in your psyche during childhood and adolescence years usually remain into adulthood. An ordinary example is children interrupt adults without saying excuse me prior to being taught to do so. Without correction, they do it as teens and adults 30-55 years old! If listening and comprehension skills were undeveloped during childhood, more often than not, those skills will be undeveloped in adulthood. Prior to entering the jail, there were multiple signs in all caps that said NO CELL PHONES allowed in the building! How does someone interpret that to mean I can leave my phone with the deputy or detention officer? That thinking is not logical. After I told the visitor no, usually the next question was can I leave my phone between the double doors (corridor)? When I answered no again, the visitor would have the audacity to get a funky attitude. Then, I would have to remind the person that the sign says not in the building. The corridor is in the building, so you can't leave your phone, cigarettes and other property in the corridor. Believe me when I tell you that this situation occurred every week. This is why it is critically important for parents to understand the importance of instilling reasoning skills, good manners and good habits in their children during the early and late childhood years. In another instance of low comprehension skills, a twenty-six-year-old inmate housed on the medical floor requested to take a shower even though he had a gauze bandage wrapped around his arm. Unbeknownst to me, it was his first day on the floor. After entering the stall, he asked "how am I post to shower with this thing on my arm?" I said what do you mean? He said, "my arm is wrapped up in tape…I'm right-handed and I can't wash with my left hand. Do the jail provide any assistance?" Annoyed, I said, hell no the jail doesn't provide any assistance. Immediately, I thought that his baby boy's brain must have run off the tracks. Who did he think was going to help him wash? How did you wash before, I asked? He said, I didn't. Today is my first day here. Ironically, I thought, he decided to commit an aggravated assault against someone, now he has the nerve to ask for assistance. Sadly, his mind didn't process whether he was allowed to get the bandage wet before he entered the shower. I told him to get dress and go back to his cell while I ask the nurse if you are allowed to remove the bandage to take a shower. Then, he said what you mean go back to my cell? Go back to your cell means walk into your cell, I said! Just like the usual punk, he said I better take a shower today, as he closed the door.

I recall teaching a third grade class and as I stood outside of the door greeting the students, little Tyrone walked by without responding to my good morning greeting. Of course, I told him to walk out of the classroom and to re-enter the room. As he walked towards me the second time, I said good morning and that little rascal walked right into the room again without saying good morning, hello or goodbye. Immediately, that prompted a short one-on-one conversation about why he didn't say good morning and the importance of manners. When an nine-year-old boy walks into the classroom in the morning and refuses to say good morning after I've said good morning two times, that is symptomatic of improper training at home, bad manners, stubbornness, a lack of respect for adults and probably some level of emotional stress. Considering the thousands of hours that I taught in classrooms throughout South Fulton and Cobb County during the 90s and early 2000s, I don't ever recall dealing with negative or disrespectful behavior from an immigrant child. This is one of the glaring contrasts that an educator notices and it begs the question why is that? I know that it has happened, but I never experienced it while teaching. I think that we all agree that children are children! A seven-year-old African-American girl is the same child as a seven-year-old Asian or Latino girl. A ten-year-old African-American boy is the same as a ten-year-old Caucasian or Indian boy. **Consistency** is one of the most important aspects of conditioning and success, as it is with parenting and teaching children various skills and concepts. If you have ever seen Steph Curry's jump shot, it is the epitome of consistency. I'm willing to bet dollars to pennies that his accuracy doesn't come from practicing twenty weeks out of fifty-two weeks of a year. I have never met him, but I believe that his accuracy stems from consistently practicing about forty-seven weeks of the year. When you teach and require your child to say please and thank you on a daily basis, he will do so on a consistent basis for many years. When you teach your child to cover their mouth, she will do so on a consistent basis for many years. Conversely, when you don't teach and require your child to cover their mouth, your child is the one coughing and sneezing on her teacher's face and hands and the other classmates. When you teach your child through your words and actions that learning is very beneficial, your child will like school and perform well in school. A child can easily model reading a book if he often sees his parent reading a book and other information. A teenager can easily learn to say sorry or compromise if she witnesses her parent(s) sincerely apologize and compromise on an issue from time to time. On the other hand, when you don't teach your child that learning is beneficial and to be respectful to their teachers and all adults, your child becomes part of the student population that contributes to the dysfunction of the school and ends up being functionally illiterate. As a result, during the filming of a documentary and news report, a mother says that her first grade son doesn't like school without realizing that it is a glaring reflection of how she has not properly encouraged him to like school. **Without a loving and supportive environment, a child will develop a diminished sense of worth and ability**. Studies have shown that there is a direct correlation between how we feel and how we think. The process of developing a habit, good or bad, is the same. *Attitudes are nothing more than habits of thought. John Hopkins University conducted a study and found that potential dropouts can be spotted as early as the sixth grade.* This study shows how powerful habits are. Most students are properly taught in public school. Unfortunately, due to restrictive policies and lack of consistent enforcement of corrective actions and rules, many students aren't conditioned to excel academically, nor socially in school. Generally, children perform their best when they are conditioned to excel. Just like a toddler, children and teens emulate and learn what they are frequently exposed to. Therefore, we must condition students to excel academically, rather than passively hoping that they eventually become good students. Excellence and high quality are never an accident! They are always the result of detailed planning, serious and continuous effort, supervision, determination and skillful execution!

I was bubbling with pride and filled with blissful naiveté when I walked into my classroom in 2008 after the Christmas recess thinking that the bad behavior kids would stop misbehaving and make a serious effort to learn now that Barack Obama was looking like the Democratic candidate for President of the U.S. Reality hit me quickly and I was in a severe state of disappointment by the end of the day! I realized that the historical and cultural feat of an African-American possibly being elected president had no positive impact at all on many of the children, especially the ones who were failing in conduct and academics. That was one of the first times that I realized how powerful habits are. Remember, **habits are habits** and they don't automatically or suddenly change! For example, the people who go to stores on Thanksgiving or the day after and push, curse or fight someone, don't do it just because they got tired of standing in line, the other person got the last television, or the sale is great. They do it because they have a hostile mentality. They are used to being hostile! Without knowing a student or an inmate, I could look at their behavior and listen to their speech and determine whether their life was primarily based on positive or negative values. I was able to do it because a person's character is a reflection of their beliefs and actions. The kid who believed that education was important completed his classwork despite other kids around him who talked, laughed and played during the assignment. For the inmate who believed in a criminal lifestyle, he would steal another inmate's property, barter it and engage in other criminal activities despite being incarcerated for criminal activities. Depending on the inmate's size and strength or gang affiliation, he was also the inmate who had the ignorant audacity to charge other non-aggressive inmates rent for being housed in a cell in that pod. Rent was paid in the form of food, commissary or actual money. As I stated earlier, behavior is very predictable although many people are oblivious to this fact of life. The legal system surely isn't! Nor are astute citizens, educators, social workers and psychologists. That's because they know that without intense behavioral modification, all of those detrimental self-destructive habits are solidifying in the psyche of the child and adolescent and will likely persist into adulthood. If you disagree with my assertion, you should read Carter G. Woodson's *The Mis-Education of the Negro*. Simple negative habits such as walking in front of another person while he is talking, skipping in front of someone in line instead of waiting patiently, walking up to two people in the midst of a conversation and interrupting without saying excuse me if there is an urgent issue; constantly making up foolish excuses for wrongdoings, like I climbed on the table because you didn't answer me; I didn't make up my bed because I forgot or you rushed me out of my cell; I banged on the glass to get your attention--I frequently asked what do you think the intercom button is for? These foolish excuses are on the same level as elementary students. Let's say a twenty-year-old male is on probation after he was convicted of armed robbery and aggravated assault. Given his educational level, character, home, neighborhood environment and family support system, the probation system is more than capable of determining the likelihood of him violating probation. In fact, one study reported that the recidivism rate was 60% within three years of release from prison. Just think about any time you have heard a prediction, be it weather prediction, medical prediction, stock prediction, fight prediction or a failure rate prediction. *It's all based on known factors*! It isn't some willy-nilly guess. Remember, **life is a numbers game**! So, the system just waits for you (parolee) to fall into your self-destructive habits (the trap as some people call it). The depressing aspect is that it's an elementary trap. There is nothing elaborate or complicated about it. Stop playing yourself by being lazy, impatient, greedy, uninformed, envious and disgusting! One major paradoxical discovery life has shown me and jail has reinforced is that the human mind is absolutely incredible and there are talented people everywhere who make little to no attempt to accomplish anything meaningful in their lives! Thousands and thousands of people are satisfied with doing nothing or the bare minimum. The million dollar question is do you engage in more positive habits than negative habits? The probability of completely eliminating years and years of detrimental thoughts, beliefs and actions is very low because they have been cemented into the person's character! *The longer you have been trapped in a dysfunctional* *and painful lifestyle*, the harder it is to create a new one. Therefore, when people say *give a seventy-year-old man a chance because he might improve, I don't think that they have an understanding of behavioral conditioning and the impact of sixty-five years of conditioning*! At a certain point in life, you are who you are and that's who you will be until you arrive at your grave site! Besides, how many people experience personality transformations when they don't see anything wrong with their behavior?

Behavioral conditioning is how our character is developed. It reveals whether we were raised to feel confident and loved, important or neglected, valuable or worthless, be polite, helpful, grateful, ungrateful, rational, rude, racist, religious, atheist, lazy, diligent, dishonest, abusive, deceitful, cheap, compassionate, aggressive, learned, obedient, violent, selfish, etc. These characteristics and others influence how a person feels about him or herself. **It relates to how visible or invisible we feel.** In that sense, I reminded of Ralph Ellison's protagonist, Bigger Thomas, in the novel Invisible Man. In this story, a young Black man faces several trials and tribulations in an effort to feel important and succeed during the Jim Crow era. He attended college for awhile and then he migrated to New York City from South Carolina. Once in New York, he became disillusioned after consistently experiencing discrimination and difficulty finding meaningful employment. This experience caused him to feel a great deal of self-doubt, frustration and anger. Subsequently, he ended up participating in burning a building and destroying property during the Harlem Riots. The sad irony of his destructive behavior is that his anger and frustration stems partly from the lack of opportunities and resources (businesses), yet the hoodlums and law-abiding citizens destroyed the few resources that Black people owned. Fast forward to the twenty-first century, and again, criminals, hoodlums and other "invisible people" looted and burned property in Ferguson, Baltimore and Milwaukee. After the violence and hostility are over, do any of the perpetrators realize that they haven't done anything to solve the problems and injustices that they claim they are angry about? Have any of their family members, neighborhood clergy, political and business leaders made a concerted, organized and sustained effort to explain to the perpetrators how detrimental their actions were and that violence usually stops progress rather than help it? Past and present history clearly demonstrates that random acts of violence will not solve the problems. **The frustration, anger, pain, distrust and resentment related to the circumstances are completely justified**! Freedom has never been free. Rights and privileges have rarely been awarded just from the kindness of those in power. *However, we must strategize and execute an effective mental strategy to eliminate or drastically reduce these horrific injustices against African-Americans and other minorities.* Life is 10% of what happens to me and 90% how I react to it, according to Charles Swindoll.

Whether we realize it or not, all of us know some people or have been around some people who have demonstrated behavior that was reflective of them feeling invisible. For various reasons, some people have decided not to cope with society or that they can't handle coping with society. When I encountered repeat offenders, particularly for misdemeanor charges, and engaged in a brief conversation with them, I could easily conclude that they committed crimes to escape society, especially when they returned within a week or thirty days after being released. James Brown, Temptations (Cloud 9) and Curtis Mayfield and other prolific writers have poetically sung about the various actions that people engage in as a form of escapism. To the uninformed brain, it seems unbelievable and crazy for a person to prefer the confines of jail or prison over living freely in society. Yet, this extraordinary situation applies to a few segments of the population, like drug addicts, homeless people, unloved people and institutionalized criminals. Over the years, I've encountered many children, parents, inmates, blue collar and white collar co-workers, ordinary citizens and celebrities who exhibited behavior that was reflective of feeling invisible. In a desperate attempt to feel visible and excited to prove that they are important, relevant, popular, all-knowing, powerful, tough and cool, these people get visible tattoos on their hands, neck, face, breast, wear red and orange hair, pink and purple braids, wear extra tight clothes, indulge in excess alcohol and drugs, brag about what they have or have done, talk loudly, behave arrogantly, dress scantily and expose half of their breasts and underwear in public places and engage in all manner of foolish behavior! Can a lady get her butt and breasts over-developed, flaunt them daily through over-exposure and then logically expect males and others to pay attention to her "good character and knowledge?" No level of society is exempt from abuse. If a child is raised in a family where verbal and physical abuse, neglect and unstable work habits are commonplace, there is a high **probability** that the child will behave the same way. Since the child has grown up in this internal environment without corrective measures from the external environment, this negative and self-destructive way of life seems normal to him. *Hurt people commit hurtful acts; Racist people commit racist acts; Cowardly people commit cowardly acts; Brainless people commit brainless acts; Hopeless people commit hopeless acts; Courageous people commit courageous acts; Ambitious people commit ambitious acts;* **Loving people commit acts of love!**

For the elementary student who feels invisible, her behavior includes talking frequently instead of working silently. For the high school student and adult, their behavior involves intentionally disobeying rules, bragging, misbehaving or talking loudly in public settings or engaging in violence, which subconsciously means look at me and hear me because I need attention. For blue collar and white collar employees, their behavior includes exerting their authority in inappropriate situations. Like the character Bigger Thomas, many low, middle and high income males and females are filled with high levels of negative emotions, such as anger, rejection, low self-esteem, self-doubt, frustration, self-hate, confusion and hopelessness. These emotions are clearly evident in many students and inmates. They constantly feel invisible, ignored and devalued by officers, family, friends, school and society, in some instances. All of their unusual, abnormal and deviant behaviors are motivated by a desperate need to be accepted, viewed as important, cute, a thug, cocky, cool, different, tough, cold, a player, pretty boy, instead of handsome, smart, faithful, hard-working, honest, ambitious, compassionate, strategic, considerate, kind, helpful and humble. In most instances, one's identity is going to cause him to engage in behavior that reflects his character. Thus, if a young man feels valuable because he receives **consistent** encouragement, praise, love and discipline, he is most likely to engage in constructive activities instead of destructive activities. In an unbelievable act of foolishness and gross disrespect, a sixteen-year-old boy who was at an unruly pool party in Florida, picked up a sixty-eight-year-old woman and threw her into the pool. To make matters worse, his weak ass wasn't strong enough to carry her, so he fell on top of her on the concrete before he reached the pool. *Boy, he needed to get a good ole-fashioned ass whupping, not whipping*! That isn't normal decision-making! I contend that he did it, in part, because he felt invisible among all of those kids, so he chose to do something that would get everybody to talk about him. More importantly, his behavior is reflective of a teenager who wasn't taught to respect women, nor elders. The irony of many inmates and young people desperately wanting to be visible and different is that they do many of the same things that their peers do—have unwed babies, get over-sized butt shots and breast implants, get multiple visible tattoos, wear pants off butt, behave badly in school and public, perform poorly in school, drop out of school, behave rudely, get arrested multiple times, intentionally violate rules, reject wisdom and advice and disrespect themselves, their families and communities. When I was a kid, we called that monkey see, monkey do! It was not cool to do something just because other people were doing it. In the passage entitled *The Law of the Mirror*, by Stephen

Covey, he says that people do what people see! As a result, some inmates and some people behave in all types of uncouth and deviant behavior, engage in profanity-laced tirades, say racist comments and masturbate in public. It makes you wonder how many internal problems are they trying to compensate? Though feeling worthless, hopeless, devalued and invisible to their family and society at-large, the irony is that many citizens still don't see them, in a sense, after the senseless and horrendous crime because we see a person who has behaved in an inhuman way. After interacting with some individuals and inmates, I could see that the negative traits were deeply embedded!

Frequent amounts of publicity leads to conditioning. *Publicity creates images, desires and beliefs.* Consequently, criminals and other low-level thinking people believe that shooting someone makes them a thug or gangster. *When you have a true understanding of the purpose of a gun,* you will use it only to defend yourself, your family and hunt animals. **You will not use it to kill humans and commit crimes**! If these dysfunctional and permanent pain-inflicting misfits paid attention to the news and possessed basic reasoning skills, they would see that 4, 5, and 6-year-old children have shot a person. Consequently, this fact destroys the perception that shooting an innocent person makes you a tough guy because it shows that a person only needs the strength of a four-year-old to pull a trigger! The major difference is that the child did it accidentally and you did it because of self-hate, greed and a warped mentality! Being a thug or going hard isn't represented by engaging in illegal activities, not having a reason to live and saying I don't give a chuck twenty times a day. On the contrary, being a responsible man and going hard is demonstrated by having multiple reasons to live and having the courage, commitment, mental and spiritual fortitude to **legally do what needs to be done in order to fulfill those reasons for living!**

Due to publicity, tattoos have become very popular. They used to be relegated to a few segments of the population prior to the

90's and the tattoos weren't usually visible. By the time the millennium arrived, it seemed like everybody and their grandmother were getting tattoos and they had to show them off, either by wearing a tank top shirt, low-cut blouse or low-cut jeans. Once that was no longer cool or different enough, people began getting visible tattoos on their neck, face and head. These are what I call self-disqualifying tattoos. By getting these tatts, I believe the person has completely eliminated himself from virtually all corporate positions and a majority of other well-paying jobs. This doesn't mean that the person won't obtain a well-paying job, but he has probably reduced his options. With respect to some inmates, I concluded that they had given up on life in mainstream society. One inmate had the words certified goon tatted across his forehead and face. The ridiculous irony was that he spoke fairly proper English and was usually polite. Subsequently, if any of these inmates get the desire to reintegrate into mainstream society, they have another unnecessary obstacle to eliminate. Also, what's the deal with criminals who have ethical and religious tattoos? I've seen a few inmates who had a tattoo that said death before dishonor. This quote is nice and profound. However, one must first have an accurate understanding of what is and isn't honorable behavior! There's nothing honorable about being incarcerated for stealing money from vulnerable and elderly people, committing a violent act or multiple violent acts, not to mention committing disgraceful and violent acts against innocent people. In addition, there was a situation where two co-defendants were sending kites throughout the jail to find their homeboy because word hit the streets that he was cooperating with the detectives. This wasn't surprising to me because there is rarely honor among criminals! Whether white collar or blue collar crimes, once the justice system starts talking those football numbers, most criminals give up the information. It's adios. No more gangster thug or gangster boo! I frequently dealt with two inmates who were charged with violent crimes. One had the words "So Blessed" tatted on his neck. On several occasions, I was really tempted to ask him, blessed how? The other inmate had prayer hands tatted on his neck and bicep. What an extremely contradictory symbol for a criminal to wear on his body. I've often wondered why people who knowingly commit violent crimes against innocent humans wear that symbol. Is it because they believe in prayer? Is it because they want God to protect them while they engage in illegal activities? Is it to impress and fool others by giving the appearance that he is a religious person? *To all of the people who have visible tatts from the neck up, you are already visible and cared for by the people who truly like you. The visible tatts will not add any more substance to you as a person.*

Behavioral conditioning allows people to become comfortable with their conditions, regardless of how abnormal or bad they seem to others! This concept applies to a homeless person sleeping in the subway station in NYC, a hoarder living with roaches and rodents in their bedroom, children ducking on the playground after hearing gunshots, the lady remaining in an abusive relationship and the inmate comfortable with waving a soap-sock in the air after his cellmate has taken a sewer dump six inches away. I don't want to become an expert in spreading peanut butter on 3-4 slices of bread. While performing a security check one day, I was confused about what I saw an inmate eating, so I passed by the cell again and asked him what he was eating. He said a honey bun sandwich. What is that? He said two honey buns between bread. Then he added, when I wanna make it special, I spread peanut butter on the bread. I smiled at him and said do your thing. As I walked away, I said thank you Lord for my blessings! Also, I recall seeing a fifty-year-old man sitting on the stool in his cell around 2:15 am talking and laughing with his cellmate. He appeared to be enjoying himself as if he were in his living room at home! I have seen inmates, big and small, exert full energy playing basketball barefoot just as if they had on the latest Jordan's or Lebron's. This looks and sounds unbearable to me. When you know how hard concrete is and then factor in the heat of the ground during the ninety degrees days in Georgia, this seems even more unfathomable. Yet, it occurred day after day, year after year. For the inmate whose feet were unaccustomed to the pavement, I would see him sitting on the side touching the skin that had peeled off his feet. After recreation ended, he would limp back to his pod as if he were walking on hot coals. However, for the pro inmate, I was told that the skin on his feet was so calloused that he didn't have that issue-- "I been doing this a long time Johnson," several of them told me. An unnecessary subsequent problem would arise on the recreation yard or in the pod when the inmate with the rookie feet demanded to be taken to the clinic immediately for the damage that he chose to inflict on his feet. The jail policy states that inmates cannot play basketball without sneakers on and occasionally, officers would warn inmates not to do it because it would result in bodily injury. Likewise, inmates would risk injury by playing in their flip-flops and this was also a violation of the jail's policy. Aside from the fact that flip-flops weren't designed for basketball, they would easily tear and replacing them on a weekly basis drastically decreased the jail's budget. Another injury that happened occasionally and required inmates to be taken to the clinic involved injuries to the groin area. This was the result of them playing without underwear. As a former basketball player, this action adds an uncomfortable meaning to the term "free ballin."

One of the frustrating problems that I had with some members of management was their lack of understanding of how they were complicit in creating an entitlement mentality by allowing inmates to receive more than the rules allowed. A few Sergeants and a couple of Lieutenants would instruct officers to leave the TV on after rotation had ended, allow the "houseman" to stay out for both rotations or turn lights off when they should be on. It was important for management to recognize actions that enabled inmates, like requiring the officer to wake up inmates who slept during meal distribution or during daily medication distribution. For those inmates who received daily medicine, it was their responsibility to wake up to get it from the nurse. They would had figured out a way to wake up if management required them to or if the medicine was vital to their health. Frequently, I would walk to the cell to wake up a baby boy or adult boy so he could get his medicine from the nurse and he would grunt, whine or curse and refuse to get his medication. It was such a waste of time for me and other officers. When people or organizations permit immature and irresponsible adults to behave immaturely or in a deviant manner, they tend to do so. Conversely, when you require these same people to behave responsibly and decently, most of them do so!

Behavioral modification consists of policies and procedures that are designed to teach and obtain a particular outcome or way of doing something. Essentially, behavioral modification deals with training and transforming behavior. Given that the rationale of behavioral conditioning is that **almost all behavior is learned**, the presupposition is that negative behavior can be unlearned and replaced by positive behavior depending on the circumstances. Basically, positive behavior is rewarded and negative behavior is denounced or punished! Therefore, we must consistently encourage positive behavior and discourage negative behavior. Behavioral modification works in most cases when it is applied consistently, fairly, swiftly and consequences are strictly enforced. I've witnessed it with many students and thousands of inmates! You can go to some public schools and almost all of the students will be seriously engaged in learning and there are no substantial behavior problems. On the other hand, you can go to some public schools and very few students will be seriously engaged in learning and there are too many serious behavioral problems. Similarly, you can go some jails and the inmates frequently behave in an uncivilized manner on a daily basis. Conversely, *you can go to two jails in the Atlanta area and both of them are as quiet as a church on Monday morning.* The inmates are overwhelmingly respectful and polite like ushers at church. Once you witness that, you can't help but wonder how is that possible? It's possible because of clear-minded management that enforce behavioral modification procedures, so that the inmates obey the rules and procedures and act like decent people.

Behavioral modification is what allowed me and other officers to stand in a pod with the door locked and effectively control the actions of twenty-five inmates. Clearly, I couldn't beat all of them and probably not two of them at the same time. I was responsible for controlling over 150 men on a floor. Yet, during all those days and hours of my sixty-eight months, I never had one inmate or multiple inmates attack me as they did some of my co-workers. **Of course God protected me on high**, *but I had to protect me down low*! I understood how to interpret their verbal and body language; interpret a possible physical threat of words versus a punk just talking shid; how to speak convincingly and forcefully; when to verbally warn them versus when I needed to show a physical threat. All of this verbal and physical interaction boils down to how to command respect and obedience, which amounts to getting people to change their behavior and become accustomed to following procedures and behaving in an acceptable manner. One such case involved a baby boy who was between 20-23 years old. I don't know what his problem was, but from the first time I encountered him and gave him verbal commands, he began cursing at me as if he had seen me rob his mother. With each morning encounter at his door, he would greet me with his favorite profanities, such as witch ass ninja, punk ass ninja and chuck boy. Each day, I would write him a citation and suspend his rotation time and rec time. This baby thug forced me to sanction him for approximately three consecutive weeks. As I approached his cell one morning, the silence caught my attention. There he stood at the door for the inmate count just mean-mugging me. His face was totally twisted. As I looked into his eyes, I saw his frustration and anger. I saw that he was frustrated and angry because he finally realized that he had to respect me and comply with the rules of the jail if he wanted to receive his privileges while I was on duty! Even as I walked away from his door, I expected him to yell something foul as he had done in the past, but he was quiet as a mouse walking on cotton. Later, when I unlocked his door for rotation and he exited his cell, he obeyed the rules, which proves that most people can obey rules and behave decently *when they want to or are required*. When rotation ended, he marched his little spoiled self into his cell without saying a word. At that point, I realized that he respected me even though he probably hated me. I was fine with that because respect was always my goal. To be an effective officer, I needed the inmates to respect me. When I worked in other fields, it was important to be liked by my peers, management and some students, but *I believe that it is much more important to be respected for your character and actions*. Just as I thought the drama was over with him, I responded to an emergency call one day and when I arrived to the scene, I saw and heard baby thug disrespecting another officer. When Sgt. Schott arrived, we escorted baby thug to his cell. At some point, baby thug called his mother whining and lying. Two days later, she called the Sheriff's office to file a verbal complaint to protect her innocent baby. Baby thug told his mother that Sgt. Schott and I assaulted him, which was a baby-face lie. As a result, we had to submit a written statement to the bogus complaint alleged by the misguided momma on behalf of her bratty baby boy!

Another clear example of behavioral modification involved another disrespectful and really hard-headed twenty-year-old Black male who raised hell every week at the jail. He was so belligerent that some officers would make up a lie after they were assigned to supervise the floor that Inmate Hard-head was on. No matter what officer worked the floor, Hard-head would refuse to return to his cell, flood his cell, fight another inmate or threaten an officer. In retrospect, I don't know why management let him cause so much havoc. In any event, he was shipped to prison and later returned to the jail for a few weeks to attend court. Upon recognizing him, I noticed during the conversation that he spoke in a very calm tone and he started and ended each statement and question with Sir! At first, it was surprising. Later, it was amusing because I concluded that he had been given specific instructions about acceptable behavior at prison and probably received a healthy dosage of Act Right to go along with those instructions. Also, many of those veteran convicts are on a whole other level than these loud mouth talking baby thugs in the county jail. Hard-head behaved like a respectful young man until he returned to prison. Several other baby boys demonstrated a 180-degree behavioral change too. This proves that behavioral modification works in most cases.

Undoing years of negative behavior requires intensive and consistent counseling, training, supervision and probably relocation in many instances. Hence, **"it's easier to build strong children than to repair broken men,"** said Frederick Douglass. Depending on the age of the person and the depth of the dysfunction, it can be corrected. The probability may be very slim. More importantly, it requires an unwavering determination from the person to want to achieve the transformation! In Tyler Perry's movie I Can Do Bad by Myself, Taraji's character says toward the end of the movie, "can you teach me how to love?" Her main ability to learn how to love lies in the fact that she recognized and admitted her flaw. She recognized that she didn't know how to properly give love and affection. Her second step will be to practice the actions that her future husband teaches her about giving affection to him, her niece and nephews and to herself. **Transformation**, particularly substantial transformation, is usually a diligent process that takes place over the course of years. It's important to your maturity to be willing to modify or change your beliefs or thinking style when shown the right way or a more effective way! If you spoke to Chef Jeff, I imagine that he would tell you that behavioral modification played a major role in him transforming his style of living as a victim to living in victory. Behavioral modification is one of the primary aspects of transforming low-income and low-performing students into high-performing students when they are placed in a conducive environment for learning, such as certain public schools, charter schools and tutoring programs. Their families are still low-income, yet the kids begin to perform on the same academic level or above those students who come from a much higher economic level. Poverty is an indicator, not a determinant. There is a huge difference in the meanings. These wonderful students are proof and a reminder that **poverty doesn't determine academic ability**! It never has and it never will!

Modification

Growth emanates from pain, whether positive or negative. The only difference is that in order for growth to come from a negative experience, **you have to seek out the positive lesson and want to do better**! You have to search for the message in the mess. In the song "Wanna be Happy," Kirk said —"if I keep doin' the things that keep bringing me pain, there's no one else I can blame. If I'm not happy, wasted time but now I can see, the biggest enemy is me, so I'm not happy… …cry yourself to sleep, shout…it won't change a thing child until you understand…if you're tired of things not changing…" When you go to jail, mental growth comes after you realize that you are responsible for making the bad choice that caused your incarceration. Also, mental growth comes after you realize that freedom is one of the greatest assets you have and you should use that asset to engage in productive behavior! I clearly remember the elders frequently saying it's okay to make a mistake, but don't make the same mistake twice. As a loving parent, do you tell your child that you feel disappointed or sad when he gets a bad grade? You should! It's okay to tell a child that she or he is not doing well, but here is what you and I are going to do to fix the problem!

Thus, you will train your child's mind to understand that setbacks and failures can be transformed into success in the future! Positive transformation usually involves some level of discomfort or pain. Like exercise, muscle growth comes after you endure the pain and continue exercising. Thus, growth comes from working through the pain, not avoiding it or quitting!

I believe that a person must have three main qualities in order to accomplish a goal or transform their life. The first quality they must possess is desire. She or he must feel a burning urge to want to do that thing or improve their life. However, **desire without commitment and effort is useless**! Some people argue that a person lacks desire when he doesn't put forth the commitment and effort that is necessary to accomplish the goal. Nevertheless, you must utilize desire, commitment and effort to: control your child; help your child behave and perform well in school; improve your employment skills; control your spending; improve your finances; control your weight; exercise regularly; improve your health; eliminate your bad habits; improve your general or specific knowledge. I believe that desire is the mandatory quality for everyone who overcame some adversity, wants to achieve a goal and for everyone who has ever achieved any level of success!

Chapter 9

Choice

We should all agree that life is a continuous series of choices, whether we make them consciously, subconsciously or someone chooses for us. The continual positivity or negativity that you experience in your life is mainly determined by the choices you make, which is heavily dependent upon the level of your reasoning skills. Attempting to travel through life without good decision-making skills is like trying to be a good chef with impaired vision, hearing, smell, touch and taste. **We have choices that our ancestors hoped and prayed about! We have choices that they could only dream about!** One of the most important choices we make is how we behave on a regular basis and in any given situation, for all of our choices come with results. Generally, when we make the right choices for the right reasons, we end up with beneficial results. One intriguing aspect of life that you should realize is that the longer you live, the more your life is shaped by your choices. The older you get, the more responsibility your choices hold. Choices begin in the very early stages of childhood and they are one of the most common ways small children begin to assert their independence. Children begin to choose what toys to play with, what food they like to eat and don't like to eat and what clothes to wear, etc. As they enter their middle and high school years, their decisions become more important, as they choose positive or negative friends, who to date, how much effort they put into doing well in school or dropping out of school. Hopefully, the child's early childhood and adolescence years were filled with good visual examples, positive affirmations and helpful lessons from their parents and family members.

During one weekend of my sophomore year in college, a few friends and I experienced some consequences that changed our behavior. We went to two parties in one night and got drunk. Unfortunately for AB, he began vomiting in his sleep while he was lying on his back. Fortunately, someone had the knowledge to know that we needed to turn him on his side so that he wouldn't choke on his vomit. That meant that our hands had to touch the vomit in order to turn him over. He continued to vomit for what felt like an hour. We decided to carry him to the shower to keep him awake. Now, all of us smelled like vomit, sweat and liquor, but funk was the overwhelming odor. The cold water shocked all of our systems. Blessedly, all turned out well. Consequently, we swore off beer and liquor for weeks and AB never got drunk again in college.

Regarding situations that we are faced with, we almost always have three choices: we can reject them, we can accept them and embrace them or we can accept them and vow to change them. Your choices will determine your actions and your actions will determine your results, in most cases. Those results will be closely associated with the positivity or negativity of your actions! A lot of choices don't have an immediate impact, which causes young, immature, narrow-minded or stubborn people to ignore or disregard the possibility of future negative repercussions. Later, when the consequences arrive in the form of unnecessary medical bills, payments are due, responsibilities must be met, retention notices are delivered, termination notices are given, shots are fired and prison sentences are handed down, people begin making excuses, boo-hooing, screaming, fighting, lying and scapegoating. What can be done to undo the embarrassment, pain and trauma of a negative situation? This is why it is very important to develop forethought. Obviously, major decisions have big ripple effects. Although small choices may not have as big an effect, there are still effects that go beyond your sight, just like you don't see the last ripple from the rock that you threw into the lake. As I stated previously about choices affecting grandparents, your choices, whether intentional or unintentional, usually impact other people. Far too often, males and females choose to engage in relations completely focused on what they want in the moment, what they think they can handle and what makes them feel good, without any consideration of the detrimental effects that their child and others will experience. It's important to realize that the choices you make today will likely determine the comfort, discomfort, joys and sorrows of your tomorrow, weeks, months and years to come. It's our responsibility to consider which choice is most beneficial for our lives. In considering which option to choose, I think that there are two major ways to consider your decision. You should consider the short-term advantages and disadvantages and the long-term advantages and disadvantages. Secondly, when making important decisions, a person should always consider whether the risk is worth the reward or consequence, for there will always be a reward or consequence. For example, choosing to go to jail multiple times or for long periods, drastically destroys one's possibilities of obtaining beneficial situations. Also, when a fool jumps over the counter at a fast food restaurant and robs them of three hundred dollars, how long is that money supposed to last? Not long! So, he is likely to commit another robbery soon, thereby increasing the **probability** of his demise. In regard to intervention, I'm wondering whether anybody who knows him believes that his life is more valuable than three hundred dollars. *More importantly, does he believe that his life is more valuable than three hundred and a 5-15 prison sentence?* That is the million dollar question because it is his mentality that will determine whether he continues to engage in positive, negative or straight self-destructive behavior. It's his choice!

The choices you make have a lot to do with the people you associate with and the quality of life that you have or don't have. One morning while I was performing a work detail with a twenty-three-year-old Inmate Worker who was incarcerated for a misdemeanor probation violation, he shouted to another inmate "my brother got his time today." What did he get, said the other inmate? "He got 50!" I said damn, what did your brother do? He told me that his brother was in a gang and got hit with RICO charges. Also, he said that his brother was "throwed off" (mentally unstable or prone to foolish behavior) and that's why he stopped hanging with him. He said that his brother began to do wild things once he joined the gang. I joking replied, so your mother fed him different food than you. Then, the inmate worker told me that his sister was locked up with serious charges also. Apparently, she ate the same food as the other brother. Subsequently, I realized during our conversation that he didn't seem fazed or saddened by the revelation that he would never be able to socialize with his brother as a young man in the free world. Luckily for him, he made the right choice to stop hanging with his brother. I don't know whether he realized it or not, but the lesson I concluded from his story involving his siblings was that **some situations in life may require you to choose between your family and what's right**. Life is a series of lessons. The value of the lessons depends on us recognizing how to benefit from them.

Who you associate with regularly and perhaps occasionally, gives an accurate reflection of your values and mentality. I think that it is fair and appropriate for others to form character judgments based upon our associations. Of course, those judgments may not be totally accurate, but they will contain a fair amount of accuracy. There used to be and still should be a negative stigma attached to socializing with criminals! This moral principle applies to frequently socializing with rude, foolish, racist, mean and unethical people. If I regularly or occasionally associate with a pimp, it's reasonable to conclude that I don't respect, nor believe in treating women decently! If I regularly associate with a guy who has 3-4 unwed children by 3-4 ladies, he logically assumes that I support his dysfunctional lifestyle and low-level views regarding motherhood and fatherhood. One of the main reasons why gang members and criminals feel comfortable engaging in criminal behavior is because they frequently encounter family, friends, officers and others who still socialize with them as if they don't care that they murdered a baby, innocent person, raped a lady or beat an elderly man. Anytime you readily socialize with someone who engages in deviant behavior, you reinforce that negative behavior and the person forms the belief that their behavior is acceptable!

One of the frequent comments and source of tension among inmates was "why do I have to suffer for what another man did?" Well, the simple answer to that is you are responsible for carefully choosing your friends and environments. Sadly for you, you are in a jail where your likes and dislikes have no bearing on the policies and procedures and worst than that, sometimes, no bearing on the misbehavior of the baby boys and adult boys you live with. Therefore, when one of the boys commits a gross violation, everybody suffers the consequences and your privileges are suspended. Inmates and even some of my co-workers often grumbled about how unfair life is, rather than make the decision to develop a plan to improve their personal situations. You would think that common sense would make them aware that frequently grumbling, pouting and complaining will not improve your situation and it won't make you feel better (I don't think). In the words of Red Man, it's time for some action! It's time for some unrelenting positive action. Obstacles are conditions for success! Obstacles are the ingredients that make your story unique to you and fascinating and inspiring to others! *You may have experienced tough times, however, your attitude is still your choice!* Often, it's a blessing to be able to make a choice, whether major or minor. As Americans, I believe that many people take their ability to make choices for granted.

Chapter 10

Disobedience and Disrespect of Authority

The greatest obstacles to improvement are disobedience, igno-rance, denial and the illusion of knowledge! Simply because you are a parent or an adult, it doesn't mean that you know the answer to many common issues or the right thing to do in many common situations. Also, it does not mean that you have good decision-mak-ing skills, nor does it mean that you are knowledgeable in important areas, such as education, parenting, positive social development, good nutrition, (sending kids to school with tall container of Kool-Aid for a morning snack) and exercising for health (obese children in school who don't have a medical condition), etc. Simply because you are over twenty years old, it doesn't mean that you are capable of handling your finances in a responsible way; It doesn't mean that you would not benefit from the guidance of a mentor or elders; It doesn't mean that you have the knowledge and the ability to improve from low income to middle income; And it certainly doesn't mean that you are capable of responsibly handling all of the duties of providing for a child or family! *He who doesn't know, yet asks questions, is ignorant for a short time. He who doesn't know, yet asks no questions, is ignorant for a long time!*

I always encourage children, teens and young adults to think before they speak, so they didn't embarrass themselves without knowing they embarrassed themselves by making jack-fool statements! As a child, you have to be trained and guided in all areas of life. Don't forget that you were comfortable walking around with number one and two in your diaper until you were potty trained by someone! As you mature and develop experience, reasoning and performance skills, the fewer areas you will require training and guidance. If you understand this principle as an adult, you will be willing to accept training, guidance and advice in areas of your life that require knowledge or development. While discussing an issue with a knowledgeable and experienced 40-50-year-old person, you shouldn't be implying or saying that the elder is wrong and you are right based on your experience and you are only 25-30-years-old. Giving you the benefit of the doubt, your experience began at twenty, which means you have 5-10 years of experience. In contrast, the elder has 20-30 years of experience, which means 2-6 times more experience than you have. Logically speaking, isn't it highly more likely that the elder person will be accurate? When we receive knowledge and wisdom from an experienced person, it is very important for us to be obedient and believe even though we don't see it or understand it. **Isn't that the definition of faith**? How many 20-30-year-olds would feel happy if they were left at home or on the job with a 5, 10 or 15-year-old child in charge? None! That's exactly how the elders feel. Maybe people, especially teens and young adults, would be more receptive to being obedient if they had an in-depth understanding of learning relationships, such as parent-child, teacher-student, mentor-mentee or an apprenticeship.

Have you ever wondered why some people are so disobedient or down-right hard-headed? If you work in education or law enforcement, you know exactly what I'm talking about. After working in both fields, it has crossed my mind thousands of times. Too many civilians and inmates suffer from CGR! No matter how many times you provide instruction, advice, money, guidance and constructive criticism, some people are hell-bent on doing it their way. What kind of assistance can you provide to a young adult or adult who consistently disobeys solid instruction and wisdom? Subsequently, they end up in a financial scheme, distress, domestic abuse, debt, evicted, pregnant, divorced, drug addicted, homeless, expelled from school or incarcerated. Then, they ask, beg and sometimes demand help. On what planet is that logical? Sometimes, teens and young adults dramatically claim *"let me live,"* so they reject and ignore advice and wisdom from loving parents and caring and experienced people. Their guidance and wisdom will save you from heartache, disappointment, lost money and time that you may never be able to restore. I understand that times and procedures change and you are grown, so you want to do things the way you want to or the new way. Provided that you were raised by loving and supportive people, either parents or grandparents who instilled good values in you, I understand that you might choose to expand your views, tweak this or that or modify some procedures. However, I don't understand why some adults totally disregard the fundamental practices and beliefs of their parents or grands, particularly when those practices and beliefs have placed them in solid conditions in their latter years. Adults disregard practices like establishing a strong faith, requiring their children to complete chores, teaching children good manners and to always respect adults, saving for emergencies, spanking children or other forms of discipline, and choosing a responsible partner. The more things change, the more they stay the same! Often, it's not what you know, but who you know. Common courtesy and decency will always be valuable assets, along with respectful behavior, a strong work ethic, honesty, patience, kindness, knowledge, reasoning skills, discretion, trustworthiness, enthusiasm, a pleasant demeanor, short and long-term planning and various other positive attributes.

As previously stated, it's *very important to nurture and train children early to accept guidance and critiques.* This skill will help teens and young adults to realize that being forewarned is equal to being forearmed. Then, they will be more equipped to avoid or prepare for situations, protect themselves and resolve situations effectively. As concerned parents, grandparents, educators, family members and citizens, we are not trying to stop you from living and experiencing life. However, we are trying to stop you from making unnecessary bad decisions that are likely to cause undue stress, harmful results or long-term negative effects. Parents, grandparents, old-timers and bosses see that you are about to walk on black ice in your situation. Just as driving on black ice is dangerous to your health, so is walking on it! You end up in a very slippery situation that makes it extremely difficult to control your body and emotions, which makes it difficult to stop before you spin out of control and crash. Selling marijuana or prescription pills in high school is akin to driving on black ice. Going for a joy ride in a stolen car or dating a guy who has been convicted of a violent crime is akin to driving on black ice. Committing a robbery or experimenting with potent drugs is akin to driving on black ice. Invading someone's home and you don't know whether they are home with a weapon is akin to speeding on black ice! In time, disobedience always brings some degree of consequences or tribulation. It's harmful and possibly dangerous to be around people who have a tendency to be disobedient and make piss-poor decisions! Frequently, *experience is the clearest demonstration of the truth, consequences and teacher of lessons!* Through the lessons, punishment or continued suffering, people eventually change their practices or their lives end while feeling a great deal of disappointment.

Being consistently disobedient is a habit or an aspect of conditioning that almost always begins in childhood. Quite often, conflict isn't the result of a lack of understanding, particularly with spoiled children, adult boys and stubborn people. They just want to do what they want to do! Most inmates often resent and sometimes reject officers telling them what to do on a daily basis. Just like boys playing sports or engaging in almost any activity, boys resent and sometimes reject another boy telling him what to do. However, the major difference is that the officer is fulfilling his job responsibility, but the inmate is behaving like an adult boy by not acknowledging his responsibility to comply with the rules and procedures of the jail, thus negating the inmate's constant mantra of "I'ma grown ass man." When officers enter a pod and we yell get down on the ground and a few inmates stand around as if we aren't talking to them, some strong actions will swiftly follow. In an attempt to get inmates to clearly understand their obligation, I frequently asked inmates, if I walked into your home or parents' home, could I do what I want to do and ignore what you say to me? Could I sleep on the kitchen table, wash my dog in the kitchen sink or smoke weed in your mother's face? Hell no was always their response! Obviously, if it is wrong for me to violate your home and I would "get dealt wit," then it is wrong for you to violate my workplace home and when you do you must "get dealt wit." Despite this clear and simple analogy, some inmates insisted on being disobedient even when it was disadvantageous or jeopardized their safety. For example, meal distribution was a bad time to be disobedient. After the call has been made to exit the cells for breakfast, for some strange reason, some baby boys would remain in front of the mirror in their cell *brushing their hair with a potato chip bag instead of exiting their cell to receive their breakfast meal.* There are a few factors that make this behavior clearly abnormal. First, I would imagine that very few people brush their hair before they walk into their kitchen to eat breakfast when they are staying home. Secondly, there are no females to impress because there are only males in the pod and female officers usually didn't participate in the breakfast distribution. Most importantly, there are time constraints that require inmates to exit their cell promptly. Once I pass by the cell a second time and the boy is still brushing his hair, I shut the door because his behavior indicates that he is willfully disobedient, disrespectful and he wants to eat when he gets ready. Now that I've locked his door, he will receive his breakfast several minutes later. Perhaps it's a bloated sense of ego or coolness that causes a baby boy to want to look cool to other males during the crack of dawn hours. Whatever the reason, it just seems abnormal to me! Another time in which it was disadvantageous to be disobedient involved certain medical situations. In this particular case, a nurse arrived to the floor to deliver some antibiotic lotion to two inmates. After I escorted the kind and soft-spoken nurse to the cell, she explained to the infected inmate that his examination revealed that he had scabies. She explained to the cellmate that the disease is very contagious and in order for him not to catch scabies, he must use the same lotion treatment as the infected inmate. She told both of them to take off their clothes and rub the lotion all over their bodies and between their fingers and toes. Just like a mule, the unaffected inmate whined about having to use the lotion and refused to use the lotion because he determined that he didn't have the disease. Also, he asked multiple silly questions about why he had to use the cream after the nurse had given him a full medical explanation about the disease. After about ten minutes of whining to the nurse, I told the nurse that he refused treatment and we had to exit the cell. After exiting the cell, I told the nurse that it wasn't our responsibility to plead with a forty-year-old man to accept medical treatment. Additionally, I had too many other duties to complete than to spend unnecessary time listening to an adult boy spout irrational statements. Furthermore, sometimes you have to allow more time for thought to a person who is stubborn or has undeveloped reasoning skills and I knew that once his butt started itching, he would surely accept the lotion.

As I stated earlier, teaching your child to be obedient is one of the most important traits for a parent to instill in their child.

There is absolutely **no beneficial reason to allow a child to be disobedient**. It's abnormal for a child to be consistently disobedient when receiving instructions. The first thing that behavior indicates to most adults is that the child doesn't realize that he is a child! The second thing that behavior reflects is that the child hasn't learned the importance of *obedience*! As a parent, you fail to realize that there are going to be some situations in life where people are not going to repeat directions 3-4 times. Yet, you have allowed your child to develop a habit of disobeying directions the first time! As parents, many of you do yourselves a tremendous injustice by not instilling obedience. By doing so, you deliver a grave injury to your child and you commit a devastating disservice to society! Additionally, some people contend that you block your child's blessings by raising a disobedient child in that you eliminate the desire for positive people to associate with your child. Who wants to deal with a consistently disobedient and disrespectful child? **Stop means stop** the first time that the command is given! If your son hasn't learned to obey this command by the time he is 3-4 years old, he is on the verge of being problematic in public (pre-school and elementary). If your son hasn't learned to obey this command by the time he is seven, he is problematic. If your son hasn't learned to obey this command before he reaches thirteen, he will probably not be inclined to obey this command in a law and order situation. Only God knows what will happen then! In law enforcement, stop means stop! **It means don't move!** Stop means to cease doing that action right away or not do it anymore in the future. It is a very simple, yet powerful instruction. During my first year as a detention officer, I witnessed how important this directive was. I was excited and nervous to see the SWAT Team arrive at my post with two German Shepherds to conduct a search for weapons and other contraband. To my surprise, Sgt. NoMess told me to exit the tower to search the cells with the SWAT Team. Man, was I filled with nervousness and pride. As we entered each pod, two officers with booming voices gave verbal commands to inform the inmates of what to do and what not to do. Three of the commands instructed the inmates to sit on the floor with their hands in their lap, don't get up and don't make any sudden movements when the dogs walk by to search them. Sure enough, just as the shepherd was approaching an inmate, he got up and the shepherd barked and bit him in the butt. When the Sergeant asked him why he got up, he said that he was tired of sitting down. Indeed, this incident was the epitome of a hard-head leading to a sore butt. His decision to disobey directions led to unnecessary medical treatment. Sgt. NoMess told me to take the inmate to the clinic. Of course, the inmate moaned and whined all the way to the clinic while telling me how he was going to sue, get all of the jail's money and get all of the officers fired.

One of my frequent challenges throughout the years was to get inmates to stop walking towards me during a conversation. Sometimes it was challenging to get inmates to understand that I could hear them from 4, 6 or 10 feet away. Part of the challenge with this procedure stemmed from the inconsistency among officers. Plenty of officers allowed completely unfamiliar and violent inmates to stand in their face or within close distance while talking to them, as if they were having a conversation at a barbershop or cookout. There is a concept known as personal space between two people and this concept is known as protective space for law enforcement officers. For those of us who were given good home training, we utilize this etiquette. On the other hand, there are quite a few people who aren't aware of this important concept. Inmates frequently got mad at me because they assumed that I was disrespecting them or thought I acted like I was "too good" to allow them to get close to me. Most likely due to habit, inmates were used to having conversations within close distance as a citizen. However, they were now inmates, which completely changes the dynamics of the relationship. First, we are talking in a volatile environment. The inmate may be hostile from the shock of getting arrested or feeling angry that he was unjustly arrested (didn't do nothin' wrong). Secondly, it is a safety hazard because I don't know the inmate, so I have no knowledge as to whether he is a violent person, has a hot temper, fragile ego or wants to gain a reputation. Oddly enough, it was also a safety hazard because quite a few inmates had halitosis. To my misfortune, I've had more than a few inmates confidently speak to me and their breath was so hot and malodorous that I could feel the heat and funk of the words on my lips, travel up my nose and make my eyes water! Who knew that human breath could be that potent and travel in such a way? It's a really unbearable, shocking and creepy experience! As disgusting as this sounds, sometimes this situation really posed a safety risk during pill call because I felt the need to turn around or take a few steps backward, but then I would be too far away to react if the inmate attempted to touch or harm the nurse. Most importantly, it was a violation of training procedures to allow an inmate to stand within striking distance during a conversation. Frequently, inmates would say something derogatory along with "don't be afraid, I ain't gonna hurt you." Unbeknownst to inmates, defensive training teaches officers to maintain a safe distance. If an inmate wasn't at least sixty-five-years-old and walking with a severe limp, I never allowed an inmate to talk to me while standing in my reactionary gap (otherwise known as personal space). I've seen too many detention officers and officers on the street get sucker punched or tackled by a suspect. Officers have been seriously injured and killed by **neglecting their training** and giving an inmate or suspect the benefit of the doubt. Countless times, I have witnessed and heard about inmates disrespecting male and female officers by saying lewd comments, brushing against them, or walking a foot or two in front of or behind the officer, which was an invasion of the officer's protective space. In certain situations involving strangers or law enforcement, common sense dictates that you take a defensive or offensive position when you don't know the intentions of the other person. To not take such an action, possibly dooms you to

209

a sneak attack, especially if you haven't been trained mentally and physically to defend yourself from a defensive position. Even if you have been thoroughly trained, you still may not be able to recover from the sucker punch. The golden rule is better safe than sorry.

Citizens need to help create *stronger juvenile laws* that will focus on protecting the public's welfare by incarcerating violent and repeat offenders! Sometimes, it is necessary to protect a person from him or herself. Some people have to be controlled in a closed environment because they lack the mental ability to co-exist peacefully with children and adults outside! If you don't believe that harsh consequences are necessary and appropriate for certain situations, ask any city officer about his frustrations from dealing with repeat offenders, including juveniles. Ask any inner-city teacher and they will tell you about their frustrations from dealing with consistently disobedient and disruptive students! Whether you are aware of it or not, there is a segment of the population for which please don't, please don't do it again and stop are not effective for them. The statistics clearly reveal that the juvenile laws are outdated and aren't responsive to the severity of today's crimes. For those people who claim to be seriously concerned about rehabilitating juveniles, they should develop some practical strategies about how to steer them in a positive and productive direction before they get involved in criminal activities. Also, they should develop some strategies to rehabilitate them while they are incarcerated because some of them need to be incarcerated because of the violent nature of the crime or being a habitual offender. When a teen has been arrested 16 times or 35 times, you can't rationally explain to me that the legal system isn't an indirect participant in their ultimate downfall. Furthermore, by continuously upholding these nonsensical laws, the DA's office and judges are knowingly and carelessly endangering the welfare of the citizens! I submit that the judges and prosecution attorneys should be the primary people leading this change movement. In the case of an Atlanta teen who was arrested for carjacking, the teen had been arrested sixteen times before that arrest for felony offenses. Where is the accountability on behalf of his guardians, extended family and lastly, the legal system? Can you imagine his thoughts about the aspects of manhood? Can you imagine that he has no aspirations of having a productive and happy future? Can you imagine the level of disrespect and disruption that he inflicts when he attends school? Can you imagine the level of danger that he presents to all of the good students and teachers who encounter him? As I mentioned before, making bad choices is like gambling. It is just a matter of time before the teenager craps out! Then, we may see a public outcry from his family. This boy is a prime example of the difference between leniency and appropriate punishment. When a person continues to engage in callous and illegal behavior, it is a clear sign that he has not received the necessary counseling and punishment to deter his negative behavior. A child learns at an early age that touching the fire or hot stove provides painful feelings. This lesson is usually learned after one time. Even the most recalcitrant person stops the behavior, which proves that *stern and sometimes harsh consequences are more effective at preventing and shaping positive behavior than being lenient.* People who are lenient inadvertently or purposely reward unhealthy behavior. This applies to disruptive students and unruly inmates.

Chapter 11

Law Enforcement

Inherent in law enforcement is a great deal of physical risk and personal liability. Law Enforcement Officers deal with the four worst groups of people in society: the *Illiterate, Dysfunctional/Ignorant, Mental Disorders and Violent.* This steep level of liability is a fact that most officers get accustomed to and then it slips to the back of their brain until she or he is faced with a liability issue. Then, many officers begin to question the worthiness of the job, from a personal standpoint. It also causes some officers to be reluctant to enforce the rules firmly, particularly if the infraction is minor, it causes the officer to question the level of support of the agency and it decreases confidence and morale. As a detention officer, you are frequently surrounded by immoral people who have no boundaries in terms of their values and behavior, yet you are constrained by very strict boundaries. These same boundaries are the very ones that can cause you to suffer severe physical damage or tremendous financial loss if the rules are not interpreted in your favor or if the people in the decision-making position have ulterior motives, such as scapegoating or grandstanding for public image and personal gain. It is truly an on-going existence of being caught between a rock and a minefield.

I've witnessed countless expressions of frustration, anger and dejection contrasted with expressions of happiness and playfulness. Indeed, Corrections is an extremely unique profession in that the emotional conditions of the inmates run the gamut on a daily basis! Every day an officer has to be prepared to deal with these varying emotions. A good officer will anticipate situations that will cause certain inmates and pods to be difficult to deal with. For example, when commissary isn't delivered on the expected date for some unforeseen reason, this will cause frustration among the inmates. On the other hand, you can get commissary every day when you don't go to jail. The proper mindset before entering a situation is often necessary to help determine your actions and allow you to respond appropriately, control your stress level and be able to decompress afterward. Otherwise, I might over-react in response to the vile behavior. In many instances, when considering an inmate's behavior, I had to remind myself of the scripture-"Father forgive them for they know not what they do!" (Luke 23:34) In most instances, the inmates were clearly aware of their actions, but I'm not sure if they were aware of how self-degrading some of those actions were because they weren't taught how to always acknowledge and respect a lady's presence; they weren't taught how to behave like a gentleman because they weren't raised by a gentleman; they weren't taught how their actions could jeopardize their health or terminate their future possibilities. Based on my years of experience of working with stubborn and irrational people, *one thing I know for sure is that you can't convince an irrational person that their thoughts are not rational during a general conversation*! How do you tell an idiot that he is an idiot? How do you tell an incompetent person that he is incompetent? How do you tell a lady that she doesn't know what she is doing? To accomplish any of these goals, it requires a significant amount of intensive counseling and negotiating in a calm setting and even under those circumstances, it may not work. However, officers are usually faced with this challenge in a general encounter or unforeseen encounter and most of us lack the basic knowledge and frequent training to adequately deal with such a situation. A verbal conversation can escalate to a physical assault in a couple of minutes or seconds! In regard to detention officers, it can escalate over a few days, which leads to a setup, a sudden attack or kidnapping of an officer. Too often, officers encounter situations with complacency, which means that they don't have any action plan and that is something that **an officer should never ever do**!

The *systems (jail and public education) are heavily flawed and everyone is painfully aware because the flaws are evident and range from minor to severe.* Yet, too many people choose to ignore the problems. I imagine that the flaws are ignored because those who have the power to improve the situation don't care because the flaws don't directly affect them! With respect to education, I doubt that any of the Superintendents over failing districts have their children enrolled in one of the public schools in their district. Then, there are those who probably believe that the flaws are too daunting to resolve. As a result, the majority of employees are unsympathetic because they feel that leadership is uncaring, so they show up every day with a whatever attitude hoping to avoid the pitfalls and landmines. With respect to the jail, the Lieutenants and Captains don't have to work the floors, so they hardly inspect the floors to see exactly what types of behaviors the officers have to combat every day. Believe me when I tell you that it is extremely troubling and stressful working with loutish people who are accustomed to behaving loutishly. Eventually, you realize that there is a subculture that is comfortable with ass-backward behavior! As an officer who happens to be a conscientious citizen, you realize that this type of behavior is shocking and extremely disturbing to your spirit because you are unaccustomed to that type of behavior. This situation is exacerbated when you are supervised by management personnel who think that it's easier to allow uncouth people to behave in all types of insidious ways, as long as it doesn't happen in front of them, than to control their behavior by enforcing the rules! In regard to long-term employment in law enforcement, is it possible to not develop a cynical attitude and maintain an optimistic attitude despite working in an environment of severe ignorance, dysfunction, violence, mediocrity, immaturity, unethical and unsophisticated people? It seems to me that cynicism and pessimism inevitably seep into the consciousness of too many officers!

There is a clear difference between a professional working relationship and a social relationship. Jail is certainly not a social setting, so I always felt some sense of discomfort around officers who regularly socialized with inmates. Initially, it was shocking to me. Part of the cause of the confusion was that some of the officers were friends with the inmates prior to their incarceration and others were excited about having friendly relations with them, but didn't understand how it compromised their professional relationship. I never understood why a person would want to be friends with a criminal, especially a violent or career criminal. It made me question the integrity of the officer's character. More importantly, it caused me to be cautious regarding the level of trust I had in the officer. It seemed to me that the younger "officer friendly," usually in his or her 20s, maintained a friendly relationship with criminals because it boosted their ego to be friends with a thug. The older "officer friendly" maintained a friendly relationship with criminals to prevent them from giving him a hard time in regard to complying with his commands. Even after I had worked there for several years, some instances of socializing between officers and inmates, such as them laughing, discussing video games and dapping, caused a troubling feeling within me! Do you demonstrate to a person that you disapprove of their behavior by socializing or not socializing with them? Officers cajoling inmates creates a sense of normalcy in the minds of the criminals. Thus, the misinterpretation in the minds of the violent criminals that their behavior is acceptable. The conclusion is dead wrong, but based on his interaction with the officers, it is logical. Despite whether a person is innocent or guilty, officers are commanded to maintain a professional working relationship, emphasis on the word professional. In some instances, officers have knowledge about some inmates who almost certainly appear guilty, yet they still socialize with the inmates! Therefore, when the officer behaves in the aforementioned manner even though he knows that the inmate killed a baby, raped four ladies or beat and robbed an elderly lady, the officer's behavior doesn't demonstrate to the inmate that his actions were horrendous. What sense does it make to have a social conversation with someone who committed such a horrendous act and is there any benefit to doing it? I feel almost one hundred percent sure that the officers who behave in that manner would not behave like that if the victim had been their sister, father, mother, brother or child! Thus, the importance of understanding the meaning of empathy. Ultimately, it's up to the officer to determine how she or he interacts with the inmates based on their interpretation of professionalism. However, that decision is heavily influenced by the management style of the jail. This was one of the most difficult aspects of working as a detention officer. I'm convinced that this philosophical difference is what leads to unethical and dangerous behavior on the part of officers, such as aiding criminal activity, drug and phone smuggling, etc.

On one occasion, I was assigned to work the "hole" (Segregated pod) with Officer Lah. He was a self-described tough guy who walked around with his chest out, head high and always talked like he wasn't afraid of the inmates and he could control any situation. The more females present, the tougher he talked. My gut told me that I might be in for a long shift. Immediately, I knew something was not good when we entered the pod and all of the inmates asked him how he was doing and where was Officer D, but most of them cursed at me. Whenever inmates are excited to have an officer work their floor, that's usually a definite sign of a soft officer, also known as "Officer Friendly." This thought was confirmed when he volunteered to feed all of the inmates, which allowed me to do another task instead of providing backup while he was serving the trays. Since I always took my job seriously, I paid close attention to him and remained alert. As a result, I heard him having a social conversation with each inmate, as if he were a personal waiter trying to improve his chance of getting a good tip. Yet, the most sickening words I heard Officer Lah say was "good luck in court today... I wish you the best." What common sense officer who possesses a strong amount of courage and dignity would utter those words to disrespectful and violent criminals who were most likely guilty of one or more counts of murder, rape or child molestation? The inmate was guilty of assaulting an officer and that's why he was housed in the hole. Before I worked with Officer Lah, I doubted his bravado because his comments were usually braggadocious and I could tell that he was talking it, but never lived it. Now, I knew for sure that it was all a front to impress the female officers and to be accepted by the male officers. More importantly, my inner safety bells were ringing because I never felt comfortable working with an officer who felt more compelled to console an inmate rather than a co-worker! *Working with the enemy is almost as dangerous as sleeping with the enemy.*

Inmate manipulation is one of the most frustrating and can be the most dangerous aspect of supervising inmates. Well into my fourth year of work, I received an assignment to work with Officer Natural Cut on a medium security floor. Initially, I felt reluctant because she was a member of the "officer friendly" crew, but I decided to give her the benefit of doubt. Halfway through meal distribution, Sgt. Snipes called me on the radio and told me to report to the Sgt.'s office immediately. Unbeknownst to me, Officer Natural Cut had been manipulated by the baby boys and listened to their whining while I was working instead of monitoring me as policy required. Then, she called Sgt. Snipes and lied by telling him that I was agitating the inmates. This situation caused my blood to boil for several reasons. First, Sgt. Snipes completely accepted Officer Cut's assertions, which was evidenced by him verbally attacking me when I arrived at the office and reassigning me to another post. The second issue that pissed me off was that he didn't ask me to explain the status of the situation before he verbally attacked me. Had he asked me to explain the status of the situation instead of focusing on exerting his authority, he could had realized that it was a normal situation in which the boys were just having a tantrum and she didn't want to deal with it! The third problem was that he didn't use any basic reasoning skills! One of the main principles of logic teaches you to always consider the source! To make a determination based on a faulty source can only lead to a faulty conclusion. Inmates are generally dishonest, conniving and manipulative. These factors should be acknowledged prior to engaging in a discussion and investigating all complaints! To attack an honest and hardworking officer diminishes their respect for the opposing person and decreases employee morale. Most of my peers and supervisors were aware of my reputation as an officer who enforced the rules consistently on a daily basis. I was firm, but fair. I didn't tolerate any blatant or gross disrespect. I never bothered inmates because I didn't want them to bother me. I have the same philosophy for dealing with civilians! One of the lessons that was solidified that day was follow your instincts. I should had contacted Sgt. Snipes and requested another partner or assignment when Officer Cut arrived at the post.

Similar to Officer Cut was Officer Yap. That's her code name because she loved to talk to inmates. She would talk to inmates about almost anything. Her officer friendly habits were bad because she liked to baby the boys by giving them extra sandwiches, food and even unlock an inmate's door when he was supposed to be on lockdown. A couple of times, she asked me to give an inmate another chance after he blatantly violated rules. After a 20-30 minute discussion one evening about beliefs and examples of how improper babying by females creates bratty boys and adult boys, she still wasn't convinced of the negative effect of babying adult boys. It irritates me when a person fails to understand how rewarding negative behavior reinforces the exact negative behavior that caused the person to end up in a negative situation or land in jail. For example, I told her about the ways K-5th grade boys whine, pout and have tantrums when they don't get what they want. As a result, she should had been able to see that these 17, 30 and 40-year-old boys did the same thing. Also, I mentioned to her how some inmates will ask a female officer about an issue that the male officer has already denied. It's the exact form of manipulation that boys at home do after their father has denied their request unless the mother and father specifically tell their son not to try that foolishness. Later, she responded by telling me how she believed that officers and sergeants "make inmates act aggressively and damage property." I told her that a person can't justify ignorant and violent behavior because of words that he disliked. Isn't that the same excuse that a man uses for *justifying* why he beat up his girlfriend or wife? The punk says, I didn't like the way she talked to me or she disrespected me, so I beat her. Regardless of whether the officer or sergeant speaks to the inmate in a rude manner, the inmate can't rationally justify stuffing blankets and other objects in the toilet and flooding the cell or breaking the sprinkler and flooding the entire dayroom. When is a person justified in damaging property that doesn't belong to him simply because he is upset? These types of fundamental philosophical differences made working as a detention officer more problematic and dangerous. Many of the inmates have committed violent acts, so feeling overly sympathetic is a job hazard in this profession!

In addition to friendly officers, good officers should feel concerned about the mental and physical fitness of an officer! These two primary areas directly impact whether an officer performs their duties in an ethical, effective and prudent manner. The main reason why we should be concerned is that our safety is directly or indirectly tied to the actions or reactions of our co-workers. Since we work hand-in-hand with each other, we are aware of an officer's competence, strengths, weaknesses, work habits, beliefs, demeanor and integrity. However, I believe that management is ultimately responsible for knowing the fitness of their officers and maintaining awareness of the fitness of the officers, which they are responsible for supervising! When an officer has poor decision-making skills or commits a terrible act, it casts a negative light on all of the officers and decreases the credibility of the good officers and the entire Sheriff's or Police Department. In the case of an *eighty-four-year-old African-American woman* in Oklahoma, I'm sure that she was extremely shocked to get pepper sprayed in her home shortly after the officer arrived. Then, they laid her on the floor to handcuff her as if she were a fit thirty-year-old combative female. The elderly lady didn't appear to be hostile nor combative. Based on my training and experience, **there is no way on God's green earth that a person should be an officer** *if they can't control an eighty-four-year-old woman or man*. That person is definitely mentally and physically unfit to be an officer with life and death authority. Additionally, if an officer doesn't have the reasoning skills to verbally diffuse a situation or use minimum hand restraint to control a very elderly citizen, again that person is not qualified to be an officer because she lacks the minimum mental and physical skills required for the job! In my opinion, this gross act of injustice was compounded by the fact that the Chief didn't immediately denounce the actions of the officer during his interview. Hiring the wrong people as officers or maintaining the employment of people who shouldn't be an officer and then justifying their wrong actions are counter-productive to establishing and maintaining trust and a solid rapport with the citizens!

Chapter 12

Importance of Terminology

Terminology is very important in regard to conveying an effective message! Too often, people convey incorrect information or messages by misusing words and not knowing the correct meaning of words. This situation occurs every day among ordinary people and professionals, at businesses and social events and in ordinary and emergency situations. Generally, poor communication and comprehension skills stem from a low vocabulary. In many instances, a person's education level is directly related to their comprehension ability. In fact, whether formally or informally educated, a person's vocabulary range determines how well or poorly they communicate, understand basic conversation, rules, procedures, laws, etc. Some college educated people have a limited vocabulary and some non-college educated people have an extensive vocabulary. Frequently, people think that you are being petty or uppity when you inform them that their word or words don't express the information correctly. The purpose of the correction is to receive accurate information because these miscommunications or mixed messages sometimes cause unnecessary issues that result in minor

or severe actions. To avoid an unnecessary problem, a mutual understanding can only be achieved by effectively using words that both
parties know the meaning of. This fact was revealed one morning
after I escorted an inmate to the dentist. Upon leaving, he asked if
he could see the doctor about his wound care. I said no because the
clinic operates by appointment only. Everybody sitting here has
an appointment. He said, "I know, but I'm here, so can't they do
it now?" I said, did you hear me say that they operate by appointment only. He said, "yeah, but I'm here!" Then I said, you must not
know what by appointment means, to which he responded "y'all
don't give a shid bout a ninja!" I just shook my head as I continued walking and I thought, does he really not know the meaning
of by appointment or was he just trying to manipulate his way into
having the doctor examine him. A similar, but more striking misunderstanding happened after midnight when I was conducting a
security check. Inmate Calf pointed to his jaw and mumbled some
words as I visually observed his cell. I asked him to repeat what he
said clearly and that's when he said his tooth was killing him. After I
completed my security check, I escorted him to the clinic to see the
general nurse because it was the weekend and the dental clinic was
closed. Nurse Jones looked in his mouth with a flashlight and said, it
looks like a cavity in your tooth. Have you had it addressed before?
Inmate Calf responded, "what chu mean!" Nurse Jones responded,
have you had it looked at by a dentist? He replied, "nah--my head
hurts and I can tell somethin' ain't right!" After waiting for a few
minutes, Nurse Jones returned and gave him one Tylenol and one
Ibuprofen and told him that they should help eliminate the pain. He
responded, "what dat post to do," which caused the nurse to respond
with a quizzical, pardon me, Sir. So, Calf loudly replied, "what dat
post to do, the pills?" Oooh, she said. The Ibuprofen will make the
pain go away for a while. The reason for quoting the inmate is to
raise the question of the probability of this twenty-year-old obtaining a decent job in mainstream society without understanding the

meaning of basic terms and utilizing that type of broken English. I can't forget the time that an inmate gave me a Work Order Request Form and it said "call maytanunce cuz my fossit dont werk" or the time an inmate gave me a Medical Request Form requesting to be taken to the clinic "cuz my stamick hurt." An inmate's lack of education has always had a strong correlation to his incarceration, as well as to the *probability* of him becoming a repeat offender (recidivism).

Specific words describe your actual thoughts and those thoughts reflect your actions! I've ridden my bicycle down steps, which is kinda dangerous. It happened because I thought I hope I don't fall, instead of what if I fall? I hope I don't doesn't cause the brain to fully consider the negative consequences. What if I fall causes the brain to carefully consider the negative consequences. Often, a criminal doesn't think at all or at the very least, he thinks I hope I don't get caught, rather than what if I get caught, what if the homeowner is home and has a gun; what if the homeowner has experience shooting a gun? What if is a big difference from I hope I don't! Likewise, thinking about what you have to do may feel more stressful or troubling as opposed to thinking about what you have the freedom to do! Whether incarcerated, living in a third world country or non-democratic country, many people don't have the freedom to do all of the things that we can do in the U.S. Despite your limitations, it is a blessing to consider the many different opportunities that are available in the U.S. So, I'm prepared to work wherever I have to work to keep me from yelling "potatoes for one pancake, I got eggs for shank, grits and eggs for a sack, got a sausage for a biscuit, got a tray for an item or **cookies for cole slaw on Father's Day**!

Has anyone else given some thought to the phrase "I did what I had to do?" This seems to be a common statement among rappers and criminals. A correct understanding of the definition of the words "had to" means that some action was mandatory or you had no choice because no other options were available! I know that Georgia Power won't give you lights for free, but that doesn't mean you can't stay trap free. Just because you don't have money or had difficulty finding a job, it doesn't mean that you "had to" commit a robbery. There are many, many other legal and reasonable options that are available. First, you should consider that the consequences and dangers of selling drugs far outweigh the possible benefits. Secondly, you could go to family and friends to ask for temporary help. If not, you could go to the nearest church or pantry and request food and toiletries. Thirdly, you should meet with someone who is more experienced than you are and perhaps older, to determine whether you truly can't find employment or you aren't able to obtain the income that you think you should earn; whether you need to enroll in programs to improve your education and job skills; whether you need to work two jobs to survive until you can implement a plan to progress a little better; whether you need to use social services until you can improve your skills. These are just a few of the many options that are available. Imagine that everyone who has had their utilities turned off, everyone who has been evicted, everyone who didn't have food or money at some time in their lives committed a robbery or engaged in some other illegal activity to get money, we would live in an extremely dangerous society.

With respect to being an officer, one unnecessary issue I had to deal with every now and then was related to the misunderstanding of the word *friend*. My job responsibility required me to interact with an inmate in a professional manner. As an officer, just because I dealt with you for six months to two years, it doesn't mean that we are friends. We are acquaintances. Even if I compliment him about his good decision not to react violently in a certain situation, it is still a professional relationship. I'm not trying to befriend him. Sometimes when I explained to inmates that we were not friends, but acquaintances and this was a professional relationship, they would get really offended. Perhaps, due to their lifestyles and circumstances, many inmates were unfamiliar with a professional relationship. Another misunderstanding that new officers had to deal with involved the term "Houseman." When I began working at the jail, there was an unwritten rule of allowing one inmate to stay outside of his cell longer than any other inmates. Generally, he was allowed to stay out for 1-2 hours longer than his rotation or for most of the day. In exchange for this privilege, he was responsible for keeping the dayroom swept, mopped and cleaned and he received extra food. This inmate was called the "Houseman." All of the officers and inmates were aware of this unwritten rule. Every now and then, an inmate would twist this nice arrangement by disobeying a new officer, female officer, weak officer or an officer he perceived as weak. For example, the officer would tell the inmate to return to his cell and the inmate would say I'm the houseman. As you can tell, the first problem in this dialogue is that the officer didn't ask the inmate who he was. This happened to me on two occasions. The first time it happened I said to the inmate, I recognize that you are the houseman, but you are still an inmate. So, you need to go to your cell now. The second time this happened to me, the inmate said why? I paused and then said, you don't have the right to ask why. You are an inmate and your responsibility is to follow directions! On a few occasions, an inmate would refuse to return to his cell and the officer would have to call for assistance. I found it amusing and confusing that some inmates behaved as if the title of houseman gave them the civilian right to disobey an order and not return to their cell.

While working as a Compliance Officer for the State of Georgia, my responsibilities included investigating complaints of housing discrimination. Numerous times, I dismissed complaints after a brief investigation revealed clear violations of the lease agreement by the tenant. As you can imagine, these dismissals came as a shock to the tenants and it upset them. At first, I was surprised to learn that quite a few tenants believed that they could do whatever they wanted to do to the apartment because they paid rent. Additionally, I was really surprised that several tenants thought that renting meant that they had the same rights as owning a condominium or house. Frequently, these tenants said comments to me like, "I don't like them (leasing agents) going in my apartment anytime they get ready," or they told me that I have to remove the green paint and put the original color back on the wall or why do I have to ask them for permission to change the bedroom door in my apartment!" In one instance, this man lived in a condominium complex and he wanted to make changes to his unit like his friend did. When the condo association told him that he couldn't, he filed a housing complaint with the state alleging discrimination because he thought that they had denied his request to make changes because of his race. However, he hadn't given any thought to the fact that he was renting his unit and his friend had purchased his unit! Usually, I would begin the conversation by explaining to the man or woman that you don't own the apartment. Renting or leasing property does not mean the same as buying property or having purchased property. Therefore, you don't have the right to make unauthorized changes to property that you don't own. I explained that X company owns the apartment complex and the leasing agents work for the company that owns the apartments. Oddly enough, a similar unnecessary misunderstanding occurred when I began working at the jail. During cell inspections and searches, several inmates would make ridiculous comments like "get out of my room, you can't go in my room without my permission, that's my uniform, or you can't touch my stuff." All of these statements were accurate toward another inmate, but not toward an officer. Often, I would ask them who did they buy the room from. Some were confused and didn't know how to respond. Others replied, "chuck you talkin' bout, I didn't buy no room!" Then I replied, if you didn't buy this cell, it doesn't belong to you! Also, the uniform has county jail written on it, so that should be your bright clue that it doesn't belong to you either and since you have more than the allotted amount, I am confiscating the additional uniforms. In fact, everything inside of the cell was subject to search and seizure. This disillusionment of ownership on the part of a lot of inmates led to unnecessary verbal and physical altercations.

It's very important to realize and understand that *all English speaking people do not understand and comply with directions and commands in the same manner*! It's as if there is a dialect that must be spoken in order to gain a mutual understanding. (see Utube video of rapper T.I. being harassed as he attempts to pump gas in peace) I don't like giving verbal commands more than two times, whether I'm speaking to a student, inmate or family member. **Directions are meant to be followed the first time they are given, not the second, third or fourth time**! Certainly, in an urgent or emergency situation, an officer doesn't have time to repeat commands four or five times. This issue is related to the day that the officers received a speech in Roll Call from Lieutenant Shorty regarding "inappropriate language" and profanity. In regard to the issue of so-called "inappropriate language," as described by Lt. Shorty, one must consider that language that is inappropriate in one setting, may be appropriate in another. When verbal commands require compliance, yet they are disobeyed, it's necessary to change your style of communicating and that involves changing your tone and words. For example, violent and aggressive inmates who reject authority don't usually comply with courteous and mildly spoken words without a show of force! Yet, most of them do respond to assertive words, profanity and in some respect, they give more respect to the officer who communicates in a manner that they relate to! If the officer doesn't check the inmates verbally, they are likely to "try" the officer physically. Then, you end up with an assault or attempted assault of the officer. This situation reminds me of the pivotal scene in the wonderful sports movie Any Given Sunday. During Pacino's pep talk to Foxx, he says *"when they look in your eyes, they gotta believe!"* Whenever inmates threatened me, I believe that when they looked into my eyes to see if I was a punk or intimidated by them, they saw that *I meant exactly every crazy word that I said to them.*

Words and actions work together. When an inmate refuses to be guided by words, he must be guided by actions. Once inmates saw fear in an officer's eyes and body language, they would abuse him in the same manner that they would devour the Hosea Thanksgiving dinner. Once inmates begin calling the officer "Officer Scary", he would have serious difficulty getting them to obey his commands. Inmates would curse at the officer and engage in all kinds of she-nanigans like hiding in different cells, throw paper balls at him, spit on him and even stand in front of the exit door and prevent him from exiting the pod. This situation was contagious like sharks smelling blood in the water because sometimes the smallest or weakest inmate in the pod would try the officer later. Then, little junior criminal might do something like call the officer several pro-fane names or threaten to kick the officer's ass while knowing full well that he wouldn't bust a grape in a fruit fight! Simply because an officer is passive and continues to treat the inmate decently even though he is behaving in an uncivilized manner, doesn't mean that the officer should be abused. Yet, these types of incidents occurred because jail and prison are environments where kindness is often interpreted as weakness. Some inmates are so predatory that they will attempt to take advantage of any situation. I recall an incident where an inmate had been released from the mental health floor and was reassigned to a general population floor. Upon reviewing his ID bracelet, I noticed that he spoke very slowly and looked like he was in a daze. After I let him enter the pod, I noticed that he had difficulty finding his cell location on the mezzanine level even though they are clearly numbered. Then, I saw 3-4 inmates gravitating towards him. I knew from experience that he would be abused within the next few minutes, hour or by the next day. Therefore, I immediately notified Sgt. Fake so she could determine alternative housing for the inmate. Sometimes, on the high-security floors and particularly on the maximum security floor, inmates would get upset and throw food, juice, wet tissue, toilet water and urine on the floor of the pod to cause an officer to fall or just to be nasty. There were several times when they threw urine and feces on an officer and even on a couple of sergeants. Generally, this type of behavior was reserved for an officer of small stature or for an officer who was mild-mannered and the inmates perceived him to be soft. Based on the officer's vocal tone and mannerisms, the inmates' predatory instincts were usually right. This assessment was dangerous because the same way bad news and threats traveled around the jail via word of mouth and kites, safety news traveled regarding an officer's reputation. Thus, inmates knew which officers to **not try** physically or throw objects at. If they threw urine or feces on the wrong officer, there would be a meeting. No talking, just bodies and furniture moving! *It is illogical to expect passivity to be capable of controlling violent aggression, especially in a closed environment where the offenders prey on weakness!* In this atmosphere where kindness and civility are misinterpreted as weakness, an officer has to be very wary of how he or she presents himself or herself. Based on the circumstances, the language must be assertive, the rules and consequences must be firm, swift and consistent in order to maintain an appropriate level of compliance, respect and decency!

Profanity/Effective Communication

I knew how to curse before I began working at the jail, but those inmates taught me how to be a professional curser! I earned a Rosetta Stone advanced degree in profanity! If this sounds offensive or unprofessional to some, perhaps they would have a different opinion if they understood the dangerous environment and the various serious situations an officer encounters when surrounded by murderers, rapists and other violent criminals on a daily basis. This abrasive language is a tactic that is in alignment with training that officers receive and it is known as Verbal Judo. Remember that I said it is in alignment with the training, not that the training taught us to use profanity. The goal of the communication training was to teach officers various terms and styles of communicating to help us control, negate or de-escalate various types of situations. I used to work with an officer who would ask inmates interesting questions whenever they started talking sideways or making threats. He would ask questions like have you ever drank Ensure through a straw for breakfast, lunch and dinner? Have you ever had a headache last all week? Do you know what you would sound like with no front teeth? I found the questions to be very funny! Also, I thought they were appropriate responses to inmates threatening to whip his ass or throw urine and feces on him. Somehow, his words would always pause them, whether they immediately understood his questions or not. It's imperative to understand that effective communication requires you to speak in the language and tone that the inmates will understand and obey. For example, Officer McBook sounded like a professor when he spoke to the inmates. Consequently, many inmates used to ignore his commands and he would have to repeat them 5-6 times before they complied. His normal style of communicating was ineffective. It took him about two years before he realized that he needed to change his vocabulary and make his commands simple, short and assertive! Typically, most inmates disobeyed and disrespected officers who spoke in a passive tone. So despite the harshness of an officer's language at times, getting inmates to comply with words is better and safer than using hands and weapons to gain compliance. Please don't misconstrue what I'm saying, as I'm not suggesting that profanity should be commonplace or occur without cause, but it can be an effective form of communication. I've shut down quite a few intimidation attempts, verbal altercations and verbal threats by using some heavily accented street vocabulary! I take pride in the fact that I only had to use my protective weapons a few times during my tenure. Part of the reason is that I spoke to inmates based on the situation. At times, I had no problem telling inmates this is a like it or not situation!

Characterization/Misunderstanding

It's all about the characterization! One's knowledge, experience, environment, values, integrity and motive determines how she or he describes a situation. If he believes in a dog-eat-dog world, he will probably not say anything against his criminal-minded friend. If he believes in white nationalism, he will say that affirmative action is reverse discrimination. If she believes that it is the school's sole responsibility to educate her child, she will likely say that the school isn't doing its job. If she believes that people should respect her regardless of how she dresses, she will probably argue about her right to wear skin-tight uniform pants around inmates, have her girls half out during Sunday service or take her child to school in her pajamas and house slippers. People have a tendency to describe their behavior or a situation in a way that is favorable to their desire. In this particular instance, despite the adult boy having been arrested multiple times, a neighbor told the news reporter that "the guy was a good dude." He said that the guy was just "trying to make a living and the cops would hassle him for selling low-level drugs." The neighbor's statement suggests that selling low-level drugs was not illegal and the cops should not have arrested the guy. This statement is a clear reflection of the neighbor's distorted morals and mentality. I don't think that this type of neighbor would be helpful in resolving the guy's legal problems. Too many family members and friends describe their father, son, uncle, cousin, brother, priest, mother and sister as good, harmless and helpful people, yet victims are left to cope with horrible crimes every day. All of these criminals can't be "good people!" If so, there are a lot of senseless and horrendous crimes being committed by "good people." I've seen their behavior and heard their conversations. Believe me when I say that many of them are not good people. As a civilized society, we must pay close attention to *individuals and groups of people* **attempting to rationalize abnormal and destructive behavior**! Also, I don't want to hear another person emphatically say "I didn't learn a damn thing in school" or "school ain't teach me nothing." If you didn't learn a damn thing in school, that's a sad reflection of you and your parents! This statement provides a false description of the schools that she or he attended in that it implies that not one of the teachers provided any competent and caring instruction. It's virtually impossible for a student to go through K-12 being obedient and diligent and not learn and develop multiple skills that are beneficial in life.

Regarding the U.S. government, lawmakers may say that a policy provides health coverage to all citizens, but the verbiage will demonstrate a difference between access to health coverage and access to health care. A policy that provides access to health coverage, yet has negative clauses and loopholes within the law, ultimately doesn't provide access to health care. So, although an insurance company offers insurance, if the average American can't afford the premiums or meet the health requirements, then they don't have access to health care because they can't go to the doctor. Likewise, although the U.S. government provides citizens the right to vote, yet provides a provision that allows states to decide the requirements a citizen must possess in order to vote, the government has provided the means for voter suppression. Specificity of words is critically important!

Have you ever given much consideration to how people describe you, whether you are a coach, teacher, principal, detention officer, manager, mother or father? Do they describe you as mean, bad, unkind, unfair, or unqualified because you enforce the rules and don't let them do what they want when they want to? Then, these same people describe someone else as cool, nice, funny, qualified, smart, helpful or friendly because that person allows them to do what they want when they want to practically every time. The problem with the positive and negative description is that almost no consideration is given to whether the behavior or situation is right or wrong. Enforcement of legal and fair rules by a person does not warrant a negative characterization. Children, teens and immature adults usually want what they want. However, the determining factor should almost always be what's right or wrong, not who is right or wrong! During my lengthy teaching career, I enforced the rules regarding behavior and academic expectations. Somehow, quite a few students labeled me as mean and rigid. Some of their parents had the same view. This perception didn't disturb me because I realized that their expectations were skewed. The primary functions of a caring and rational teacher do not include forming social friendships, permitting disruptive or self-destructive behavior, giving good grades that a student didn't earn or not expecting the best effort from each student.

During my tenure as a detention officer, many inmates, and sad to say, some of my co-workers thought and said that I was mean, unfair and rigid. Many inmates complained about me and officers with similar work-styles who enforced the rules. I didn't mind that inmates complained about not being able to watch TV or not having gone outside for ten consecutive days because of cold or rainy weather. If they truly appreciated going outside, they should had appreciated their freedom and stayed legal. This scenario was played out during a mild day during the Day shift. An inmate made a hand gesture towards the TV. I said, are you asking me to turn on the TV? He replied, yeah. I was just wondering if you would turn on the TV for a "brotha." Since I was familiar with him, I said weren't you watching TV at home about a month ago? He said, yeah, about fifty days ago. I said you must not appreciate watching TV at home and your freedom since you came back here. He replied, I got into a situation, but "I'm supposed to be going home and look at how y'all treat a brother. I betcha I gotta wait 4-5 hours before I get released." I excitedly responded by saying *how can you complain about how we treat*

235

you before you consider how you treat yourself! They should make you wait 4-5 hours every time you come in here. The audacity of him to expect rush delivery service to exit jail. His attitude was very typical of the mentality of an immature, irresponsible and irrational person. **Jail should be uncomfortable**. Jail isn't supposed to be comfortable and convenient! Inmates shouldn't leave jail and feel that the experience was okay and cool. One of the uncomfortable aspects for many inmates was the procedure that required all inmates to return to their cell if the inmate who committed the violation refused to return to his cell. Such was the case one night when I instructed a nasty inmate to return to his cell because my female co-worker told me that the inmate began masturbating as she was walking towards him in the pod. To my surprise, a full-bearded, gray-haired seventy-year-old man began spouting foolishness about me "not being man enough" to make the nasty inmate return to his cell. He said, why do we have to be punished? I said, Sir, you have gray hair and so do I and I know you understand how authority works. So, just comply with my words and return to your cell. Inmates frequently said, "I don't like you Johnson or worse, I hate you Johnson." If I had a dollar for every time I got cursed out, insulted or verbally threatened, I would be able to buy a house on Star Island in Miami or in Country Club of the South. By the way, it is foolish to threaten a person because your words convey your intent to harm him and it may cause him to overreact, which could be very costly to you. If you are in jail or prison, it will cause the officer to always distrust you.

Once when I was handcuffing about eight inmates to take them to the Transport area to be taken to court, I clearly remember an inmate saying *"there you go Johnson, chaining us up like the slavemaster."* Admittedly, this comment stopped me in my tracks because it was shocking and very insulting to me based on the history of African-Americans in the U.S. Furthermore, this early morning butthole comment came from a half-gray-haired man who was a repeat offender and had committed serious felonies. He looked like he grew up right after the civil rights movement, so he should have had better sense than to make that kind of degrading comment. On a different level, another irrational comment that was frequently stated by the boys to the officers was "you killing my rotation." This phrase referred to all inmate activities that had to stop whenever the officer was performing a security check or another procedure. Once in a while when this phrase annoyed me, I would tell the adult boy, when you decided to commit an illegal act and got arrested, you killed your rotation! You chose to risk your freedom and now it's gone! All you can do now is charge it to the game. In most instances, their comments never bothered me for two main reasons. First, I wasn't hired for them to like me. I believe that it is important to strive for people to respect you. Once you are confident that you are performing your responsibilities in a correct, decent and honest manner, you don't worry about whether people like you or not. The job description said nothing about a popularity contest, so it would have been immature and irrational for me to feel some kinda way about them disliking me. Secondly, I always enforced the rules consistently and fairly. I had a reputation for being firm, but fair. I knew that it was important to be consistent because inconsistency weakens your authority and breeds disobedience. Again, an employee who enforces legal and fair rules shouldn't be described by negative words or have a negative perception. Yet, you must realize that perception is determined by an individual's morals, life-experiences and reasoning skills or lack thereof! Oftentimes, you can show and tell people the truth, but many of them prefer to believe their perception!

Dichotomy/Paradox of Words

Words are profound and impotent! Some of us are familiar with the saying **there is power in words.** Energy flows after words are spoken. That energy is usually positive or negative, depending on the nature of the conversation and the impact will be constructive, destructive or neutral based upon the age, maturity and knowledge of the participants. Negative, disparaging, degrading and inflammatory words have the ability to damage and destroy twenty-year-old friendships, long-standing relationships, short and long-term marriages, small and behemoth businesses, race relations and dynamic international coalitions. Therefore, you can clearly understand that negative words are powerful enough to damage the undeveloped mind of a child between the ages of 4-17. Have you ever heard a mother, father, grandparent or sibling tell a child shut up, you drive me crazy, you so stupid, you gettin' on my nerves or you so bad? *Negative words spoken to a child on a consistent basis will likely cause the child to have a negative self-image and stunt his or her ability to develop confidence in his abilities.* Once a boy has spent years in that toxic environment, this dangerously negative perception becomes **embedded in his mentality and often remains into his adult life**. The horrible manifestation is demonstrated by his devaluing of other humans, including his children. Negative words are toxic enough to cause people to experience long-term depression, addictions, commit single and group suicide, commit senseless and violent acts, march and protest to spread hate or even start a war. Hence, the term war of words. Conversely, positive words have the ability to create wonderful relationships, small and behemoth partnerships, dynamic international coalitions and wonderful children who grow up to be wonderful adults! Words are strong enough get people to March on Washington, tear down the Berlin Wall and create a Million Man March and cause over one million brothers and sisters to stand in harmony in Washington. Words are powerful enough to get people to march from Selma to Montgomery! Words provide inspiration, confidence, strength, instruction, guidance, hope and comfort. Clearly, all of us know how we feel good or flattered when someone says nice words to us, such as you look beautiful, you look handsome, I like that fragrance, nice outfit, you did a great job, your hairstyle looks nice, that was nice of you, etc. All children have fragile egos and it isn't until their parents, family members, teachers and coaches begin frequently telling them I love you, we love you, I am proud of you, you are special, you are smart, you can do it, and I believe in you, that children begin to feel important and confident in their abilities. Consequently, it's extremely important to the positive development of boys and girls to **consistently expose them to encouraging words and actions to solidify their self-worth and confidence in their ability to perform tasks during their formative years**. Then, they will likely face their educational and social challenges with confidence and enthusiasm in their ability to succeed. Confidence and enthusiasm are important aspects of achievements. As children continue to strengthen their confidence during their formative and adolescence years, they will have the ability to successfully combat teasing, verbal bullying and negative peer pressure because they have been **consistently** shown that they are valuable. Therefore, they will be less likely to follow a negative group just to fit in, feel accepted or cool. Should the kids feel weak, embarrassed or overwhelmed by a situation, they have been filled with enough confidence to ask an adult for guidance and know that they are no less special.

It's very important to expose children to more encouraging words than discouraging words, as well as misguided words. So, Dear Momma, just because the father left home or the father never lived with you and his son, you should had not started calling that boy or young man the "man of the house." By doing so, you created a misperception in his mind, which sets him up for failure or unnecessary difficulties later on in life. *It's important for his growth process to live his boyhood years being called a boy and being treated like a boy.* We need to stop trying to appease children and appeal to their ego just to obtain their cooperation by calling 10, 13 and 19-year-old boys man. They are not a man, aren't even close to manhood and surely can't handle the responsibilities of manhood. I frequently heard teachers and administrators call 8, 10, and 13-year-olds young man. That is how people create the perception of being a man in a child's mind. Why? They are boys and we should call them as such. Those are boys by virtue of their age and maturity. Some parents and adults choose to address them as man or young man, but when he gets beat up or is standing in front of a judge, he is conveniently labeled just a boy. You can't have it both ways! There is nothing negative about calling a boy a boy. Frequently, I would hear 17-25-year-old inmates get angry and say I'm a grown ass man, which usually made me laugh. Then, when I spoke to them in grown man's language, I received a boy's reaction! Frowning, pouting, whining, stomping feet, yelling and throwing objects inside a cell doesn't seem like grown man behavior.

On the contrary, **words are powerless**! Hence, the profound and enduring slogan "talk is cheap." What substantial benefit does a lady receive from a man who tells her "I love you," but regularly neglects her? What meaningful benefit does a child receive from a father who tells him "you know I love you," yet he hardly spends any quality time with him? With respect to relationships, words are ineffective without supporting actions. For anyone in late childhood, adolescence and early adulthood who was consistently nurtured with words of love, confidence and encouragement, negative words cause minimal or no impact on their daily life activities. Childhood includes harmless teasing and jonesin'. When I was growing up, many kids would frequently recite the rhyme sticks and stones may break my bones, but names will never hurt me. Sure, as a child or young adult, you may feel blue for awhile, but it won't last long and it surely won't have a lasting impact. The reason why negative words, assertions and characterizations don't have a negative impact is that the person's mental and emotional foundations were solidified during their childhood and adolescence years. **They are confident of who they are and know without a doubt that they are valuable and loved**! They know that the negative characterizations of a friend, boss, relative or a group of people cannot determine the outcome of their life unless they allow it.

For sure, law enforcement is a field in which a person has to have thick skin, solid reasoning skills and be totally secure in their self-worth, as you will be disparaged and called all types of insulting names. On one occasion, an inmate shouted "damn Johnson, ya old ass look like Danny Glover and of course, other inmates laughed. As I walked out of the pod, I thought to myself, Glover is a multi-millionaire and I'm a multi-thousandaire. We are both free men who eat very well, wear clean clothes, reside in clean and comfortable houses and sleep in clean beds that are much larger than a bunk bed. Not to mention, I don't wash in the same shower that twenty other men use. Therefore, how could the joke be on me? Why should I feel some type of way? During another encounter with an adult boy, he exhibited his elementary and boyish mentality by saying "is this the best job you could get? You can't get no better than this cuz you ain't no good." I replied, it pays more than the job you have now! He said no it doesn't. These foolish comments were meant to antagonize me. First of all, it's difficult to antagonize a mature, knowledgeable and confident person with foolish comments because the person knows that there isn't any reason to consider the foolishness! Also, a wise elder told me that you shouldn't spend time talking into the ears of foolish people, so I didn't argue with them. As a newbie, you get cursed out every day until time passes and you establish your authority with the inmates. Then, the disparaging remarks decline. I've been cursed out forward, backward, up, down, sideways, with southern twang and without. I had to ask myself am I a punk ass because he called me a punk ass? Am I a witch ass ninja because he said so to the other twenty-five guys standing around? No, not hardly. Since my mental and spiritual foundations are solid in my understanding of manhood, I was able to easily ignore those insults. I brushed it off because I knew that I was on my way to my destiny. How idiotic and childish is it for inmates to yell insulting remarks and call me derogatory names while standing behind cell doors. They probably don't realize, nor care that they look like a test creature in a laboratory—tattoos on their neck and face, strange hairstyles and colors, yellow-gold colored teeth and missing teeth, all the while begging for extra food and supposedly the joke is on the officer. Yet, all the bitterness, rage, vulgarity and frustration inside them, *won't provide them the freedom, respect, admiration, accomplishments, self-esteem and money that they desperately crave*!

Powerless people often fight power with their words, according to the erudite professor, historian and prolific orator Dr. Michael Eric Dyson. This is a weak and useless action, for words alone can't conquer power. It seems to me that descriptive words which evoke strong emotions that lead to strategic planning that evolves into strategic actions are best suited for combating powerful people, corporations and injustice. How many times have you seen or heard of a person speaking disrespectfully to a judge? Yet, it doesn't stop the person from going to jail. How many times have you seen or heard of a person speaking disrespectfully to a leasing agent? Yet, it doesn't stop the person from getting evicted. How many times have you seen or heard of a person speaking disrespectfully to their boss? Yet, it doesn't stop him or her from getting suspended or fired. How many times have you seen or heard of an inmate speaking disrespectfully to a detention officer? Yet, it doesn't stop him or her from getting their privileges revoked. Even after the inmate gives me the middle finger because he wants to return to his cell immediately after he handed over his breakfast meal as payment for the bet he lost, his door is still locked and he can't return to sleep right away because of his asinine behavior. Officers get the last move, which is a lesson that you would think inmates would learn quickly and adapt, but sadly that's not the case in many instances.

Chapter 13

Truth

Truth without love is brutality
and love without truth is hypocrisy

—Warren W. Wiersbe

Whenever you tell a person something that contradicts their belief, their situation or positive view of themselves, their ego automatically feels a sense of attack, anger or disappointment. In psychology, this is known as cognitive dissonance. At this time, defensive mechanisms will generally kick in. The only exception to this reaction is a mentally mature person who has the mindset that he wants to know about his flaw, so that he can eliminate it or improve upon a weakness. Before telling someone the truth, you should determine if the information is necessary, is it beneficial and whether you can say it in a compassionate way. If yes is the answer to the prior questions, you should tell him or her the truth. You should also be willing to help the person if you can. Sharing information is a critical aspect of establishing and developing professional and personal relationships. Yet, this information is useless and harmful when it lacks honesty. Be subtle whenever possible, **but still speak the truth**. Once someone has identified the areas where you are lacking in skills, the next move is to discover tools you can use to strengthen those areas. In most instances, *I subscribe to the philosophy of hurting a person with the truth is better than making them happy with a lie!* "*The truth can hurt you; Or the truth can change you; What will truth do to you?*" says the prolific Kirk Franklin. While growing up, I frequently heard the expression "the truth will set you free." Experts say that the first step towards resolving a problem is admitting that you have a problem. Thus, you must admit the truth, regardless of whether the problem involves your combative attitude, mood swings, hard-headed children, disrespectful child, lazy son, fast daughter, womanizing husband, academically low-performing child, careless spending, etc. If mom has a 20, 30 or 40-year-old boy, it's important for her to acknowledge it and begin taking actions to wean him off. Her actions should benefit the 20 and 30-year-old, but I'm not sure if there will be much improvement in a forty-year-old adult boy.

I believe that *political correctness has contributed heavily to the moral decay in society*. In an effort to be politically correct, **too many people act as though everything is relative and there are no more absolutes**. These people often attempt to avoid personal accountability and justify right and wrong, good and bad to justify their agenda through idealistic or false interpretations. I believe that it is **reasonable, justifiable and necessary to have and enforce decent standards**. All leaders are responsible for setting and enforcing standards. Standards can be low, moderate or high. Principles and standards are related to a process. Generally, a process is a way of doing something based upon principles, which ensures that a standard is achieved. A process provides specific procedures, which provide continuity. It is senseless to have standards, but not enforce them. This applies to all leaders and agents for the leaders, such as Property Managers, Correction Officers, Detention Officers, Wardens, Sheriffs, Parents, Principals, Teachers, Pastors and CEOs. In most instances, high standards should be consistent and uncompromising. A church should require its members and guests to wear appropriate clothing and not have inappropriate body parts exposed. Schools should require students to dress appropriately, speak proper English, not tolerate bullying and other forms of negative behavior and not allow known gang members to attend classes. It's okay to tell a child that he is not doing well in school, but here is what you and I are going to do to fix the problem! It's more important to tell the parents that their child is doing badly and this is what we are going to do to get him or her to perform well by this date! We really need you to assist us in our efforts by doing these specific things. A *comprehensive and documented plan of action involving the parent(s) should be implemented.* This unwillingness to be truthful was at the heart of the **2009 Atlanta Public School CRCT cheating scandal** that involved one hundred seventy-eight teachers and thirty-eight principals at forty-four schools. Simply because administrators and teachers refused to tell the truth and deal with the truth of the extremely low-performance levels of the students, they compounded the situation by attempting to get slick and change the answers and test scores. What reward did they receive for their irrational reasoning and slickness? They received jail time or termination notices. Furthermore, after all of that negative and illegal behavior, **the children are still sorely academically deficient**.

Over the years of working in various fields, I have encountered and formed relationships with a lot of nice people in terms of being friendly and having good manners. So, the difficult challenge is to persuade some of these people to not argue for the sake of argument and to accept the fact that their ideas, beliefs or actions may be wrong or have a negative impact. Too many people reject information because they don't like it or it offends them, instead of logically determining whether the information is accurate and logical! Moreover, they should determine whether the information can be helpful for them. Many times, people choose to believe what they want to, rather than what is true or appears to be true based on the facts or reasonable standards. Some situations are indefensible! When your position defies logic, then it makes no rational sense to defend it because **you lose your credibility in the process**! In regard to honesty and legal training, I was always taught that the **facts are the facts and the truth is the truth**! When an officer shoots an unarmed man in his back or with his hands in the air or at his side, **it's illogical and insulting for the officer to allege that he feared for his life and for the police department and district attorney to try to justify deadly force!** When an officer shoots a child within three seconds of seeing him, it is a horrible example of piss-poor decision-making skills and probably combined with racist beliefs. Clearly, nobody had been injured and nobody was in imminent danger, so there was no compelling reason to use deadly force! **You can't make a wrong right!** *It doesn't matter who you get to explain it or what intellectual or slippery method they use to explain the reasoning*! You may legally get away with the unjust act, but all of the righteous people and the universe know that it was wrong! However, you can right some wrongs through various actions like admitting that you made a mistake, accepting responsibility for your actions, providing a sincere personal or public apology, eliminating and implementing corrective policies and procedures, replacing a service or product for free or providing financial compensation. *Nevertheless, wrong is wrong and it is high time that management personnel, police departments, prosecution offices, predominately white juries, politicians and concerned citizens start admitting the truth*! **The health of our society is dependent on it!**

As a matter of basic common sense, it's important for people to realize that other people don't need you to verbally admit something for them to know the answer or truth. As the saying goes, small children and fitted clothing always reveal the truth! Whether common or uncommon knowledge, it's okay to admit that you don't know something. *You don't know what you don't know! And when you don't know that you don't know, rest assured that those who do know, know that you don't know. However, when you know that you don't know, it's important for you to seek out the information, ask for assistance and be willing to accept instruction from those who do know.* Whatever you know or don't know is what you are comfortable with. Typically, whatever you are comfortable thinking, doing and believing is where you want to stay because doing something differently or thinking and believing different information, despite being right or beneficial, moves you out of your comfort zone and it requires courage and effort. It requires you to seek a new normal! **Everything that we say and do reveals facts** about our upbringing, beliefs, habits, knowledge and skills! I don't need you to admit that you have bad writing skills. Based on my knowledge and training, I can easily make that determination by looking at what you wrote! I contend that there are far too many disconnected and disillusioned fathers who don't **consistently** provide positive attributes to the lives of their children. More than likely, you and a few family or friends will strongly profess that you are a good and nurturing parent and not grossly negligent. However, I can tell that you are a bad and grossly negligent parent by listening and looking at your child. I rarely saw fathers walking in the school halls with their sons and daughters. I also didn't see more than 2-3 of them proudly attending PTA or PTC meetings for the entire school year. I know the immediate defense is just because I didn't see them doesn't mean that they weren't taking care of their parental responsibilities and spending quality time with their son(s) and daughter(s). The gaping hole in that defense is that you don't always have to see something to know that something is true or not! For example, I know that many fathers weren't spending quality time with their children and teaching them good values like obedience, manners, self-respect and honesty because their children were in my class and throughout the school and they didn't exhibit any of those values! Therefore, the appearance and behavior of the children revealed the truth! **I saw and heard the neglect**! I heard the rude and disrespectful comments from the children. I saw the frequent ashy faces, hands and bodies (no lotion or vaseline in the home, said the children), dry and knotted hair, crust in eyes and around the mouth, morning breath due to not brushing teeth or no toothpaste in home, wax oozing out of both ears, sad, angry and depressed expressions in the morning and sometimes throughout the day, hungry upon arrival (no food in home or mom didn't wake up to fix breakfast)! *The proof is in the pudding*!

A kindergarten teacher knows that you haven't spent quality time teaching your daughter how to spell her name because she is struggling to write the letters of her name five minutes after the worksheet has been placed on her desk and it is a fifteen-minute worksheet! Why give the child a name with eight letters and you don't spend the time to teach her how to spell her name? As I mentioned previously, I knew that the boy's mother didn't properly supervise his academics because he struggled with addition, subtraction and multiplication in the fifth grade. He should had been proficient in those areas by the end of the third grade. Teachers don't need some parents to admit that they haven't taught their child proper hygiene because the teachers smell the students! There are more than a few fifth grade teachers who can attest to the issue of malodorous scents wafting through the classroom and hallways, especially when the warm weather arrives in April and May. I can only imagine how these funky scents are magnified in middle school. In regard to inmates, I don't need them to admit that they have irrational beliefs and habits after they tell me that they don't see "nothing wrong with robbing and assaulting innocent people" because "I gotta feed my family." That sounds like what a caveman would had said and we are thousands of years removed from that period.

When seven out of twenty pre-k kids eat their entire lunch with their fingers, Houston, we have a problem. This doesn't even include the four who picked up their plate to slurp the juice and lick it! So, it doesn't matter to me how animated the parents get when they tell me that Shirley, James and Robert eat with a spoon and fork at home because if that were true, they would not eat with their fingers at school. Actions always reveal the person just as light reveals what's done in the dark. Just because a person denies facts, it does not make the facts untrue! Many people unwittingly believe that they have to admit the truth in order for others to know that something is true. With most situations, we determine the truth by the evidence and the actions of those involved. For example, we can tell by his actions at work that he doesn't want the job. Some people deny being a weed smoker. The truth is revealed by their clothes smelling like weed and their fingertips being burnt yellow in color. Despite your management title, the employees know that you lack interpersonal skills by your abrasive treatment and unprofessional behavior towards most of the staff. A lady doesn't have to admit that she is suffering from depression or her self-confidence has been crushed. When a lady is well-dressed and she keeps her hair and face looking nice and then she begins to gain or lose weight and begins looking sloppy, she is exhibiting two of the major signs of depression. Ladies, do you need a guy to admit that he is interested in you or can you tell? Some people deny being angry, argumentative, depressed or insecure. Yet, they exhibit all or most of the behaviors of a person who is angry, argumentative, depressed or insecure because it is in their mentality and spirit. This is the same concept as the blood test revealing drugs in the system of the suspect, despite him yelling or sincerely proclaiming that he wasn't on drugs or drunk! **Truth lies in actions and facts.** We must address difficult truths (problems) and make a whole-hearted effort to resolve them collectively and individually! When I worked in law enforcement, it seemed as if crime, grief, dysfunction, violence and suffering appeared every day in some form or fashion. When I wasn't at work, these elements captured my attention on the local and national news stations. **When do people get tired of needlessly damaging and destroying other people?**

Chapter 14

Silence

"We will have to repent in this generation not merely for the hateful words and actions of the bad people, **but for the appalling silence of the good people!"**

—Dr. King

At first glance, this statement may not seem deep, but I think it is extremely profound, provocative and relevant! **Collectively, we must actively and continuously denounce violence and absurd propaganda, policies and activities.** Not only do some inmates sleep a lot, but citizens like to sleep also. This allows a vast amount of people to ignore their daily problems. In regard to negative aspects of society, some people say that too many citizens are asleep with their eyes open. All of us are guilty of being asleep during some period of our lives. *However, the crime is becoming aware of your slumber and not engaging in the necessary actions to correct the issues that you were sleeping on.* Essentially, adults are asleep when they ignore the challenges of their children, the changing of local and state laws that have a negative impact on their property tax bill, zoning laws, voting rights, environment, school budget and policies like zero tolerance in school. This **policy is absurd** because it punishes a child without allowing mitigating circumstances to be considered in the conclusion! A student who defends himself in a fight should not get suspended! I would be interested in seeing if the policymakers would allow someone to beat on them without fighting back.

Did anybody happen to see the Facebook post that went viral regarding Chauncy, the Mississippi teenage boy who stood in a Kroger parking lot asking strangers if he could carry their groceries to their car in exchange for donuts (food)? Fortunately, Chauncy's plea touched the heart of one man. The man decided to take him into the store and buy him groceries and then drove him home. Subsequently, I saw a Mississippi news report that stated **47% of the children live in poverty**. *This story begs the questions of how long has this statistic existed? How and why is this condition acceptable to the parents, academic leaders, business leaders and politicians of the state?* The abnormal normal is that too often, *we turn a blind eye to crime, drug selling, unethical behavior, unusually high poverty levels, high illiteracy levels, irrational rules* (cell phones in middle and high school classrooms; don't deduct points for major grammar and spellings errors in essays/papers) and *then act like we don't know what's going on, who did it or why it happened.* In 2017, there were at least five people who witnessed the fanatic who called baseball player Andrew Jones a ninja. Did any of those people find it offensive enough to call the authorities and point out the racist fanatic? Did the Red Sox organization find out who the fanatic was? If they did, did they ban him from attending any future events held in the stadium? Many times, a person or people know who committed the egregious act, but we don't tell. We know the priest whose behavior seems a little strange around boys and in some instances, we know the priest who has molested boys and we did not report it and did nothing to prevent it from happening again. We know who committed the murder, shot the women and children at the cookout in Philly and who robbed the bank because we saw his face and tattoos. We know who is selling drugs in the neighborhood, recruiting and forcing children into gangs and who killed the girl in the school bathroom in Delaware. We know the teacher who fondled the girl in Gwinnett County high school and was allowed to keep his job--we know the teacher and the administrators who made that very bad judgment and nobody protested enough to get him fired until much later. We know the KKK member. We know the manager and company that employs discriminatory tactics; We know who molested the boys at Penn State University; We know who assaulted and raped the ladies at Baylor, MSU and other universities; We know the boy who stole the Yorkie from outside of the apartment in Gwinnett County because we saw his face on the camera; We know the cowardly clown who robbed and killed the lady in her apartment complex in Georgia, June 2017, because we recognize his slinky frame and janky ass walk! In some Black communities and other minority communities, residents have adopted a belief in "no snitching." Although I realize that compliance with this irrational belief may involve the safety of an innocent person, it allows the crime and violence to continue for weeks and years. I imagine there are many incidents where a person's safety isn't in jeopardy, yet people still obey the no snitching code because it is the cool thing to do! That is until you or your loved one is the victim of a senseless crime, then you are left hurting and wondering why crime won't stop and pleading with the public to provide information about the crime! Somebody has to have the courage to decide that they will report what they know about the crime because that is the only way to drastically reduce crime. Supervising criminals day after day, year after year, often had me singing Kindred the Family Soul's Far Away-"**tired of crooked cops and tired of black folks complaining that crime don't stop!"**

What we fail to realize, discuss and then **enact change on a national level is our acceptance of abnormalities as normalcy!** The violence in Chicago, Oakland, New York, Atlanta and other inner-cities, teen pregnancy, single-parent households, illiteracy, child neglect/abuse, children fighting and loitering in public areas and police brutality is out of control. How do we convince parent(s) or guardians **not to involve their children in criminal activities?** In 2012, a lady who was 39 weeks pregnant took her two daughters to Walmart to steal items. Apparently, she thought that the police wouldn't or couldn't arrest her because of her pregnant condition. Clearly, she's ignorant of the law and had no clue about the statute of limitations, so the police department is going to arrest her shortly after she gives birth. How do we convince parent(s) or guardians that it is inappropriate to allow their pre-teen child to get a tattoo? Also in 2012, a Cobb County mother took her ten-year-old son to get a tattoo in remembrance of his brother who died. What happened to honoring a person's memory in your heart and mind, making a collage, writing a poem or song? *When I consider the extent and frequency of harmful behavior that exists in minority, rural and affluent communities, I conclude that much of it is the result of broken men and women!* As a lay person, almost all of us lack the essential knowledge and skills to effectively repair a broken person. Consequently, we decide to accept, ignore, avoid or deny their abnormal, unstable, self-defeating and destructive behavior, which allows them to suffer in silence or inflict their pain on another vulnerable person. We may even try to pray it away. However, when we don't engage in any strategic works to combine with the prayer, the prayer is usually ineffective. Faith without works is dead! It takes courage to hear about our character flaws, admit our flaws and then accept guidance about how to solve our flaws to improve our lives and **prevent the flaws from existing and causing severe damage from generation to generation.** We also need courage to put forth the effort to find and engage in actions to eliminate our flaws. The same is true for our weaknesses and fears. For instance, when you know that your brother, baby daddy, cousin or best friend is involved in a gang and participates in criminal activities, how does it make any sense to allow your child (his) or any child to be around him in public? It doesn't matter if it involves two minutes on the porch, a ten minute car ride or a backyard party, **the risks are too high**! Part of the gang culture is *hunt and get hunted*. When these unloved, undisciplined, irrational and dysfunctional puppets begin shooting, they don't usually just aim at the designated person. They just shoot! If a young teen or adult boy makes the sad decision to risk his or her life, it is their choice. If the adult boy gets mad and has a tantrum because he is not allowed to be around his child outside, so be it! He has to learn to live with the consequences of his choices. If you run in the jungle filled with snakes, lions, liars, tigers and bears, what is the likelihood that you will be attacked? What is the likelihood that you will be killed? High! It's just a matter of time. As rational and responsible family members or friends, it is our responsibility to protect and guide our children 24/7-365. **As rational and responsible family members, we are completely responsible for the safety and well-being of our children.** We cannot afford to be silent or passive on this issue! This is extremely important to the future of our families and communities. *The world is a dangerous place, not because of those who do evil*, **but because of those who look on and do nothing**, said Albert Einstein.

In order to improve race relations and society, we need conscientious Caucasians who possess integrity and sincerely care about humans to publicly speak out against racial discrimination and injustice instead of being silent! This silence fosters the perpetuation of the racial divide and animosity between Caucasians and African-Americans and other people of color and it prevents racial harmony.** Apathy, righteous indignation, fear, willful ignorance and willful indifference will no longer be an excuse for not acknowledging racism, confronting your racist family members, friends and elected officials. Also, it is important for these same individuals to **consistently** provide tangible support to the legitimate organizations that fight for human equality and to eliminate racial discrimination. Too much racial discord has occurred since 2009 to assert plausible denial. Either it was excessive force or it wasn't! It requires six bullets to stop a man or it doesn't! It is a hate group or it isn't! The policy is discriminatory or it isn't! The school or company utilizes discriminatory practices or it doesn't. When we witness public and workplace discrimination, we must report it and denounce it! When we witness police brutality and misconduct, especially officers, we must report it and denounce it! When we witness political misconduct, we must report it and denounce it, regardless of the office level! When we witness or suspect child abuse or neglect, we must report it and denounce it, **so that we attempt to reduce the damage to the lives of the children**!!! Please remember that whatever we tolerate, we perpetuate!

Conclusion

As an African-American man who was raised by a proud, strong, hard-working, loving and religious African-American father, I am seriously concerned about the illiteracy, irrational, self-destructive and violent behavior among African-American males! When I was growing up in the 70's, there was this smooth R&B song called **Show and Tell**. ... when I wanna say I love you. Although I liked the song because it had a smooth melody and nice words, I didn't realize how powerful the message was. Show and tell is how we must raise our children. **It's important that we show and tell our children that we love them very much**. Both parts are necessary and one doesn't usually work well without the other. In fact, I would argue that **showing is more important than telling because as humans, we need positive demonstrations to emphasize our value**. This sense of nurturing from a loving spirit will remain in the memory of a child for a lifetime. My Aunt Adele was that way and I did not spend much time with her growing up, *yet I vividly remember her beautiful smile and gentle and loving spirit*! An important fact that is sadly overlooked about children and human behavior is that **all children** want to *feel loved, understood and a sense of belonging. If you provide these qualities,* **they will do anything good or bad that you tell them to do!**

I heard a wise Atlanta pastor say that one of the worst things that can happen to you is **for God to take his hands off your life**! I thought that was a profound statement. Likewise, I think that one of the worst things that can happen to a person is for loving people to stop supporting them! **Nurturing, supportive and loyal relationships are essential to a productive and happy life! From birth,**

nurturing is a need for every human being! People need to be cared for mentally, emotionally, physically and spiritually. Once you learn about human emotions or various types of personalities, you will recognize that there are people in your life who want and need to be fed recognition, security, affection, hope, knowledge, guidance, constructive criticism, discipline, quality time and encouragement. This is especially true of children! *Some fundamental core skills and qualities that every child and adolescent should have* are effective reasoning, listening and communications skills, good manners, obedience, patience, a strong work ethic, dignity, honesty, confidence, self-control, empathy and faith. **Faith will guide you and sustain you** when your reasoning doesn't seem to provide you a rational reason for your situation. **Children must be taught to be obedient and develop a work ethic similar to the strength of our ancestors.** There are fifty states, as well as various countries where a young adult can flourish. *It's pure madness to reach the tender age of 17 or 25 and be sentenced to spend the majority of your life incarcerated simply because you didn't have the wherewithal or confidence to believe that you could utilize your mind and body in a legal endeavor and live fruitfully!* This is very alarming considering the multitude of extraordinary and ordinary accomplishments achieved by African-Americans and other minorities. To a large extent, a person can obtain an average or above-average lifestyle by simply mimicking the actions of an identified person. For those who aren't inclined to attend college, go to a trade school. Read information about blue-collar millionaires. It seems as if there will always be a need for a technician or maintenance engineer to repair pipes, electrical items, alarm systems, water heaters, heating and ac units, cars, trucks, trains, planes, buses, computers, elevators or install carpet. However, all of these professions require fundamental skills, such as a solid work ethic, respect, obedience, honesty, comprehension skills and timeliness.

One of the best things that a person can receive in life is *a completely fair opportunity*. People need the opportunity to receive an education in a school that maintains a conducive environment for learning, compete for a job, scholarship, position on a sports team or academic team and receive general information that can be used to benefit their life and family's life. Opportunity gives you the chance to improve yourself and develop independence! Since the founding of this country, adults have always desired the right to take care of themselves and pursue various opportunities of their choice. African-Americans **traveled hundreds and thousands of miles at night without a map or GPS, but rather by following the stars and landmarks to reach a perceived better opportunity**! Now, many people rely on GPS so much that they can't drive fifteen miles without using it and still get lost! *We've designed and built homes and cities without attending architectural colleges or classes and sometimes without a high school diploma! Therefore, it is virtually impossible to convince me of what "we can't do or why we don't have!"* I couldn't be persuaded because of the incredible and inspiring accomplishments of our ancestors and recent ancestors, such as Reginald Lewis, Bob Johnson, Sheila Johnson, John Johnson, Earl Graves, Arsenio Hall, Earvin Magic Johnson, Byron Allen, Brenda Wood, Monica Kaufman, Fredrika Whitfield, Ed Bradley, Ed Gordon, Roland Martin, KD Bowe, Rosalind Brewer, Lisa Price, Cathy Hughes, Oprah Winfrey, Tyler Perry, Michael Lee-Chin, R. Donahue Peebles, Sean Combs and Jay-Z. Spike Lee paved the way for John Singleton, Ice Cube, F. Gary Gray, Tyler Perry and Will Packer. I remember seeing Michael Baisden sell his first book at a super club in Decatur. Then, we have Barack and Michelle Obama! The few names listed here don't nearly begin to scratch the surface of the many, many accomplished people within the African-American race, notwithstanding the multitude of unsung heroes and sheroes! I listed some historical accomplishments, pioneers and achievers, in part, because I believe that one detrimental aspect of ignorance is that **if we don't know that greatness is possible, we won't bother attempting to achieve it.**

We have and still do accomplish too many ordinary and extraordinary feats for people to convince me that most poor children lack the ability to perform well in school and that we don't have the ability to **create more safe homes and communities for children, especially poor children**! We need to focus on effective ways of consistently honoring ourselves, family and ancestors. If we honor these three groups, we will most likely honor other members of the human race, even strangers! **As compassionate and concerned citizens, do we sincerely want to cherish, honor and protect our children**? *Can we create more scholars and trailblazers? Can we significantly reduce the amount of unloved predatory misfits? Can we increase the amount of caring, considerate and supportive people among us? Can we develop more boys into men?* Yes! The compelling question is what citizens and organizations are going to do the work? One of my favorite scriptures advises us to be **doers of the word**! Far too many of us are just hearers of the word. For those doubters or haters, I challenge you to research the achievements of the *five Detroit girls* from University Prep Science and Math school, for they won gold in the under 14 category of the KFC All-Girls National Chess Championship; Rebecca Schmitt was the 2017 Valedictorian of Maynard Jackson High School in Atlanta. This is a great accomplishment in-and-of itself. When you consider the fact that she was temporarily homeless while her mother was very sick, then you truly realize that her journey was extremely extraordinary and inspiring. In another extraordinary feat, according to CBS News, eighteen-year-old Raven Osborne of Gary, Indiana, graduated in May 2017 with her *high school diploma and college degree.* This is an extraordinary accomplishment by an extraordinary child who came from an ordinary family. Raven attended 21st Century Charter High School where the students are **required** to take college classes in order to graduate from high school.

    We have not because we reason not! We have not because we believe not! We have not because we understand not! We have

not because we work not! We have not because we obey not! We have not because we ask not, plan not, expect not, require not, honor not, respect not, sacrifice not, prioritize not, unite not, organize not, and mobilize not! We wait not, **submit not--everybody can't lead and sometimes it's more important to follow than lead!** Have you ever heard of a powerful leader without dedicated followers? *Quality leadership experience is gained after quality follow-ship experience!* We seek not, apprentice not, humble not, commit not, discipline not, persevere not, analyze not, and strategize not. **We recall not the ingenuity, tenacity, dignity, integrity and legacy of our ancestors** and the everlasting prolific words of our Creator! Like our ancestors, w*hat we accomplish in life is based less on what we want and more on how much we are willing to do to get it.* If you realize that you aren't aware of the concept of *self-determination*, then this is your shout out. We have to take some time to think about what reasonable and practical actions we can take to achieve self-sufficiency and our own comfort level. **FAITH without WORKS is dead**. At a minimum, progress is always a two-step process! First, you have to believe and then you must take some action! Our history clearly and demonstrably shows that *we are extremely ingenious, resilient, beautiful and accomplished.* **It's our responsibility to be aware of it, own it, honor it, represent it and reflect it in our daily lives!**

Despite the sadness and madness that happens on a daily basis, I'm grateful for the victories that we have won. **I'm especially grateful for the victories of my parents, relatives, friends and extended ancestors.** *Brother Carr gave us a powerful testimony when he sang I Almost Let Go!* There is a profound lesson in why he didn't let go. Countless other courageous people and our ancestors didn't let go. Not only did many of them not let go, but quite a few of them managed to significantly improve their conditions, their children's conditions, as well as the conditions of the fifty states of America! **Just as our ancestors decided, I decided that I'm gonna run on and see what the end is gonna be!**

May we all be consciously aware that "**children are the living messages** we send to a time we will not see!" Let's send the future children who are mentally and emotionally healthy, intelligent, ethical, compassionate, humble, loving, innovative and peaceful!!!

About the Author

Mr. Johnson was born in the Bronx and raised in Queens, New York. He is a graduate of Morehouse College.

His passion for teaching children began after a few years of substitute teaching and fully expanded after he began completing long-term substitute assignments. He has eight years of experience teaching children from K-12th grade. He spent five years and eight months as a detention officer at the seventh largest jail in the Southeast observing and supervising males and females between 17-65 years of age. Consequently, he has seen students go from school to jail. This unique combination of work experience evolved into a mission! Furthermore, it has afforded him the opportunity to *witness and identify common characteristics that are exhibited by students and inmates and multiple factors that contribute to students becoming inmates.* Mr. Johnson has thousands of hours of hands-on experience with many types of personalities! He has taught and supervised people who had ADD, ADHD, bipolar disorder, schizophrenia, bipolar schizophrenia and plain ole hard-headed. Based on his breadth of experience, he knows the signs of immature children, baby boys and adult boys, **mild and severe child abuse**, unbrushed teeth, funky body odor, sour clothing (washed without soap or detergent and not dried properly), defensive behaviors, defeatist mentality, victim's mentality, false bravado, dysfunctional behavior, mental illness behavior, illiterate behavior, as well as functionally illiterate behavior. He knows how to interpret behavior well and effectively deal with negative behavior! He knows how to train children and adults to think logically and behave appropriately.

Mr. Johnson's philosophy is grounded in the principles of **purpose, empowerment, transformation and familial obligation**. Through educational and social programs, he hopes to create an honest and broad dialogue that will create a cooperative spirit, which **inspires people to become active participants** in programs designed to benefit children and the future of the United States. The BellJohnson Foundation is on the way!

Contact info:

Eric Johnson – Facebook
Bjfnow – Instagram
Bjfnow – Twitter

www.ingramcontent.com/pod-product-compliance
Lightning Source LLC
Chambersburg PA
CBHW071824020726
47502CB00004B/1230